Center Stage

The Backlot Series – Book 2

Kimberly Page

Center Stage

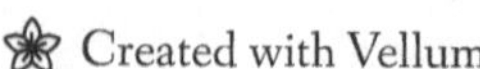 Created with Vellum

*For those who know everything worth having
lies on the other side of fear.*

author's note

Dear Reader,

Welcome back to Hollywood! While Grant and Sophia's story is fictional, it explores very real challenges that many of us face like the fear of taking risks, the weight of others' expectations, and the courage it takes to be vulnerable.

Some of the themes in this book touch on difficult subjects. For example, Grant's story involves the loss of a parent and its lasting impact on a family. There's also talk of the subtle (and sometimes not-so-subtle) misogyny that still exists in many industries, particularly entertainment. While I did my best to handle topics with care, I understand they may be triggering for some readers.

What I love about romance is how it allows us to explore these deeper issues while still delivering hope and joy. Through Sophia's journey, we see how success doesn't shield women from having their achievements questioned. Through Grant, we witness how childhood trauma can shape our adult fears about love and loss. But most importantly, through both of them, we see that healing is possible when we're brave enough to let others in.

I hope their story resonates with you, makes you laugh, maybe makes you cry (in a good way!), and reminds you that sometimes the scariest leaps lead to the most beautiful landings.

P.S. Like its predecessor, this book would earn an NC-17 rating for strong language, alcohol use, and steamy scenes. Grant and Sophia definitely make good use of that pool house! 😉

Paparazzi - Lady Gaga
Sparks - Coldplay
This Town - Niall Horan
Heat Waves - Glass Animals
Friends - Chase Atlantic
A Sky Full of Stars - Coldplay
Eyes Wide Open - Sabrina Carpenter
Late Night Talking - Harry Styles
Delicate - Taylor Swift
Adore You - Harry Styles
I Think He Knows - Taylor Swift
Shameless - Camila Cabello
PILLOWTALK - ZAYN
Bloom - The Paper Kites
How Does A Moment Last Forever - Celine Dion
Cell Block Tango - Chicago Soundtrack
Rewrite The Stars - Zac Efron, Zendaya
Heaven - Julia Michaels
The Way You Look Tonight - Frank Sinatra
Guys My Age - Hey Violet
Speechless - Dan + Shay

Electric Feel - MGMT
Feels Like - Gracie Abrams
Stay - Zedd, Alessia Cara
boyfriend - Ariana Grande, Social House
This City - Sam Fischer
Without You (feat. Usher) - David Guetta
I miss you, I'm sorry - Gracie Abrams
You Are The Reason - Calum Scott
Fairytale - Livingston

one

. . .

Sophia

TWENTY MINUTES UNTIL SHOWTIME, and my bladder picks now to revolt. As I shift from one stiletto-clad foot to the other, the distant hum of voices filters in from the red carpet leading into the Dolby Theatre, home to the Oscars. The afternoon sun casts long shadows on the pavement, its warmth doing little to ease the anticipation coursing through me. Nearby, a cluster of assistants and security personnel mill about, their movements purposeful yet unhurried, creating a strange calm before the storm.

My silky pale blue Prada dress slides beneath my palms as I smooth out invisible creases. The dress is a work of art, hugging every curve exactly how my stylist promised, guaranteed to land on tomorrow's best-dressed lists. But the back view nags at my brain. Those pleats better behave for the cameras, and that seam along my hip? Definitely pulling a millimeter tighter than at this morning's final fitting. My stomach flips, partly from that cleanse—which, for the record, absolutely works—but mostly from those persistent butterflies that crash every red carpet like uninvited paparazzi.

My hands clasp in front, and I take in the surrounding scene. The glaring lights, the fake smiles, the strangers who'll dissect every choice—the dress, the makeup, the precise angle of hair falling over my shoulder—it's all familiar territory. My body has starred in countless tabloid headlines and sparked endless online speculation.

A flash catches my eye—some early photographer testing their settings. The unspoken rules of the red carpet play through my head—chin down, shoulders back, smile bright but not too bright. My stylist's voice echoes in my thoughts, *"Channel Grace Kelly, not Real Housewife."*

"You're on in two minutes," crackles through a nearby radio, and my pulse skips into double time. The deep V of my dress needs a quick adjustment to keep the girls in check, and my heels click against the hard cement as I step forward. Wyatt catches my eye and wanders toward me, his hands stuffed in his pockets, wearing that signature big brother grin that's gotten me through every awards show since I was twelve. I'm up next, and the spotlight—with all its blinding expectations—awaits.

"I'll meet you at the end of the press line," Wyatt says.

"Tell Blair I'm going to need her help after this," I say.

Wyatt leans in for a hug, his grin easy. "Will do. Break a leg, Soph." He plants a quick peck on my cheek before stepping away.

At the same time, I notice Grant Hall at the edge of the staging area, his presence as commanding as the rumors suggest. My toes tingle—blame it on these ridiculous heels or on the way the head of Wonderland Studios carries himself with such effortless authority. He's close enough that I could count the silver strands at his temples if I weren't pretending not to notice him at all.

The pre-carpet shuffle drags on. I exchange air kisses with familiar faces, nod at publicists, and trade industry small talk with line monitors. It's the unglamorous intermission before the main show—the part *E! News* doesn't broadcast. Last year, I walked this carpet as a surprise nominee, bright-eyed and clueless. Tonight? Tonight, I'm returning as a winner, and suddenly, every detail matters more.

Funny how fast things change. One Oscar win can transform you from "that girl from the kids' network" to someone whose every expression might land on tomorrow's *TMZ*. The pressure sits differently now. Each twist and turn needs to be calculated, each step precise. Glide, don't stomp. Keep the face serene, the eyes forward. God forbid I react to anything—Twitter would explode.

A production assistant appears with a mirror for one last check. The routine highlights the absurd double standard of it all. In about two minutes, male directors will field questions about their artistic vision while I'll be asked to name-drop designers and show off my shoes. But that's a battle for another day. Right now, it's showtime.

The red velvet path stretches before me, a gauntlet of flashing lights and shouted demands.

"Sophia, over here!"

"Give us a twirl!"

"Who are you wearing?"

At least the Oscars try to keep it civilized—smile, pose,

move on. The real circus waits in those cordoned-off interview hubs at the end of the line.

I shift into my signature over-the-shoulder pose as Grant steps onto the carpet behind me. Even with the careful spacing between celebrities, his presence fills the air. His black tux fits like a dream, all broad shoulders and lean lines, catching the light with each movement. The mix of chestnut and silver in his perfectly styled hair only adds to that effortless polish. Behind sleek black-framed glasses, his warm brown eyes survey the scene with practiced ease. He radiates old Hollywood charm—the genuine kind, not the manufactured version this town mass produces.

His breath hits my neck before his voice does.

"You look incredible."

His scent engulfs me—crisp and clean, with notes of coffee—and suddenly, these practiced poses feel a lot less steady. I pray my smile doesn't broadcast the embarrassingly massive crush I've been nursing since Blair introduced us at the *Pink Slip* premiere last year. That night, Grant had completely shocked me. Most executives see right past you, already scanning the room for someone more important. But Grant? He'd locked in like I was the only person worth talking to, asking about everything from my childhood roles to my favorite books.

Over the past year, I've collected little moments that prove he's the real deal. He remembers every crew member's name and actually listens when they stop to talk to him. As long as his schedule allows, he'll take a meeting with anyone, not just the top elite. Those small kindnesses aren't for show. Now he's bought my first producing project, and we start filming next week. Dreams really do come true in LA sometimes.

"Want to do a few interviews together tonight? We could tease your new project," he whispers, still close enough that I'm sure the photographers are having a field day.

"Sure, if you think Lucas would be ok with that?"

Lucas, Wonderland's PR mastermind, runs a tight ship when it comes to press strategy, though with his model looks and athletic build, he could easily be in front of the cameras instead of managing the narrative behind them.

"He'll be fine. We can stick to our excitement about working together." Grant pauses and then adds softly, "Do you mind if I put my arm around your waist?"

The unexpected thoughtfulness makes my chest warm.

"Of course."

His hand settles around me, firm but respectful, as he draws me closer. The cameras explode in a frenzy of flashes.

"Eyes forward. Smile for the camera," he murmurs, his tone low and commanding.

I angle into my best pose, letting myself lean slightly into his warmth.

"Good girl."

The words send an unexpected jolt through my entire body, settling into a very specific and surprising ache down south. Well. That's...interesting. Seems I have a praise kink. Or maybe it's just a Grant kink.

"Dad!"

Grant's warmth disappears as he steps away, his attention completely captured by a small girl running toward him. He scoops her up with practiced ease and settles her on his hip like she's his whole world.

"Hey, nugget! You look like a beautiful princess." He kisses her cheek, and the tenderness of the moment makes my chest do funny things. "Hazel, meet my friend Sophia. We're working together on a brand-new movie."

His daughter gazes at me with eyes that mirror Grant's exactly—same warm brown, same depth. She offers a shy wave, her tiny fingers curling in a way that melts my heart instantly.

"Hi, Hazel," I say, waving back. "I'm honored to meet you. I've seen your pictures all over your dad's office."

A soft giggle disappears into Grant's shoulder just as a stunning brunette appears. The woman slips her arm through his and settles her hand on Hazel's back. The easy way Hazel leans into her touch speaks volumes.

My dress suddenly feels like a boa constrictor. Of course Grant has someone this gorgeous in his life. So much for Blair's intel about him not dating. Maybe he doesn't date because he doesn't need to.

"Oh, Sophia Ford! I loved you in *The Great Alone*! Kristin Hannah is one of my favorite authors. She can do no wrong. You were incredible. So deserving of that Oscar!"

Her genuine enthusiasm makes me feel guilty for the jealousy churning in my stomach.

"Thank you," I manage, accepting her warm handshake.

A PR assistant waves us toward the interview hubs before introductions can continue, and we're swept into the press line. Grant takes point with the first reporter, describing our project with the kind of passion that made me fall for it in the first place.

"It's a survival thriller wrapped in a deeply personal story. The protagonist is a big-city executive forced to return home to care for her mother, and suddenly, she's dealing with a potential landslide that could destroy the entire town. It's not just about physical survival but also about the emotional weight of holding on to what matters most. We wanted the stakes to feel incredibly real and relatable while still delivering those nail-biting moments people love in a survival drama," Grant says, sounding both polished and passionate.

"I also think *Survivor* is about the lengths we go to for the people we love," I add, my voice soft but sure.

The weight of Grant's gaze hits me like a spotlight. When I dare look his way, the intensity in his eyes steals my breath —too raw, too real for this circus of cameras and microphones. Something unspoken passes between us, drawing taut like a wire about to snap.

A reporter's polite cough breaks the spell. Heat floods my cheeks as I wrench my attention away.

"It sounds fantastic! It's going to be agony waiting over a year to see the film!" the reporter exclaims, oblivious to the charged moment that just passed.

Grant shifts back into his polished, charming demeanor, thanking her for her kind words as we're ushered toward the next interview. I follow, trying to steady my breathing and shake off the lingering effect of his gaze, but it clings to me, persistent and unshakable.

We move through the rest of the interviews until I'm pulled

aside for solo comments. I'm in mid-answer for the dreaded "Are you dating anyone?" question (the answer is always no, in case you're wondering) when I spot Grant rejoining the brunette and Hazel. The sight shouldn't sting, but it does.

By the time I finish, the crowd has thinned, and I find Grant waiting near Wyatt. My stomach flips. Did he wait for me?

The hope vanishes as Hazel runs over, waving something in her hand and chattering excitedly. The brunette guides her up the stairs just as I approach.

"Good luck tonight, Sophia. Enjoy the show," Grant says, flashing one of his practiced, charming smiles.

"You, too, Grant." I match his tone and grab Wyatt's arm as we climb the stairs.

"What a perfect little happy family," I whisper, my tone tinged with longing.

Wyatt's questioning eyes zero in on me, his confusion plain in his gaze.

I laugh lightly, blowing it off. "It's just not something you see a lot of in Hollywood. It's...sweet."

He doesn't push, thank God.

"Let's find our seats," I say, already moving on. "But I have to pee first."

two

. . .

Grant

"SO, THAT'S SOPHIA?"

My sister's face leaves no speculation as to how giddy she feels about meeting the Oscar winner. I'm sure my face looked the same when I realized we were on the red carpet together, a stroke of luck that I don't think Lucas could've planned better if he had tried.

I can't seem to shake the memory of my hand against Sophia's hip just moments ago—the smooth satin of her gown and the warmth of her body still buzzing in my fingertips. Without thinking, my hand tightens at my side as if trying to hold on to that sensation. I force it into my trouser pocket, determined not to dwell on the scent of vanilla and magnolia or jasmine or whatever lingers whenever she's near. I make a mental note to remind Lucas I may have gotten a bit cozy with my arms around her, so he should ensure that the press and trades know it's nothing but a working relationship. Nothing intimate. Just friendly.

She has this particular smile—her "photo op" smile that

doesn't quite reach her eyes. But I've seen another one, a private one, that lights up her entire face and nearly stops my heart. Every time I'm around her, I seem to lose just a tiny bit of my grip on the whole "No Dating" rule.

"A little star-struck, sis?" I ask, hoping to divert my own swirling thoughts.

"Definitely. And even more excited that she might be dating my brother!" She mentions that last part quietly so Hazel doesn't hear, but it brings me to a full stop.

"What?" I look down at Hazel to see if she's paying attention. "Why would you say that? It's the absolute furthest thing from reality that I've ever heard. Never going to happen."

"Ok, ok, calm down. I've just never known you to willingly introduce Hazel to other women."

She's not wrong, and now I wonder if my reaction is another clue that I may have a tiny crush on Sophia Ford.

It doesn't matter, though, because I just bought her project, and she's asked me to act as a mentor. Besides, relationships aren't for me. Hazel is my one and only. I don't date, and I'll never get married. I've known since I was a teenager that love isn't worth the risk. I saw what losing my father did to my mother—how she fell into a grief so deep that she never really crawled back out. One day, you have this epic romance; the next, you're left broken. I'm not putting Hazel or myself through anything like that.

It was a fluke that my fling with Geneva ended with her pregnant. I'm grateful she was just as uninterested as I was in trying to make a go of a relationship. And I managed to get the best gift of my life out of the deal. Hazel, my pride and joy, the smartest, strongest, most beautiful six-year-old you'll ever meet. I'm not biased. It's the truth. Everyone tells me that, so I know I'm not exaggerating. Bragging, maybe.

I never wanted children, and I'm definitely not what people refer to as husband material. I'm good at analyzing things and making decisions. I stick to facts and leave emotions out of it. But the day Hazel was born, a new level unlocked in my heart, and I was a goner. She's the only girl who will ever have all my heart, soul, and attention. Yes, Sophia is incredible in many ways—smart, talented, kind— but I can't risk it, especially not for someone at least a decade younger and in a totally different phase of life.

"Hazel saw her, and it would've been awkward not to," I mutter, feeling my sister's gaze on me.

She just nods like I'm full of it. "Just because Mom and Dad didn't have the fairytale ending, doesn't mean it doesn't exist. I wish you'd get over your hang up on love."

"It's not just Mom and Dad. Geneva cut things off as soon as she found out she was pregnant."

"Bullshit. You two were never serious, and you can't hold it against her for chasing her career. You did the same thing when you were her age, and look how great it turned out for you."

Geneva is currently the model you see on every major magazine cover. She's on her way to being the next Gisele or Heidi. Our agents set us up for a few publicity moments, but there was some chemistry, so we took advantage of it. We both knew it wasn't serious. She travels the world for her career, and I escape into different ones for mine. We had already parted ways when she realized she was pregnant, and looking back, I was lucky it happened with her. She's level-headed and doesn't play games. This pregnancy could have derailed her career, but she figured out how to adapt and use it to her advantage.

When Hazel was born, we discussed our options, and to Geneva's credit, she was honest about her desire to continue growing her career. In her line of work, age is a factor, and at the time, she was twenty-four years old—prime modeling years. We decided Hazel living with me would give her the stability and routine kids need. I took on full custody, and Geneva works hard to keep in touch and visit Hazel as often as she can.

"We start on *Survivor* next week, and she's asked me to be her mentor throughout the process. She may be around a lot over the next few months, so I didn't think it would be that big of a deal. Introducing her, I mean."

"You're going to be her mentor?" My sister raises one eyebrow, as if every word I say validates her suspicions.

"It is my job to make sure the film is successful."

"Sure, but since when do you mentor people?"

"It's literally my job to help filmmakers out," I say, though it's usually more about budgets and deadlines than the cozy, personal guidance I seem to be offering to Sophia.

She squints with a head tilt as if she's trying to determine if that's total bullshit. In my defense, I do mentor a lot of people. Ok, maybe it's more of an advisory role I tend to play. And by advisor, I mean I tell them what they can and can't do. But with Sophia, I want to help.

"Well, I like her," Sarah says. "And I think it would be fantastic if you realized while you were mentoring her that maybe you'd like to date her, too."

"Never going to happen."

I just shake my head and keep walking toward the theater, but my mind drifts back to Sophia's body in that soft silk dress, the material clinging to every curve and dip. I can imagine how my fingers would glide smoothly over every inch of her ivory skin, my hands finding all the places that might make her sigh or moan—a veritable treasure in my palms. But Sophia isn't the casual type. She has that blend of worldly confidence and endearing awkwardness that suggests she's not into meaningless flings, and I'm the guy who doesn't do relationships.

"Are you talking about Sophia?" Hazel asks.

"We sure are. I was just telling Aunt Sarah that the movie starts shooting next week."

"Awesome, Dad. Maybe I can come to the set with you one day."

"We'll see, nugget."

I smile down at my perfect girl. Sarah is right—I am over-protective of Hazel when it comes to who she meets. If I date —and let's be honest, I have needs—I establish boundaries and expectations well before making any arrangements. There's absolutely no need for any woman to meet my daughter. Hazel already has a mother and doesn't need another one.

I scan the event and feel the electricity hum through my bones. I love this stuff. I'm surrounded by the most creative storytellers in the world. The imagination and ingenuity seem contagious, and I believe this right here is what makes the world a better place. The ability to reflect, explain, or escape the world in a way that can change a person—or the entire world—is humbling. I'm a lucky idiot who stumbled his way into this business, and I'll never take it for granted. It's where I'm meant to be.

Now that Hazel is getting older, I want her to experience the same feelings of possibility and hope. That's why I'm excited about bringing her to events like this. Plus, I love spending time with her and will take every extra minute I can get. She may not decide entertainment is her path, but she'll never for once believe she can't achieve whatever she puts her mind to.

"Thanks for coming tonight. Hazel wouldn't be able to enjoy this without your help. I appreciate it."

I wrap my arm around Sarah's shoulder and bring her in for a side hug just as I catch Sophia's eyes on us. Sophia gives me a curt smile and turns quickly before I can wave back. Something about that expression—her face closed off, her lips pursed—tells me she's wearing her fake smile again. Maybe she's nervous.

"It's tough, you know, all these celebrities and fancy gift bags. You owe me for sure," Sarah teases with a laugh, hugging me back.

I take another look around at the buzzing energy of the attendees before we walk into the theater for the show. My eyes search for that dark-haired, blue-eyed princess who seems to have a spell on me, no matter how much I deny it. It's the most a woman has been on my mind in years.

three

. . .

Sophia

I'M SCARFING down the biggest plate of fries, making up for what I missed prepping to fit into my Oscars gown. It was worth it, but oh, how I've missed my salty friends.

The bustling lunchtime at The Front Yard is all cozy booths, soft jazz music, and the constant clink of silverware on china. Sunlight peeks through umbrellas shading the outdoor dining area, illuminating the pastel-colored walls and highlighting exactly how much I've already eaten.

I'm antsy, too. Tomorrow is the first day of filming for my new project, and my brain won't stop flitting between best-case scenarios—landing critical acclaim by lunch—and worst-case ones, like me face-planting in front of the entire crew.

"You ready for tomorrow?" Blair asks, reaching across to pluck a fry from my plate before I can stop her.

I fake a slap at her hand. "If you wanted fries, why didn't you order fries?"

She smirks, brushing salt off her fingertips. "I'm not like

you. I can't eat whatever I want and maintain this girlish figure."

I roll my eyes. Blair is knockout gorgeous. She has the kind of body that belongs on posters boys pin to their bedroom walls. I shove my plate over to her, partly to share and partly so I won't keep mindlessly eating because of nerves.

"I'm just ready to get the first day over with," I say. "It's always awkward. No one really knows the cast-and-crew dynamics yet, but by day two, things feel normal."

"You're leading the day off, right?" Blair snags another fry.

"Actually, I asked Grant to say a few words first thing. I thought he might like to meet everyone, plus"—I lower my voice—"I could use a little visual credibility from the boss."

Blair stills and looks up at me right before she takes a sip of her iced tea. "Grant is coming? Tomorrow? In person?"

"Is that weird?" I ask, frowning. "What's the problem?"

She's sitting across the table from me, next to my brother. Wyatt glances at her, and they do that silent brow-wiggle communication I've seen a million times.

"Stop it," I say, pointing a fry at them. "I can see you two talking about me with your little wiggle-waggles. Spill. Am I missing something?"

Blair's cheeks color. "No, it's just that...Grant is involved but also busy. It's not unheard of for him to show up, but it's not the norm."

"It's great, though," Wyatt chimes in, leaning back in the booth. "He seemed kinda smitten with you at the Oscars. Maybe that's why he's dropping in."

"Wyatt," I groan, "he was with someone else that night, remember?"

Wyatt arches a brow. "The brunette?"

"What brunette?" Blair asks, with confusion across her face.

"Someone that was almost as excited to see Sophia as he was. She was a bit star-struck. Kept talking about you in *The Great Alone*, right?"

Blair snaps her fingers. "Hold on. Was her hair wavy, about this long?" She gestures under her chin, and I nod. "Looked like a nineties Sandra Bullock?"

"That's the one," I say. "She seemed really close to his daughter, too."

Blair leans back with a smug look on her face. "That was his sister."

My heart does a traitorous little flip. So, Grant wasn't there on a date after all. Maybe he *was* flirting with me. Heat warms my cheeks, and I distract myself by sipping from my straw.

"Oh, good to know."

"Hey," Wyatt says, "I was only teasing about him crushing on you. He's way too old for you. Please tell me you aren't interested in him." I can see the conflict of wanting me to be happy with the torture of wanting to keep me sheltered all over his face.

"I'm not."

"Why not?" Blair asks.

"Blair..." Wyatt says.

"I'll admit he's hot. And I have a crush on him in the most innocent 'it will never be a real thing or go anywhere' type of way. But I've learned my lesson with Hollywood men. Nope. No way. Not for me."

"Never say never," Blair says. She gives me a knowing wink, and I just shake my head like she's insane.

"Just because Connor was a dickweed, it doesn't mean everyone is," Wyatt says. "You know it wasn't even his idea."

"That's exactly my point. There was an entire team behind him, dreaming up our relationship. His PR people, producers, and lord knows who else. If it was just Connor, I might be able to chalk it up to one bad guy."

I still feel a flush of embarrassment whenever I think about it, and it's been three years since we broke up—or, more accurately, since I found out our eight-month relationship was basically a storyline. Connor had been my co-star in the last season of *Code Crusaders*. We spent countless hours together. We were the only two "kids" on set, and it was his first real acting gig. I was the seasoned pro with a few shows under my belt. At first, I thought we genuinely clicked. I was the one showing him the ropes, introducing him to people, and falling for him.

Turns out, when you cuddle up next to a teen-network sweetheart, it's a fast track to bigger roles and media attention. He got exactly what he wanted. As soon as the show ended, I learned the truth. He'd never felt that way about me. It was all a carefully orchestrated step on the PR ladder, a plan I knew nothing about.

It stung worse than my very first heartbreak, and that one had been pretty bad, too—a fellow up-and-coming actor from a sitcom on the same network, he stole my v-card. Back then, I chalked it up to being young, dumb, and starry-eyed. That was mostly a pride thing. I'd believed him too easily, and I felt stupid later. But Connor? That was real heartbreak. That's the wound that left me with trust issues and an instant no-thanks policy for dating in the industry.

"I'd be fine if you never dated again," Wyatt jokes, motioning for the check. Blair smacks his arm, and he laughs.

"Well, for now, I'm focused on this film," I say, straightening my back. "I've worked really hard to get here, and for the next few months, I won't even have time to think about anything else."

It's true, even if I sometimes wish things were different. I glance at the midday crowd standing in line by the hostess stand—a mix of well-dressed studio assistants grabbing takeout salads and older couples waiting for a seat. It's such a normal scene, yet my life feels anything but normal.

I watch as Wyatt helps Blair out of her seat and how she places her hands on his jaw before giving him a light peck on his lips. His hands fall to the small of her back, and she tucks in closer to him as we walk out of the restaurant. I know they'll have a lively conversation on the way home while he touches her thigh or she wraps her fingers through his. It's simple, and some days, I crave those same moments, too.

four

· · ·

Grant

"I WISH you would've talked to me about this before you agreed to it," Lucas says as he escorts me to Stage Twenty-Six. It's the first day of production on the *Survivor* film, and thanks to my ill-timed commitment to Sophia, I'm walking across the lot before I've had coffee, trying to figure out exactly what I'm going to say.

"I know. Let's just get through this."

It's quiet this early in the morning, and the calm before all the creativity that comes to life within these stages gives me a rush of excitement. Everything here feels full of promise and hope. I can't explain the thrill of driving through the gates and stepping into what's essentially a huge metal barn. One day, it's transformed into a basketball stadium, and the next, it's a church. It's magic.

I've missed being out here, missed the smell of sawdust and paint from the studio mill, the tents with rows of food from craft services, and production assistants zipping by in golf carts to grab the morning coffee orders. I'm not sure when my days started blending into hours of back-to-back meetings, but it's been a while since I set foot on a stage on day one of filming.

Normally, I don't attend first-day productions, but when Sophia asked me to open the day with a few words, I couldn't say no. Part of me is excited about this movie—it's a risky bet for the studio, but I've always been drawn to stories that rely on human connection and raw emotion over superpowers and explosions. Another part of me just wanted to see Sophia. It's more than just physical attraction. Her excitement is contagious, reminding me of how I felt when I first moved here from New York. Ambition wrapped in curiosity, sprinkled with pure anticipation—that feeling doesn't surface much in my usual executive meetings.

"Ok, well, just keep it simple," Lucas coaches, scrolling through his phone while he talks. "Wonderland is home to the most talented creatives... We aspire to be the most innovative, exciting, and fun place to tell stories... We wouldn't be here or successful without all of you... You know the drill."

I nod absently. We round the corner toward Stage Twenty-Six, and I spot Sophia standing outside the door with her phone pressed to her ear. She's dressed in black yoga pants and a faded gray sweatshirt, and her hair is pulled back in a loose ponytail. It's only the second time I've seen her casual, and the glimpse of this relaxed side of her feels oddly intimate. My forward momentum stalls for a moment as I'm transfixed by how natural and effortless she looks in this outfit—every bit as captivating as she was in that glamorous ballgown.

She holds up a finger, signaling for us to wait while she

finishes her call. I can only imagine the adrenaline running through her right now. First day at the helm of a movie you'll bring to life. She's starring in it, too, which can be tricky, but I'm excited to see her impress everyone.

Her gaze flicks over toward me and then quickly away, her brow tight like she's caught in a tense conversation. She paces a few steps, nods, and then says something quietly into the phone before ending the call. Slipping her phone into the front pouch of her sweatshirt, she draws in a breath, and her expression brightens as she turns to us. Still, there's a trace of leftover worry in her eyes that I can't quite place.

"Sorry about that. Morning!" she says, flashing a quick smile.

"Hope everything's ok?" I ask, sensing there might be more behind her forced cheer than she's letting on.

"Oh, yeah, nothing to worry about. Trying to talk Wyatt into dinner with the parents."

I'm compelled to press her further, though I'm not sure where this surge of curiosity is coming from. Then Lucas jumps in.

"Morning, Sophia! Is everyone here? We won't take up much of your time—in and out."

Usually, I appreciate Lucas playing the handler role, but today, his impatience grates on me. A flare of irritation burns through my veins, mixed with a pang of confusion over why I suddenly care so much about lingering here.

I hold the door for Sophia and Lucas and then follow them inside. The stage is organized chaos, but it's the kind that fills me with life. Once we're settled, Sophia steps forward to command the room with a calm, confident grace.

Her words flow with such warmth that it feels like she's speaking directly to each person here—lifting them up and making them feel vital to the process.

When it's my turn, I offer the standard corporate spiel. I'm aware of how stiff I sound by comparison, and I make a mental note to tell Lucas that I need to appear more human in situations like this. I'm sure he'll come back at me with a reminder that there better not be a next time. Despite that bit of awkwardness, I do have an early meeting with the streaming team that I need to get to, and disappointment creeps in again at the thought that I can't hang around all morning.

Once opening remarks are over, Sophia walks me to the exit. "Thanks again for being here. This was so great—it really sets the tone that we have full studio support." She rests a hand on my arm, her gratitude palpable.

It's a simple gesture, but I feel it more than I should. Her smile radiates like sunshine, reminding me of what's at stake. We're here to make a movie, nothing more.

"No problem," I say, and we fall quiet for a moment. My hands shift to button my suit jacket, my usual power move. "Well, I'll let you get back to it."

"You know..." She hesitates, biting her lower lip as if to stop herself. "You're probably busy, but you could stay for the first read-through if you want."

I glance from her to the cast and crew mingling around a cluster of tables. I must have paused too long because she's already waving it away.

"It's ok. You're busy. I know I've already taken up a lot of your time. Next time."

I am busy. But apparently, I can't resist being around her. I hold up a finger, asking her to give me a minute, and head out the door to talk to Lucas.

"Hey, I'm going to stick around for a bit. Listen to the first read-through."

"You're kidding, right?" Lucas says.

"Not at all."

"You have meetings."

"I'm aware."

"You have meetings with Gavin Goldberg," he reminds me, exasperated.

I take a measured breath. "Lucas, can you link up with Emma and handle any adjustments? I'll text her now and let her know my schedule is shifting. You'll be fine."

He exhales sharply but nods, agreeing to disagree with me. He's a good guy, and I wouldn't want to do this gig without him, but some days, I just need him to go with the flow. He's so wound up.

"Fine. Just...try to stay out of any selfies. I'm sure people will post on their socials. I can manage any calls that come in from the press."

"Thank you, Lucas. I appreciate it."

When I return, I see Sophia at the head of the table, an empty chair beside her. She gestures me over, and a ripple of nerves sparks inside my chest.

"Hey, after this, do you want to grab lunch at the craft services tent?" she asks. "I promise I won't keep you all day. You can leave right after."

I check the time and remember my afternoon obligations.

"How about we pop over to the executive dining room instead? It's closer to where I need to be."

"Perfect."

Somehow, it really is. It's shaping up to be one of the best days I've had in a long time—and I still haven't even gotten my first cup of coffee yet.

five

. . .

Sophia

I DIG into my braised short ribs, barely pausing to chew before asking, "So, what did you think of the morning? I mean, be honest. I can take it."

My words come out muffled, but I don't care. I'm starving, and apparently, filming makes me eat like a linebacker.

I glance at Grant and almost laugh at how calm he looks, sitting across from me with that perfect posture, his sleeves rolled up just enough to showcase those strong forearms. His glasses sit slightly lower on his nose, and the way he glances at me over the frames makes him look both serious and unfairly attractive.

Meanwhile, I'm shoveling food into my mouth like I haven't eaten in a week. Not exactly glamorous, but it's not like he's thinking about me that way. And even if he did, we're colleagues, and he's a good decade older than me. That thought helps me relax—lets me be more of myself. No Hollywood persona, just Sophia.

Grant smirks, his dark brown eyes glinting with amusement. "Hungry?"

"Don't judge me."

"I would never."

His gaze lingers on me, and I find myself staring at his mouth. He has a beautiful mouth—soft, full, expressive, with those little lines at the corners when he smiles. I'm so distracted that I don't notice the smear of sauce on my lip until his brow quirks.

"You've got a little something," he says, motioning to his lip. I swipe at my mouth with my napkin, but he shakes his head. "Not quite."

Before I can react, he leans forward and brushes the pad of his thumb across the corner of my mouth. The touch is light, barely there, but it sets off a spark I didn't expect. My breath catches as his eyes meet mine, and for a moment, the space between us seems to vanish.

Then, just as quickly, he sits back, brushing his thumb against his napkin like it was nothing. "All clear," he says, his tone casual, but his gaze flicks away, betraying the tension.

"Thanks," I manage, trying to ignore the way my skin tingles where he touched me.

"Honestly? You were great this morning," he says, seamlessly steering the conversation back. "Natural. I've seen a lot of producers fumble through their first day, but you handled it like you've been doing it for years."

My stomach flips, and it's not because of the food. It's the way he says it—like he believes in me more than I do.

"Really?" I ask as heat rises to my cheeks. "I don't know

what I'd do without your guidance, though. This is a whole new ballgame for me. I can act all day, but producing?" I shake my head. "It's a lot."

When I started acting, I was enamored with the idea that I could transform into anything I wanted. I could pretend to be happy, sad, or angry. It was so fun to shift into a character who was a teen with psychic powers or a secret FBI hacker. The more I was around the magic of TV and movies, the more I learned about how it all came together.

In the beginning, someone handed me a script and told me where to stand, and then I played the part. It didn't take long before I thought about what I would've done in the script or how I would have blocked a scene. I shadowed some friendly directors and producers and realized I might enjoy creating movies as much as I enjoy starring in them.

When I signed with Blair, I told her it was a priority to expand my experience to behind the camera, and I can't believe she made it happen so quickly. Well, she and Grant.

"You're doing fine. And I'll be here if you need anything."

"I appreciate that more than you know. Is it wrong to admit that I'm nervous?"

"Not at all. If you want, I could...spend more time on set. You know, make sure things are running smoothly." The way he says it, it's almost like the words surprise him.

My brow furrows. "Seriously? You'd do that?"

He shrugs like it's no big deal, but there's a flicker of uncertainty in his expression. "Yeah, why not? I'm invested in this, too."

The quiet intensity in his voice tightens something in my

chest. I nod slowly. "Ok. I mean, having someone like you in my corner...it means a lot."

We lapse into a comfortable silence until I ask, "How's Hazel, by the way? It was great to meet her."

Grant's face softens, and for a moment, the weight he always seems to carry melts away. "She's great. Loves first grade. She's been obsessed with outer space lately. Says she wants to be an astronaut."

I laugh, picturing tiny Hazel in a spacesuit. "That's adorable. She's so full of life. You can tell she's the best thing that's ever happened to you."

"She is," he says quietly, almost to himself. Then he looks back at me, his gaze searching. "I didn't plan on being a dad. It just...happened. But I wouldn't change it for anything."

The love and quiet pride in his voice make my heart ache.

"She's lucky to have you," I say softly. "If you don't mind me asking, is she with you most of the time?"

Grant hesitates. His eyes meet mine, and then he sighs. "Yeah. Her mom, Geneva, and I...it was never serious. She's focused on her career, and I don't begrudge her for that. I try not to talk about it too much because people can be harsh when hearing that a woman wants to prioritize her career when she has a child."

He looks up at me to see if I'm one of those people. I don't know if I am. I can't imagine having a newborn baby placed in my arms and not being there for every milestone and experience. But at this age, I can't imagine giving up a career I love when I'm starting to see all my effort pay off. Geneva was my age when she gave birth, so I understand how she might have felt.

"I get that. It's a tough balance. She's lucky she had your support—in a variety of ways."

"It scared the hell out of me. Geneva moved in before Hazel was born and stayed through her maternity leave. That helped. We also hired a nanny, who's been with us ever since. She's incredible—practically family."

"That's smart. I hear nurse nannies are the way to go."

"Absolutely. Hazel adores her."

I want to ask how much Geneva sees Hazel, but it feels like Grant has already shared more than he planned.

"What about you?" he asks. "Do you want kids one day?"

"Oh, well...I don't know. Some days, the idea of a family seems nice. My parents were great—family vacations, holidays, all that. But I can't really see myself with a partner, so it's hard to imagine having kids."

"Technically, you don't need a partner."

"Just a nurse nanny, right?"

"Exactly," he says with a grin. "But for what it's worth, I think you'd make a great mom. The care and attention you've given this production is impressive."

"Thanks, Grant. I appreciate that."

We lapse into an easy silence, and I realize how natural it feels to talk to him. It's like we've known each other for years, even though we haven't.

I take another big bite, and Grant chuckles. "You're going to need a second lunch just to keep up with your appetite."

Grinning, I swallow. "What can I say? I'm working hard. Gotta fuel the machine."

He laughs and then takes a bite of his sandwich.

I pause, reaching out to touch his arm. "But seriously,

thanks for everything. I know you've got a million things on your plate."

He looks at where my hand rests on his arm and then back at me, his gaze steady. "Some things are worth making time for."

six

. . .

Grant

I'M STILL DISTRACTED on the drive home, just like I have been all afternoon. After my assistant, Emma, moved things around to accommodate my morning whimsy, I spent the rest of the day speeding through meetings so I could take a few moments to reflect on sitting next to Sophia during the table read and while we ate lunch.

I shouldn't be surprised at how easy it was to talk to her, considering there was an ease about her during some of our first interactions, but I guess I was skeptical. It's not often I'm interested in women on a deeper level.

Don't get me wrong; I care deeply about the talent in this town and the people I work with. Some of them are my closest friends and confidantes. But there is a very platonic aura in all of those settings. I was drawn to Sophia the first time we met—physically, emotionally, intellectually. That kind of trifecta never happens.

The vibration in my suit jacket shakes me from my daydream, and all my tension and worries disappear when the image of my daughter's ice-cream-covered lips stretched in a smile across her face appears on my display.

"Hey, nugget!"

"Hey, Dad. Can we go to the Space Center tonight and watch *Deep Sky*? My friend Charlie saw it this weekend and said it was awesome!"

"Oh, yeah? It definitely sounds like something we should see, but not on a school night."

"Oh, Dad, come on. Charlie keeps yapping about it and rubbing it in that he's seen it and nobody else has."

"Sorry, nug. You know the rules. How about we watch the trailer for it and see what we can find on the internet about it, and I'll get tickets for us to see it this weekend."

"Ok, fine. But I'm making you take me to the telescope exhibit while we're there."

She's only six and already bossing me around. I'm nervous about those teen years. I hide it the best that I can, but I'm already wrapped around her finger. If she had pushed harder, it's possible I would have caved and brought her tonight.

"Deal."

"You almost home?"

"About fifteen more minutes. What's for dinner?"

"Oh, Dad, you're gonna love it! I talked Josie into making sloppy joes!"

I can hear Josie telling Hazel to go wash her hands, and I remind Hazel to let Josie know she's welcome to eat with us before we end the call. I have a meal delivery service that we rely on most days, but Josie doesn't mind cooking with Hazel. She says it's good to teach her some kitchen basics, although the way she said it made me feel like she might be judging me a little. I can cook. A few things. Whatever. I'm good at other things.

I wonder if Sophia likes sloppy joes.

I shake my head because why does it matter? It's not like she's ever coming over to eat dinner with us. My house is my sacred space, so I try not to invite many people inside. I have a small guest home out back where I will invite a select few over for small gatherings, but we keep the festivities outside by the pool or in the open areas of the guest house.

I can hear the music coming from the kitchen when I walk in, and I creep quietly around the corner so I can catch the joy on Hazel's face. She is the light of my life, but some days, I worry if I'm enough for her. I'll give her anything she wants, but I can't give her that traditional mom experience. I tell myself she doesn't know any other way, so it's not a loss like it might be for someone who has experienced it and then lost it. Geneva has been great about staying in touch and visiting when she can, but I know Hazel wishes she were here more.

"Dad!"

Hazel runs and jumps into my arms with such force it pushes me back a step. There is nothing better in life than this little girl's arms wrapped around my neck. Her sweet scent of hand wipes mixed with strawberry shampoo and the soft waves of her hair brushing across my cheek trigger a feeling of love I never knew existed.

I smack my lips all over her face, drowning her in kisses, aiming for giggles that give me a quick dopamine hit.

"Alright, nugget, let's go eat!"

We have dinner outside since it's that time of year when the sun isn't beating down and trying to set you on fire and the recent time change allows us to still see each other.

"Ok, Dad. You first. Any struggles today?"

It's our dinner routine. Sharing our struggles and wins. I wanted Hazel to know that it's normal to have both. Some days, the struggles overtake the wins, and that is ok. It makes the wins feel that much better.

"Yes. Way too many meetings. So many I didn't even get an afternoon break and barely had time to go to the bathroom!" I lift my sandwich and dive into the messy meal. "You?"

"Charlie rubbing in the space movie. He mentioned it all day long. It was annoying."

"You're not jealous, are you?"

"No way! But I am kinda mad that he got to see it first."

"There's no prize for seeing it first, you know."

"I know. Ok, Josie, your turn."

I guess we're done with that conversation.

"My daughter had to postpone her visit again. I won't be able to see her until after her baby is born."

"You can hang out with me more if you want to, Josie."

"Oh, thank you, sweetheart. I'll definitely keep that in mind."

"Sorry to hear that, Josie. Everything ok?"

"Oh, yes, I'm so proud of her for following her dreams. I just wish they weren't halfway across the country and the ranch where she works did not control her schedule. A few mama cows will deliver over the next two weeks, and she wants to be there to make sure everything goes ok. By then, she'll be too far along in her own pregnancy to fly safely."

"Missy is going to help the cows have babies!"

"It sounds pretty exciting, but I can imagine how much you miss her. I can't imagine what my heart will feel like when Hazel follows her passion." Bursting and broken for sure.

"You cannot follow me to space, Dad. You have to be an astronaut."

The idea of Hazel in space makes me panic a little, but at the rate our world is changing, we may all be living up there by the time she's ready to visit.

"Yeah, Yeah. Josie, what's your win for the day?"

"Talking to Missy! Today, she FaceTimed to share the news, and I admit, it helped ease the disappointment!"

Hazel jumps off her chair and runs toward the house, yelling, "I'll be right back!"

She returns with a piece of paper and shoves it into my chest before climbing back into her seat.

"That's my win. I painted us hiking, and my teacher said I have natural abilities."

I can't hold back the smile as I look at her masterpiece. "I'll add it to my collection! I think this is going to be my win for the day."

"That's cheating, Dad. It has to be from your workday."

"Ok, then."

My mind drifts for a moment as I remember sitting next to Sophia at the table read, how my leg would brush against hers every time she moved to make notes.

"My win was getting to visit one of our sets today. You remember Miss Sophia?"

"The lady that looked like Cinderella at the red carpets?

I nod. "Today was the first day of production, and I was a guest speaker."

"Awesome. Is her movie about space?"

I laugh. "No, it's actually about a girl who has to move home to take care of her mom."

"That sounds boring."

"Well, it gets exciting when it rains and the mountain they live on turns into a mudslide disaster."

Hazel's mouth drops, and her eyes go wide, and I realize that the story sounds very tragic.

"She doesn't get hurt. She ends up being a hero when she helps evacuate everyone off the mountain."

"Is she a good hiker?"

"I'm not sure. But I'm sure the director will make sure she looks like she is."

"You should teach her how to hike. Maybe she could come with us one weekend."

The idea of that sends me into a panic, but it also excites me at the same time. At no point would I want a woman joining Hazel and me on our weekend hikes, but the idea of Sophia joining us sends a little buzz of electricity up my spine.

In fact, I get an even better idea.

I send off a note to my assistant, Emma, and ask her to book a scouting trip to Honey Pine Farms up in Santa Clarita. I just thought of a perfect location for the top of the mountain scene, and it involves a little hike to get to the top.

seven

. . .

Sophia

I'LL NEVER tire of driving through these gates. I wave to the security guard as he activates the barrier arm so I can drive onto the lot.

"Morning, Ms. Ford."

"Hi, Larry. Another beautiful day today!"

"You got that right. Make the most of it!"

There's a distinct energy on the lot. Stepping out of reality into a world of possibility—it's electric. I pull into my reserved spot at Stage Twenty-Six, and a smile stretches across my face when I see the name *PRODUCER* on the sign. It still feels surreal that Grant and Edie took a chance on me.

As I'm stepping out of my car, Edie pulls up, looking surprised to see me.

"What are you doing here? I thought you were headed up north today."

"I am," I say. "I just wanted to check in, make sure everything's set up for today, and see if you needed anything."

Edie quirks an eyebrow, a hint of approval in her expression. "Come look. You'll appreciate the setup—we've got the details nailed down, and I know how much you love the details."

Edie Lang is one of Hollywood's most formidable forces. Tiny but mighty, she's a sci-fi legend who started with coming-of-age films that shaped an entire generation. She's the director and screenwriter behind this project and one of the most intense perfectionists I've ever worked with. After leaving her former agency, TWA, she also signed with Blair at Tangerine Talent, becoming one of her first—and most high-profile—clients. Now I get the privilege of working alongside Edie on my first producing venture, a leap that feels a little less daunting with her by my side.

I follow her through the stage door, where the exteriors of a house set greet us. From the outside, it's all unfinished two-by-fours and plywood walls, but I know what's waiting behind that front door.

"Imagine you've just pulled into the driveway after a twelve-hour drive," Edie says, her voice low and measured. "You're exhausted. It's late. You want to see your mom, but you hope you don't. Not tonight. Hold on to that feeling when you step inside."

She pushes the door open slowly, and I peek my head around her to see inside.

"It's incredible," I whisper. No matter how many sets I work on, I'll never stop being in awe of what our designers create.

The interior looks like a rustic yet well-loved log cabin. Every detail feels lived in. The recliner in the corner with a draped blanket, the worn magazines on the end table, and the family photos on the walls. Through the opening to the kitchen, I glimpse a fridge and sink positioned under a window that seems to look out at a mountain view. It's exactly what the script described.

"It's perfect," I say. "Just like the script."

Edie smirks. "It fucking better be. I agonized over this. It had to feel worn down enough to show why she wanted to leave but cozy enough that she'd miss it."

"You're a genius," I say, pulling her into a quick hug. "I'm so lucky that I get to work with you!"

"Ok, ok, enough," she says, brushing me off. "Go check in with Grant before you're late for Honey Pine. If he gets us permission to shoot up there, this film will be unstoppable."

She's right. Shooting at Honey Pine is almost impossible, thanks to strict environmental regulations. But if anyone can make it happen, it's Grant Hall.

I leave Edie with a smile and cut through the backlot toward the executive offices on the backside of the property. My eyes linger on all the storefront façades, marveling at the special details and effects Hollywood puts in place to bring stories to life. I still pinch myself that this is my life.

As I near the offices, I spot Grant descending the stairs of the development offices next to his. The sight stops me in my tracks. His long strides carry him with an effortless confidence, and when he rakes a hand through his hair, his shirt pulls taut across his chest. It's unfair how good he looks. I've spent so much time imagining what's under those suits.

Less than a year ago, I only knew him by reputation—a powerful, unattainable figure. He's earned it for unearthing box office gold. But all I can think about right now is how much I'd like to unearth him.

"Hey, Sophia," Grant says, his smile lighting up his face as he approaches. "Wasn't expecting you yet."

His presence is magnetic, but I try to play it cool. "Stopped in early to check on Edie. The set looks amazing."

"I took a peek last night. It's fantastic." He gestures toward his bungalow. "Walk with me? I need to grab a change of clothes before we head out."

I follow him, excited to step inside the historic space. We walk inside, where his admin is set up in a cozy living-room-style setting complete with couches and chairs. She looks like part of the décor behind an inset credenza near a wall of glass that overlooks the backlot.

Down a long corridor, a door on the left opens to an office for Lucas, Grant's head of PR. Across from him is a door on the right that opens to a small private screening room, and next to it, at the end of the hall, a door opens to Grant's spacious office.

Entering Grant's office feels like stepping into Old Holly-wood, a mix of timeless elegance and modern comfort. A large conference table stands off to the left, with his desk tucked beyond it in a corner of windows. An overstuffed couch and two leather club chairs complete the comfort side of the space. There's a bathroom just beyond the living space that looks more like a spa. From here, I can already see a steam closet and what looks to be a jacuzzi tub.

"Make yourself at home," Grant says, pulling a shirt and shorts from a nearby closet. "Coffee's on the minibar. I'll just be a minute."

I grab a mug and pour myself a cup, but movement catches my eye. The bathroom door has drifted open, and through the gap, I see Grant in the mirror. He's pulling his shirt over his head, revealing a lean, defined chest. My heart races as he moves to adjust his shorts, but before I can look away, his eyes meet mine in the mirror.

I jump, nearly spilling my coffee, and spin away. "I-I was just... It was open, and I didn't mean to..."

Grant steps out, fully dressed, his smirk devastatingly casual. "It's ok, Sophia," he says, his voice low and teasing. "I'm sure it's nothing you haven't seen before."

Heat floods my cheeks, and I turn back to my coffee, willing myself to act like a normal, professional adult.

"Ready to go?" he asks, tugging his shirt into place, the flex of his arms not helping my resolve.

"Yep," I say, overly bright. "How many people can say they've seen Grant Hall in shorts?"

His knowing smile sends shivers down my spine. "Not many."

And just like that, we're out the door.

We head out to his Range Rover and start the drive up I-5 into the Santa Clarita Mountains, and thankfully, the conversation is easy.

"So, how was your first week as a producer?"

"It's been incredible. And thank you again for pulling whatever strings you have to get us clearance to check out Honey Pine as a potential location."

He shifts in almost a nervous way and adjusts the vents to direct the air on his body.

"Anything for the movie," he says under his breath. Then

he changes the subject. "I know the highlights of your career from our first lunch and your goals from our time putting together *Survivor*, but tell me the story of Sophia. How'd you get started in all this?"

I smile. It's the same story as anyone else, really, but that he wants to know it makes my heart flutter. I'm sure I'm over-reacting. I tend to read into every little thing and make it something more than it is.

"I auditioned for *Beauty and the Beast* in sixth grade and got the lead. I remember the seventh- and eighth-grade girls giving me the cold shoulder and talking behind my back, but I was too excited to care! The minute I got on that stage, I knew I never wanted to do anything else."

The memory brings a smile to my face.

"I was hooked. I auditioned for *Frozen* in seventh grade and, during spring break that year, convinced my mom to bring me down here for an open call on *The Disney Channel*. The ad was vague, inviting young actors between the ages of eight and sixteen to audition for a new live-action sitcom. No prior professional acting experience was necessary, and I just had to read a scene in front of a table of casting execs and producers."

"And you were, what, twelve or thirteen years old?"

"Yeah. Thankfully, I was too young and naïve to have any fear and just delusional enough to assume I'd be chosen."

"And you were."

"And I was."

"And that was for *Code Crusaders*, right?"

"Actually, it was for *Mind Reader*, a short-lived show about a teenage psychic." I laugh. "I know it was a completely corny show, but I learned so much about the business and acting. I had a fantastic director, and Disney accommodated an on-set school. I lived in a house with other teen actresses, and our mothers rotated staying with us, so it was like I had also inherited more family, too."

"That's amazing. Are you still close to everyone?"

"I'm closer with some from *Code Crusaders* since it was on the air longer." I shift nervously, not wanting to get too deep into specifics about that time in my life. "For others, it is sort of out of sight, out of mind. It's funny how it's such a small town but also a big place, too. There are a few I've never seen again."

"That's where you met Connor, right?" Grant says as he glances my way. The absolute last thing I want to talk about with him is how naïve I was to fall for Connor.

"Yes, he was my co-star in the last season, when my character was finally old enough to have a love interest."

"But you two dated in real life, too, right?"

"We did. It was short-lived, just while we were shooting."

"Well, I think that happens a lot. It must be easy to get caught up between the characters you play, the scenes you're in, and general proximity."

"Something like that."

I catch his head turning toward me from the corner of my eye as I try not to look at him.

"Sorry, I didn't mean to bring up any old feelings."

"Oh, no, you didn't. There's no old feelings. Unless still feeling foolish counts."

He's quiet but staring at the road with his eyebrows furrowed in confusion.

"Oh, you know, the age-old story of PR team curates relationship."

He nods in understanding. "I've had a few of those. They can be handy."

"I'm sure they are if you know they are happening to you."

He whips his head back to me so fast that I worry he's going to drive off the road. "What do you mean?"

"His team set it up with mine, but it seems my team forgot to tell me about it, and I guess he thought I knew it was all for show. Instead, I thought every bit was real—right up until he shook my hand at the wrap party." I pull my knees up and tuck my head into my hands, embarrassed to be baring my soul like this.

"What the fuck?"

"Yeah, that and what happened with my first boyfriend has pretty much set the tone for my views on dating."

"What happened with your first boyfriend?"

"Oh, that's another classic. Woo her until she gives in. Once he took my v-card, I never heard from him again."

"Jesus, Sophia. That is not at all what relationships are really like."

"Oh, really? And you know this how?" I'm teasing him—everyone knows he doesn't date, and he owns it unapologetically.

"I know how to treat a fucking woman, and it's not like that, whether you're dating seriously or not."

His voice is tight and laced with frustration, and his body language matches. His hand tightens on the steering wheel, his knuckles turning white as the veins on his forearms strain against his skin. His jaw is tense, his glare fixed on the road ahead, and the energy radiating off him is electric. My skin burns under the heat of his temper, and I can't ignore the way my body reacts.

I'm especially tingly around my lady bits. Angry Grant is hot.

"I'm sure that's true," I say, trying to sound casual despite the growing heat in the car. "But right now, I'm not willing to validate it. Besides, I'm focused on my career. I have no time for dating, much less any kind of relationship."

His grip on the steering wheel doesn't loosen, and his eyes remain locked on the road. "We've got about twenty more minutes, and then we should be there."

I guess that conversation is over.

"No rush. This is a beautiful drive. I've only been up this way a few times, and this will be my first time at Honey Pine Farms."

"You're going to love it. Hazel makes me drive her out to watch meteor showers. She tells me it's the only place you can see stars since LA has too many lights."

"She's got you there. I love that she's into all that science."

"Yeah, and all things space. She's determined to be the first woman to walk on the Moon or live on Mars—or both."

"I love that so much. She's amazing. If she has half the talent and instinct her dad does, I have no doubt she'll reach her goals."

He turns my way, and I see a flicker of pride and vulnerability in his eyes. Surely, he knows how amazing he is. That his daughter is only six years old and already plotting to make history as a woman says so much about what kind of father he is to her.

"Thanks. I hope so. We're here," he says, ending the conversation. He rolls down his window to chat with the security guard, and then we pass through the gates and make our way to the main cabin on the property.

"You ready to tour this land?" he asks.

"I'm all yours," I tell him, fully aware of the double meaning behind that statement.

eight

. . .

Grant

NO WONDER she doesn't date. She's only been with idiots. If she were mine, she'd know exactly how she should be treated.

I shake those thoughts from my head, but the more time I spend with Sophia, the harder it gets. Thank God we've arrived because I need a break from being this close to her. Her sweet scent reminds me of summer, which makes me think about her in those shorts and that tank top, or more accurately, how they'd look crumpled on my floorboards right now.

Talking to her feels easy, natural, which somehow makes me antsy. Usually, I don't feel anything for women—not beyond physical pleasure and the satisfaction of no strings attached. This...feeling...is new. Unwelcome.

I've been accused of being cold or emotionless before, but those accusations usually come from women who don't believe me when I tell them upfront I'm not interested in a relationship. I never lie about what I can offer—casual, uncomplicated fun. They always say they're fine with it, but they fool themselves into thinking they'll be different, that they'll break through and make me fall in love. When I don't, they call me cold. But I've never played games. I've always been truthful. That's just who I am.

Sophia, though, makes me wonder if I've been wrong all this time. Could she break me? Could she be the exception?

"This way." My voice comes out rough, and I clear my throat. "We'll walk through the frontier set. That leads back to the trail for our hike."

She steps ahead, and I immediately regret letting her take the lead. I hadn't gotten a good look at her outfit earlier, but now...now I'm getting the full picture. Black athletic shorts. A hot pink tank top clinging to her curves like it's painted on. Sensible Brooks sneakers. She's not trying to impress me— she's practical, grounded—and that somehow makes her even hotter. My mind wanders to dangerous places. I have to force myself to focus.

"How many sets are up here?" she asks, glancing back at me.

"There's the western town, a suburban neighborhood, and a campground with cabins. Those are fully built out—you can actually stay in them."

"Amazing. It's gorgeous up here."

She takes in the scenery with wide-eyed wonder, and I can't help but admire her. Most people in this business get jaded, but she's not. She still sees the magic, the possibility. It's refreshing.

"So, Grant," she says, breaking the silence, "I know you grew up in New York. How'd you end up in LA?"

"It's a story as old as time. A boy sees a movie he loves and decides right then to make movies. The rest is history."

"What movie?"

"I knew you were going to ask that."

"Of course! You set me up for it."

I laugh at her exaggerated irritation. She's trying to look annoyed, but that smile on her face gives her away.

"You can't judge me."

"I'd never."

"*The Breakfast Club.*"

She stops, whipping her head toward me, her jaw dropping.

"I said you can't judge me," I remind her.

"I'm not! I mean—were you even born when that came out?"

"You flatter me," I say with a smirk. "But no, it came out a few years before my life began. Caught it during a sleepover at a buddy's house. His older sister was having a slumber party movie night, and we crashed it."

"Cute."

"Something like that."

"I have to know, why was that movie the one?"

"I understood it. I felt that it was written for me. Even though I was younger than the characters, the storytelling was so authentic. It was real life. I wanted to tell stories about real life so other kids like me felt seen, understood."

I don't tell her the rest of the story—how that night changed everything for me, why I went to NYU, why I ended up in LA.

I don't want to bring the mood down, so I keep the details

about my dad dying that same night to myself. I spent the evening watching teenage girls swoon over the story on the screen, believing love was the answer to all their problems. It reminded me of my parents—how in love they were, how unstoppable they seemed together. They were an unlikely duo from different parts of society, but with a connection like no other—and undeniably meant to be.

The next morning, I went home, and my world shattered. Love didn't save anyone. Love destroyed my family. It stole the strongest woman I knew and left her a shadow of herself. Love is not a risk worth taking. I'll pass.

"Where'd you go?" Sophia's voice pulls me out of my thoughts.

"Nowhere," I lie. "Just thinking how long ago that was."

"How old were you?"

"Eleven."

Her lips press into a frown, and her eyes soften.

"What?"

"I don't think I was even born yet."

"Jesus. Way to make me feel ancient," I joke, shaking off the heaviness.

"Will you be able to make it up this hill, old man?"

"Ha, ha. Just go."

I gesture for her to lead the way again, but it's a mistake. Watching her climb the incline in those shorts is like torture. Her thighs flex, smooth and endless, and I have to force myself to focus on anything else. With every step, they taunt and tease the possibility of seeing more.

I take a deep breath and send a message along with the blood that seems to rush to my dick to chill the fuck out. This is a professional work trip, for Christ's sake. I must have grunted out loud because Sophia turns to look over her shoulder and ask if I'm alright. No, Sophia, I'm popping a boner at the thought I might catch a glimpse of that perfect peach with every step up you take.

Throughout our hike, her arm brushes against mine, or her hip grazes my leg, and these little touches are driving me insane. It's like she has no idea how much she's touching me and how crazy it's driving me.

We crest the hill, and the view is breathtaking—a perfect stand-in for a mountain town. Sophia stops abruptly, laughing as she takes it in.

"It's so beautiful, I think I just had a joygasm."

"What?"

Before I can process what she just said, she stumbles. Instinct kicks in, and I grab her by the waist, steadying her. Now she's straddling my knee, with her ass pressed against my cock.

"Careful," I murmur, stepping back quickly. "I've got you."

I steady her and then remove my hand, doing my best to pretend what just happened is completely normal and not awkward at all.

"Thanks," she says. Her cheeks flush, and she straightens her tank top, avoiding my gaze.

"Sorry about grabbing you; my dad instincts kicked in," I say, trying to lighten the mood a bit.

"Good thing. Thank you," she says, finally looking back over her shoulder at me. "It really is beautiful up here."

I point out a few places where I think we can create the scenes in which her character plays the role of a stubborn daughter who refuses to leave her home despite a mandatory evacuation and where she'll end up helping firefighters place sandbags to divert the flooding and fend off mudslides. It's also where she'll fall in love with one particular firefighter and...well, I won't spoil it for you.

As we head down the mountain, back toward the western sets, Sophia reaches out and holds on to me so she doesn't stumble again, and a whole host of feelings spreads through my body—mostly how I'd be happy to rescue her from this mountain, carry her over my shoulder like the firefighter she'll fall in love with, and find a soft place to lay her down and worship her.

nine

Sophia

I CAN'T STOP THINKING about his hands on my waist, backing into him, a certain piece of anatomy pressed against my lower back so briefly that I'm not sure if I imagined it or if it really is as big as I think. I cross my legs, uncomfortable in the front seat of his car, so turned on by the idea of Grant with his hands on me.

His eyes wandered over my body more than once, and I may not be as experienced as he is, but I know the look of desire. I shake my head and turn to watch the scenery pass by us on the highway. I need to get this little crush on Grant under control. He's been nothing but a gentleman since the day we met.

I'll never forget the *Pink Slip* premiere and how his undivided attention made me feel like we were on a date. It didn't hurt that Wyatt and Blair got caught up in long bathroom lines—or so they said. Whatever their excuse, it forced Grant and I to hang out while we waited for them. I've never had anyone so genuinely interested in me.

Don't get me wrong—everyone is interested. But it's *actress Sophia* they want to know about. What I'm wearing, dating rumors, on-set stories, all the misogynistic questions about marriage and kids. Grant spent time asking me about *me*. My hobbies. How it felt to win the Oscar. He wanted to know if I was hungry or needed a drink. Nobody cares if I'm fed or hydrated—*ever*! But all evening, he kept me close. His soft touches on my back, his fingers brushing mine when he handed me my drink, and the way he stood just behind or beside me felt...possessive. Like I was his.

We'd only spent time together three or four times before starting this production, but each moment had left an impression. At first, I was a little heartbroken to learn he had a daughter. Not because of Hazel—she's incredible—but because he didn't share that with me at first. A sting of jealousy crept in when I wondered if there was someone else in his life.

But that jealousy faded the moment I saw Hazel's photos on his desk. Her gap-toothed smile lit up the frame, and the way Grant spoke about her—so animated, so full of pride—showed how deeply he loves her. Meeting Hazel made it even clearer why she's his everything. She's smart, funny, and kind, and it's obvious she adores her dad just as much as he adores her. Knowing that side of Grant only makes me admire him more.

"You're awfully quiet over there," Grant says, pulling me out of my daydream about him.

"All the ideas are flowing."

"I thought you might like it."

We spend the next hour discussing ways to adjust the

production schedule. It'll be chaotic, but Grant's willingness to shuffle the budget makes me feel like we can make it work. I'll work with Edie on the script changes and sets, whatever it takes.

My phone buzzes, and my assistant's name flashes across the screen. She rarely calls, which makes my stomach tighten.

"Sorry. I need to take this." I bring the phone to my ear. "Hey, Jamie. Everything ok?"

"Sorry to bother you, Sophia, but there's a problem at your house," she says, her voice tense. "Any chance you are close by? I'm down in San Diego today, so I can't run by to check it out."

"Um, I think we are about fifteen minutes away. Grant and I are just getting back into town. What's going on?"

"Your house flooded. The fire department's there. They need someone to check it out."

"What? Flooded? How bad?"

"I don't know the details, but I called as soon as I hung up with the studio. Your neighbor called the fire department, then the studio. The studio called me."

"I'll head there now. Thanks, Jamie."

As I hang up, panic claws its way up my chest. What if everything is ruined?

"Everything ok?" Grant's voice is gentle, his concern clear.

"I don't know," I admit. "My house flooded. The fire department's there."

"Let's go. We'll figure it out."

When we turn onto my street, my worst fears feel real. A trail of water snakes along the curb, reflecting the late afternoon sun like some cruel spotlight.

I sit up straighter in my seat, and my breath catches when the gate leading to my driveway comes into view—wide open, likely opened by the fire department. My house sits a little further back from the street, surrounded by a low security fence and lush hedges that usually make it feel private.

"Oh, no," I whisper, gripping the center console.

The scene grows worse as we approach my driveway. Firetrucks and a plumbing van haphazardly block the street and my yard. Several firefighters are milling around the lawn. But it's not just the vehicles that make my heart sink—it's the sight of my furniture.

Half of it is scattered across the front yard. My plush armchairs, my vintage coffee table, even the rug I spent months searching for—it's all out there.

"What the hell happened?" Grant mutters beside me.

I step out, my legs shaky beneath me, and head toward the group of firefighters near my porch. Grant stays close, and his steady presence grounds me.

"Hello, I'm Sophia, the homeowner. Can someone tell me what's going on?" I ask, my voice trembling.

The fire chief steps forward. "Miss, it appears the upstairs bathroom has been leaking for some time. Water has been collecting between the floor and ceiling, and it finally gave out. I'm afraid most of the bathroom is now in your kitchen."

His words hit me like a punch to the gut. My eyes widen as I step inside. Pieces of my tub sit on my breakfast table, now half-collapsed. Chunks of the ceiling cover the counters, and water pools at my feet. The scene is surreal, like a nightmare I can't wake from.

Tears sting my eyes as I take it all in, and my arms wrap

around my middle as I try to hold myself together. This was my first real home, something I owned, invested in, made mine, and now it's destroyed.

Grant's hands settle gently on my shoulders. "Hey. We'll figure this out," he says softly.

I glance back at him, my tears threatening to spill. "I don't know what to do."

"Well, for starters, you can't stay here," the fire chief interjects. "I'm going to guess there is probably going to be mold, and this being an old house, there's a good chance of asbestos. You'll need to get water remediation in here and an adjuster to do a thorough inspection, and they can tell you what kind of damage and repairs you're facing."

I think I'm in shock.

Grant steps in and speaks to the fire chief and plumber, arranging for cleanup crews and an adjuster. Meanwhile, I sit in his car, staring blankly at my phone, trying to figure out where I'll stay tonight. The thought of dealing with more decisions feels impossible.

When Grant climbs back into the car, his determined expression softens as he looks at me. "I called someone to manage the logistics. They'll keep you updated."

"Thanks, Grant."

"I'm so sorry, Sophia. I know this is a lot, but the good news is that it's all fixable. Inconvenient, but fixable."

He's right. The destruction didn't hurt anyone, and although it damaged some of my favorite things, I don't seem to have lost anything sentimental. I can't go upstairs to grab anything until an engineer looks at the stability of the second floor, so I'm stuck in these clothes for the foreseeable future.

I'll raid wardrobe back at the studio until I can get into my closet here.

"I have a guest house," he says, his tone casual. "You're welcome to crash there for a few days. It's off to the side of my house and totally private. The driveway is shared, but other than that, you'd have the place to yourself."

I glance at him and catch the way his jaw tightens slightly, as if he surprised himself by making the offer. His fingers grip the steering wheel just a bit too hard, and there's something in his expression—hesitation? Uncertainty? It's not that he doesn't mean it, but I can sense he's not entirely sure he should have said it out loud.

"Oh, um, I can just grab a hotel. It's no big deal," I say, giving him an easy out.

He just nods and drives through the studio gates. I direct him to where my car is parked, and as I'm about to step out, he stops me.

"Soph," he says, his tone softening, "my house is literally right over there." He points toward Toluca Lake, the quiet neighborhood just past the studio.

"And you drive to work?" I tease, raising a brow, trying to deflect.

He chuckles and shakes his head. "Yes, I drive. And you're avoiding my offer."

Am I avoiding it? Or am I avoiding the idea of being so close to him? The thought of staying at Grant's house—or his guest house—sends a shiver of something I can't quite name up my spine. Excitement? Nerves? Both? Would we talk? Would I see him in passing? Would he *want* to see me?

"I can ask Blair and Wyatt if I can crash with them," I say, grasping for a safer alternative.

"You want to stay with a couple who are about to get married and just reconnected after twelve years apart?" His smirk tells me he knows exactly how terrible that idea is.

He's right. The last thing I need is to sit in the middle of Blair and Wyatt's rom-com montage.

"Are you sure?" I ask, needing to hear it again. I search his expression for any sign of reluctance.

"I'm sure, Sophia. You're welcome to stay as long as you need. There's food and toiletries already there, but I'll have the housekeeper stock up the kitchen. You'll be all set."

I hesitate, still watching him. There's no trace of pity in his voice, no sign that this is just an obligation. If anything, he seems...earnest, like he genuinely wants to help.

I nod slowly. "If you're sure?"

"I'm sure," he repeats firmly. "You can follow me home."

Home. There's something nice about how the word sounds coming from him. Warm. Solid. It stirs something in me.

I need to be careful. I'm an excellent actress, and sometimes, it's hard to separate reality from the roles I play. Acting. Delusion. Sometimes, they cross over and blur the lines.

"Ok, thanks, Grant. Give me a minute to run inside and grab some clothes from wardrobe. I'll be right out."

He nods, and as I climb out of his car, I feel his eyes on me—not in the way most people look at me, but in a way that makes me feel seen. I shiver again, this time from the chill in the air—and maybe a little from the warmth in his gaze.

ten

. . .

Grant

WHAT THE FUCK? Why the hell would I put myself in this torture situation? I instantly regret offering her the guest house. What was I thinking?

It's fine. Once we find out what the damage and repairs are, she can figure out a longer-term solution. This is just a few days; it's not a big deal. Except it is a big deal.

Fuck. What am I going to tell Hazel? She already loves Sophia. I caught her binging her old *Code Crusaders* episodes the other night. Hazel's only met her one time, but I can tell she is going to be all over this. It will be hard to keep her away.

I don't love having my lives intermixing, and I'm not sure what came over me or why I would suggest my guest house. Something crunched in my chest when I saw Sophia standing in her house. The look of hopelessness, the look of sadness. My hero instincts kicked in, and all I wanted to do was wrap her up in my arms and tell her everything would be ok and I would take care of her. Apparently, that's exactly what I did. God dammit.

I don't like how she makes me feel. I don't like that she makes me question my loneliness. I've spent thirty-six years of my life just fine without needing anyone. And then I see her tears, and I abandon all logic and sense.

I got carried away when we met last year at the *Pink Slip* premiere. I knew of her—hell, everyone in town knows of her —but I'd never met her in person. Blair introduced us, and I'd never seen anyone so beautiful before. Her skin is like porcelain, so soft and smooth and creamy. I've never had such an itch to touch someone's face before, but it's all I could think about. I wanted to brush my fingers across her cheek and then run them through that dark brown hair.

She hypnotizes you with those ice-blue eyes, and I assumed that her kindness and empathy were part of her brand, but I realized quickly that she had saved those bits for me. I'm not saying she was rude to anyone, but when we found ourselves abandoned by her brother, Wyatt, and Blair, I could see how she greeted others we ran into, and I could feel the difference in how we interacted versus how she interacts with the population at large. I felt something...special? I'm not sure what.

I begged Blair to go to lunch with me after that event so I could find out more about Sophia. Word on the street was Blair was out to sign her, and I'd always had a great working relationship with Blair and wanted to know more.

I won't lie and say that her personality or talent alone attracted me; she is undeniably gorgeous. Her beauty is untouchable. No man alive deserves her. But I also wanted to see if it might be possible to work with her.

She was an Oscar-winning actress at the age of twenty-four and came straight from a kid's television network—not unheard of, but it's definitely unusual, which tells me she's got that special something. When Blair brought Sophia along for lunch, I spent the entire time talking with Sophia and felt bad that I didn't even ask Blair about one project she was working on.

I invited her to my Hampton's party, and it was then that I knew I was in trouble. Right then, I should have put these feelings in check and locked them down. It was my intention, in fact. Come to the party, meet the people. It would be good to have her as part of my network. But then she sat down next to me, and I spent the rest of the night with my eyes on her. If Hazel hadn't been upstairs, I'm sure I would have asked Sophia to stay over.

Since then, I've tried to get back on the track of a professional relationship. That's one reason I wanted this project. I figured if we were working together, it would shift us into that friendly but strictly professional zone, but now all I do is find excuses to be part of the production meetings when I have no reason to.

I'm not sure what kind of hold she has on me, but I need to get it in check. Maybe I just need to get laid. She's not the one-night-stand type. At least, I don't think she is. She's always escorted by her brother, and the only man I've seen her connected with is that douchebag Connor. She's been pretty busy with work, so I understand how hard it is to date. It's one reason I don't.

First, I'm not boyfriend material. I've known for a long time that kids and marriage would not be part of my world. And while Hazel was the shock of my life and also the best thing that ever happened to me, I don't believe it would ever work that way with a partner.

Hazel has to like me. I'm basically all she's ever known. I raised her from the beginning of life, so her beliefs are my beliefs. Well, mostly. She is starting to exert her indepen-dence. But it's different when it's your own flesh and blood. The wildcard is when you bring someone else into the mix. They can change their mind or leave. How can you ever really know someone if you didn't raise them or grow up with them?

Maybe, when I get home, I'll flip through some contacts and get out of the house tonight. I just need some fun time to get my head shifted from the gorgeous doll following me to my house and relieve some of this sexual tension bottled up inside me. I'll be fine with a release with someone, anyone, at this point.

I pull into my driveway and wait until she pulls up next to me before I get out of the car. I'm compelled to go open her door for her, but I restrain myself. It's shit like that that I need to stop doing. I need to stop caring about her like she's mine and like she belongs to me.

"Your house is beautiful," she says as she crawls out of a Range Rover of her own. Look at us, in matching cars. Her eyes take in the mid-century, split-level home. It's a point of pride for me because it belonged to Frank Sinatra at one point.

"Thank you. I've tried to keep as much of it original as I

can. Shall we?" I motion toward the small square building to my left, where she'll be staying. You have to walk through the driveway gates to get into the backyard, where the entry to the small bungalow is accessible.

"Dad! Come look at how long I can hold my breath!" Hazel yells as soon as we click the gate closed, and I turn to see her in the pool. My sister sits on a nearby lounger, with one eye on my kiddo and another on her book of the week.

Hazel immediately dunks underwater, and Sophia and I walk over to the edge of the pool right as she resurfaces.

"Did you see? I was under there for so long!"

"I did see, nugget. Impressive!"

"Very impressive, Hazel. It was a whole 22.3 seconds long. Is that a record for you?" Sophia bends down to get closer to my daughter, and I'm stunned she was timing the event.

"I don't know. I've never timed it before, but I say the alphabet, and I can get all the way through the song now."

"Sounds like a record to me!" Sophia tells her, and I watch as Hazel's face lights up at the attention and acknowl-edgment.

"What are you doing here?"

"Hazel, don't be rude."

"That wasn't rude, Dad. I was asking a question."

"Yeah, Dad, she was just asking a question. Hi again, Sophia. I'm Sarah, Grant's sister. We met at the Oscars." My sister joins us, and Sophia stands back up to shake her hand.

"Yes, of course. Nice to see you again."

Sarah gives me a glance with a raised eyebrow, and I roll

my eyes. Thankfully, Sophia is talking to Hazel again, so she misses the interaction.

Hazel is asking if Sophia came over to swim, and all that does is force my imagination into wondering if she would wear a bikini or a one-piece. Either way, more of her skin showing would be sexy as fuck, but a tiny string bikini top to cover those small, perfect tits would be something I'd pay to see. Wait. That's not what I meant. Fuck, I'm finding someone to meet up with tonight. It's imperative.

"Sophia is going to stay in the guest house for a few days. Her house had an accident, and she can't stay there right now," I tell Hazel and my sister, since she seems extra invested in this anomaly of another woman in my backyard and talking to my daughter.

That's the other thing. I never, ever introduce women to my daughter. I mean, other than a casual "Honey, meet this person I work with" type of introduction. No women come to this house; no dates or flings are ever within restraining-order distance of my daughter. Nothing relationship-like exists in my life with Hazel, and I'll never budge on that.

Except now, I guess. But technically, Sophia is a co-worker, no matter what my sister's eyebrows say to me.

"My whole bathroom upstairs fell through the ceiling right into my kitchen," Sophia explains.

"Why?" Hazel asks.

"Seems there was some kind of a leak upstairs. I'm not sure. I'm waiting to get more details about the whole thing."

"Ok, well, my room isn't big enough for two people to stay, so you'll have to sleep with my dad."

I nearly choke on my spit as my sister bends over, roaring with laughter. Sophia looks up as a giggle escapes her lips.

"Hazel, Sophia will stay in the guest house. She's not staying with us in our house."

"Why? She might get lonely out there," Hazel replies. Then she whispers to Sophia, "The bungalow is kind of creepy, and it smells like chlorine."

Sophia reassures Hazel that she'll be fine in the bungalow and promises to come inside the house if she does get scared.

I break up the conversation before it gets any more awkward and walk Sophia over to the entry of sliding panel doors. It doubles as a pool house—hence the chlorine smell—and I replaced the regular entry for more of an indoor-outdoor living experience. I'll have to show her how to use the curtains because she'll definitely be exposed with all this glass. She's only facing my house, but that's precisely why I'll need her to use those curtains.

There's not much to show her. When you walk in, the dining-kitchen space is over to your right, and the living-bedroom space is over to your left. The coolest thing about this little hut is the oversized bathroom. It's nestled between the living and dining space and boasts heated tile floors, a huge soaking tub, a separate shower, and a little sauna off to the side. I even put in a little loveseat so you could sit down while you dry off.

"It's about seven hundred square feet, and while I don't have many guests stay here, I use it quite a bit to entertain. It's a great space to watch games and hold snacks when people come over to swim." I try to keep my tone casual and professional, though my mind keeps circling back to the fact that

Sophia Ford is about to be sleeping less than a hundred yards from my bedroom.

"This is really nice, Grant. It looks so cozy. Thank you again. You're saving my life right now." Her smile does something to my chest that I'm not ready to examine too closely.

"I hope you'll be comfortable, and it's all yours. Stay as long as you need."

I walk over to the kitchen and open a few cabinets to show her where everything is, telling her that our housekeeper can stock the pantry and fridge with whatever she likes. I'm already making mental notes to have Josie pick up those fancy oat milk lattes I've seen Sophia drinking on set.

"Oh, don't worry about it. I'll only be a night or two, max."

Something in her casual tone makes me pause. A night or two? I force my expression to remain neutral, though my jaw clenches involuntarily.

"You should have everything you need, but if you don't, I'm sure we have it in the main house." The words come out a bit more clipped than I intended. Is she already planning to stay somewhere else? With someone else? The thought of her leaving here to meet someone else makes my stomach turn.

Not that it's any of my business. She's talent. I'm a studio executive. This is just a professional courtesy, nothing more—even if the sight of her standing in my guest house, bathed in the soft evening light, makes me want to tell her she can stay forever.

She's looking through the pantry when I see her stop and pick up a box of Slim Jims. She turns to me.

"I love these."

"I know."

"Thanks," she whispers, and for a moment, I think I catch something in her eyes—uncertainty? Anticipation?—before she looks away. "This is...this is really kind of you."

I should leave. I should absolutely walk out that door and maintain appropriate, professional boundaries.

I don't realize how close I've gotten to her until I feel her hair brush the side of my face and I close my eyes and breathe in her sweet summer scent.

I feel her move, and when I look down at her, a moment passes between us. Her eyes are taking in every feature on my face. I see her look from my eyes to my nose to my lips, and then her gaze lingers there before going back up to my eyes. My hand is still resting on the shelf to her side, where I've replaced the box of snacks, and I move to push a piece of hair behind her ear. Why am I doing that? I have no fucking idea, but I want to touch her. I want to put my lips on hers. She shifts closer, and her hands rise, but I can tell she's not sure where to put them, so they fall back to her side.

"Time to eat!" Hazel screams, breaking the moment between us, and I step away quickly and turn to leave the pantry space. "Come on, Dad. Come on, Sophia. It's taco night! Aunt Sarah made the combo for us—chicken, steak, and shrimp!"

"Oh, I'll be ok," Sophia says. "There's plenty here if I get hungry. I should really start figuring out what I'm going to do for housing longer term and call the adjuster. And I want to look through all the pics we took today."

The trip to Honey Pine Farms seems like ages ago. So much has happened since then.

"Might as well eat with us since everything is ready," I tell her. "And the offer stands. You're welcome to stay for as long as you need. No pressure, but...there's no need to rush off to other arrangements."

I try to keep my tone light, but I know some of my feelings must show through because her eyes snap back to mine, widening slightly.

"I..." she starts, then stops, seeming to wrestle with something. "Thank you," she finally says. "I'll...keep that in mind."

I nod and force myself to head for the door before I say something I shouldn't. Something about how I'd rather know she's safe here than wondering where—or with whom—she spends her nights. Something about how the thought of her leaving makes me feel slightly insane.

Before she can change her mind, Hazel grabs her hand and leads her to our house, where no other woman has gone before.

eleven

. . .

Sophia

I JOLT AWAKE. Shadows flicker across an unfamiliar ceiling, and panic grips my chest for a split second before memories of last night race in. The flood. Grant's offer. The guest house.

Grant's guest house.

I groan and pull the duvet over my head, but even the expensive Egyptian cotton can't smother the butterflies that take off in my stomach at the thought of him. Of his gentle insistence that I stay. Of the way his hand tucked my hair behind my ear when he was showing me around the kitchen.

"Get it together," I mutter into the pillow. "It's just temporary. Just a studio exec helping out talent."

A studio exec who somehow manages to look devastatingly handsome even during rushed production meetings. Who has a way of making everyone—even the greenest PA—feel seen and heard.

A soft knock at the door makes me freeze. I wait, holding my breath, until I hear retreating footsteps. Padding over, I peek out. On the doorstep sits a steaming cup of coffee. My heart flips as I pick it up and inhale the rich aroma. There's a sticky note attached: *Thought you might need this. Have a great day on set. – G.*

I smile, biting my lip, until my phone buzzes. It's a text from Brandon.

BRANDON

Girl, you never called me back last night. Everything ok with the flood situation?

I stare at the screen for a long moment before typing.

ME

Staying at Grant Hall's guest house. HELP.

His response is immediate.

BRANDON

WHAT??? Can you meet me at the studio? I'm at Stage 18 today for a commercial shoot. YOU OWE ME DETAILS.

"You're living in his guest house?" Brandon's voice booms across his makeshift green room tent as I step inside. I frantically shush him, glancing around the space.

I met Brandon Grimaldi years ago when I was still finding my footing in the industry. I was young, eager, and completely out of my depth on a physically demanding set, and Brandon—already a rising star in the stunt world—had swooped in like a real-life action hero, showing me how to take a fall without bruising more than my ego. What started as him giving me a few survival tips quickly turned into an unshakable friendship. He became my mentor, my partner in crime, and another big brother to me.

He also grew up surrounded by women—six sisters, to be exact—so, while he's all man, he's also completely at ease in a room full of women. The honorary girlfriend who knows the best shade of lipstick, who will hold your purse without complaint, and who somehow ends up in the middle of gossip sessions like he belongs there. But make no mistake—he's a notorious flirt, charming his way through an ever-revolving door of casual dates, never staying too long, never letting anything get too serious.

"Sorry, sorry," he whispers, motioning for me to join him on the chairs set up. "But seriously, Grant Hall. *The* Grant Hall. The guy whose mere presence on set makes you flub your lines?"

"It's not like that," I protest weakly, clutching the coffee Grant left me. "He was just being nice. You know how he is—he probably would've offered it to anyone on our cast and crew if they needed it."

Brandon arches an eyebrow. "Honey, he's the head of the studio. He could've had his assistant book you the presidential suite at the Four Seasons. Instead, he personally offered you his *guest house*. Try again."

"It's just temporary," I insist, warming my hands around the cup. "A few days, maybe a week tops, until the restoration company sorts everything out. And it's not like I'll see him much. Unless we cross paths here at work."

"Uh-huh." Brandon's knowing smile makes me want to

crawl under the nearby makeup table. "And how did you sleep last night?"

"Terrible," I admit. "The bed was amazing, but..." I trail off, remembering how I lay awake for hours, hyper-aware that Grant was just a hundred yards away in the main house, wondering if he was awake, too, and if he was thinking about me being there. "It's just weird, you know? Yesterday morning, I left my house for a scouting trip with Grant. Now I'm living in his guest house like the plot of some cliché romance novel."

"Maybe it is," Brandon says bluntly. "Sometimes, the best stories write themselves."

"I just need to stay focused. Keep things professional. Get through this without making a fool of myself."

Brandon squeezes my shoulder. "Or maybe, just maybe, you could let yourself see where this goes? The universe literally flooded you onto his doorstep, Soph. Even Edie would say that's a sign—and you *know* how she feels about improvising."

A voice calls out and makes us both jump. "Taping in five minutes," a PA calls out.

I swear Brandon to secrecy about my living situation as I stand and straighten my shoulders, preparing to pretend my world hasn't shifted on its axis.

The sun is setting as I make my way past the driveway gate toward the guesthouse, my mind still running through today's shot list. We're right on schedule, and if we can get approval to shoot at Honey Pine—

"Sophia!"

A blur of motion is all the warning I get before Hazel crashes into me, her arms wrapping tight around my hips. The force of her enthusiasm makes me stumble back a step, and I laugh.

"You're home!" She beams up at me, and my heart does a funny little flip at her choice of words. Home. I glance instinctively toward the main house, where Grant is watching us from the patio. Instead of the awkward tension I half-expected, there's something soft in his expression that makes my chest tight.

"Perfect timing," Hazel declares, grabbing my hand. "It's pasta night. You have to stay! It's all he knows how to make." She whispers that last part, and I pull my lips together so a laugh doesn't escape.

I lift my eyes to find Grant again. The last thing I want is to intrude on their time together, but he's already pulling out another chair.

"Come on," he says, that polished smile of his making an appearance. "You've got to eat, right?"

"Well, when you put it that way..." I let Hazel pull me toward the table. The patio is strung with lights that cast everything in a warm glow, and the smell of tomato sauce and garlic bread makes my stomach growl embarrassingly loudly.

"Someone skipped lunch," Grant observes, sliding a plate in front of me.

"I neither confirm nor deny these allegations." I reach for

a slice of bread still warm from the oven. "Though I will say craft services was seriously lacking today."

"Dad never skips lunch," Hazel informs me solemnly. "He says it makes him hangry."

"Hangry?" I raise an eyebrow at Grant, who's suddenly very focused on twirling pasta around his fork.

"I have no idea what she's talking about," he says with dignity. "I am a perfect professional at all times."

The banter flows easily as we eat. Hazel bounces between topics with the delightful randomness of a six-year-old as she tells me all about the working volcano her class is building for the school's science fair and how her best friend Hannah just got a new golden retriever puppy named Pancake.

"Ok," Hazel announces when we're mostly finished eating. "Time for struggles and wins!"

"Struggles and wins?" I ask.

"It's our thing," she explains. "Every night at dinner, we each share one struggle from our day and one win. Even if it was a terrible day, you have to find one win. And even if it was a great day, you have to admit one struggle." She sits up straighter. "Want to play?"

I catch Grant watching me with something unreadable in his eyes. "I'd love to," I say softly.

"I'll go first!" Hazel clears her throat dramatically. "My struggle was that Charlie said my volcano ideas were boring, but my win was that our teacher said my design plans were really creative and different from the usual volcano projects."

"That is a win," Grant agrees. "And Charlie sounds like he might be a little jealous of your ideas."

"Your turn, Dad!"

Grant leans back in his chair, considering. "My struggle was having to push back some marketing meetings because we're behind on getting approval for the promotional materials." His eyes meet mine briefly. "My win was getting to see some really incredible dailies from Sophia's movie today."

The warmth that spreads through my chest has nothing to do with the yummy pasta and everything to do with the way he's looking at me. I duck my head, suddenly fascinated by my napkin.

"Sophia?" Hazel prompts.

"Ok, let's see..." I take a breath. "My struggle was feeling like we weren't getting anywhere with this one particular scene today. We must have shot it fifteen times, and it still didn't feel right."

I don't mention that it was a romantic scene with James or that, for some reason, I kept imagining someone else in his place.

"My win was..." I look around the table at the twinkling lights, empty plates, and these two people who've somehow made me feel so welcome. "My win was this. Right here. Coming home to..." I stumble slightly over the word. "To such a lovely dinner invitation."

The silence that follows feels charged. Hazel breaks it by launching into a detailed explanation of proper volcano construction techniques, but I can feel Grant's eyes on me. When I finally look up, the intensity in his gaze makes my breath catch.

Later, after Hazel has gone inside to finish her homework, I help Grant clear the table. We move around each other with an ease that feels dangerous, like we've done this a hundred times before, like we could do it a hundred times more.

"Thank you," I say quietly as I hand him the last plate. "For including me."

"Of course," he replies.

Our fingers brush during the handoff, and the contact sends a shiver down my spine that has nothing to do with the evening breeze. For a moment, we're frozen there, connected by a dinner plate and something much more complicated.

Then his phone buzzes, and Hazel asks for help with her math homework, and the moment breaks. But as I walk back to the guest house, I can still feel the ghost of his touch on my skin.

I'm in so much trouble.

twelve

. . .

Grant

THE STEADY HUM of activity on set makes me feel right at home. I've spent countless hours on sets just like this—the organized chaos of crew members darting about, the oversized lights casting everything in an artificial glow, the quiet intensity right before someone calls "action"—but today feels different. Today, I'm here to watch Sophia.

She's been staying in my guest house for a week now. You'd think I'd see her enough at home not to feel compelled to visit her on set. You'd be wrong.

When I arrive, she's already deep in character, running lines with James Foster, her co-star. I hang back near the monitors, not wanting to disrupt their flow. The scene they're filming is intimate—not physically but emotionally—two people dancing around their feelings for each other, neither brave enough to make the first move. The irony isn't lost on me.

"Quiet on set!" Edie's voice cuts through the bustle. "Rolling...Action!"

Sophia transforms. It's subtle—a softening around her eyes, a slight shift in her posture—but suddenly, she's not Sophia anymore. She's Maya, the character she's bringing to life. I've seen her act before, of course. I've watched her previous films and even sat in on this chemistry read, but there's something different about seeing it happen live, about watching the way she can slip in and out of character like she's changing clothes.

"I can't keep pretending this isn't happening," James says, stepping closer to her. His character, Drew, is supposed to be fighting years of repressed feelings. He's doing a decent job, but I find myself irritated by the way his hand lingers on her arm.

Sophia looks up at him with such longing that my chest tightens. "Then stop pretending," she whispers. The vulnerability in her voice makes me forget to breathe for a moment. Would she look at me that way if we ever...? I shut down that thought before it can fully form.

"Cut!" Edie calls out. "Good, but let's try it again. James, remember Drew's been holding this back for years. Everything he says costs him something. And Sophia—perfect. Keep that same energy."

Just like that, Sophia's back to herself, laughing at something James whispers to her. Her smile is different now, friendly but professional, nothing like the raw emotion she just displayed. It's fascinating watching her navigate these spaces, slipping between actress and producer with such ease.

They run the scene three more times. With each take, Sophia introduces something new while maintaining that core of emotional truth. I try not to let it bother me when James touches her arm, shoulder, or face. It's just acting—very good acting.

"That's the one!" Edie announces after the fourth take. "Let's break for twenty while we reset for the next scene."

Sophia immediately heads over to where Edie is reviewing the footage, her producer hat firmly in place. "What do you think about running that last exchange a little tighter?" she asks, leaning over Edie's shoulder to study the monitor. "We might want the option in editing."

I'm struck by how naturally she moves between roles—actress, producer, and creative partner. At twenty-five, she has instincts that usually take decades to develop. In moments like these, the age gap between us feels both significant and completely irrelevant.

"Grant!" She spots me and breaks into a genuine smile, the one I think of as distinctly Sophia. "Please tell me you're here with good news about Honey Pine."

"Would I dare show my face if I wasn't?" I pull out the signed location agreement. "We're officially approved for three weeks of shooting, starting next month."

She lets out a delighted squeal and throws her arms around me in an impulsive hug. I catch her, acutely aware of every point of contact between us. That hit of vanilla and summer floral—jasmine, I'm pretty sure—is intoxicating.

"This is perfect timing," Edie says, either not noticing or politely ignoring our lingering embrace. "We were just discussing how to handle the transition scenes. Honey Pine will give us exactly what we need for that story beat."

Sophia steps back, but her eyes are still bright with excitement. "Remember that mountain behind the frontier set? The way the light hit in the late afternoon? So perfect."

"It was." It's not a day I'll easily forget. After hours of walking the property, Sophia's mind worked overtime as she envisioned shots and scenes. Her passion was infectious—and still is.

"We should celebrate," she says. "Dinner? I'll cook. It's the least I can do since you're letting me crash at your place."

"You cook?" I raise an eyebrow, amused by this new information.

"Don't sound so skeptical! I'll have you know I make an excellent..." She pauses, thinking. "Ok, I make exactly three dishes really well. But one of them is coming your way tonight, so act surprised and impressed."

"I'm already impressed." The words come out more sincere than I intended. "With all of this," I add quickly, gesturing to the set around us. "Very impressive."

A faint blush colors her cheeks, and for a moment, I see a flash of the same vulnerability she showed in her scene. But before she can respond, she's called back to set.

"Tonight," she says firmly, already backing away. "Don't work too late."

I watch her go, struck by how easily she's woven herself into the fabric of my life. In the few days she's been staying at my place, everything has shifted slightly—like furniture moved an inch to the left. Nothing dramatic, just enough to make me hyper-aware of the change. Of her.

"She's something else, isn't she?" Edie appears beside me, following my gaze.

"She is." I keep my voice carefully neutral.

Edie gives me a knowing look. "The camera loves her, but it doesn't do her justice. There's something about her you can only really see in person. A light."

I think about Sophia's determination, her focus when reviewing scripts, the way she loses herself in scenes only to emerge more fully herself. "Yeah," I say softly. "There really is."

As I head back to my office, I try not to think about dinner tonight, the way she felt in my arms during that brief hug, or how much I wanted to punch James Foster every time he touched her face.

I fail spectacularly on all counts.

thirteen

. . .

Sophia

"TO HONEY PINE FARMS!" As I raise my wine glass, a grin spreads across my face that I can't—and don't want to—contain. The approvals have finally come through for us to shoot on location, and the relief flooding through me feels like liquid sunshine. Or maybe that's the wine talking. Probably a combination of both.

We're celebrating in Grant's backyard, with string lights creating a golden canopy above us. The soft glow makes everything feel intimate, magical, and risky. Stop it, I chide myself. He's your boss—your *very attractive, off-limits boss.*

Grant clinks his glass against mine. "To Honey Pine," he says, "and to our very persistent producer, who wouldn't take no for an answer."

I arch an eyebrow. "I prefer the term 'diplomatically tenacious.'"

His laugh rolls through the evening air, and something inside me trembles. It's not just a laugh; it's a sound that makes my skin prickle, that sends unexpected heat racing along my nerves. *Get it together, Sophia.*

The evening is perfect—just cool enough that I'm glad I grabbed my light sweater but still holding the day's warmth. Soft acoustic music drifts from the outdoor speakers, creating a dreamlike atmosphere that feels dangerously close to romantic.

"Thanks for cooking dinner tonight," Grant says, leaning back in his chair. "The pot pie was incredible."

I smile as a hint of nostalgia crosses my face. "Family recipe. My grandmother used to make this every Sunday after church. Taught me everything I know about cooking. And about feeding people's souls, not just their stomachs."

He raises an eyebrow, intrigued. "Big family?"

"Not exactly." I laugh. "Just my brother and me. But my mom's side? Total chaos. Tons of cousins, aunts, uncles—family that takes up entire parks for reunions, where someone's always cooking, always talking." I take another sip of wine and then pause. "Speaking of family, Hazel's mom is pretty fascinating. I saw the news. The new face of Ralph Lauren."

Grant's expression softens. "Geneva's incredible. She travels a lot with her modeling career, but she's relentless about staying connected with Hazel." His pride is evident. "Last month, she was shooting a campaign in Paris and still managed a daily video call. Sometimes multiple calls."

"That sounds challenging," I say, genuinely impressed. "Balancing a high-profile career with parenting can't be easy."

"We've built a solid co-parenting system," Grant explains.

"With this new gig, she'll be based in New York now, so less travel and more opportunities to see Hazel."

I can see the deep love and respect he has for Geneva's role in their lives. "You must have had great role models in your parents," I say casually.

Something shifts in his eyes—a flicker of pain quickly masked.

I wait, sensing there's more. Sometimes, silence invites conversation better than questions.

"My dad," he says finally. "He passed away when I was eleven."

The words hang between us. Not a request for pity, just a piece of himself, offered carefully.

"That must have been hard."

He nods. "It was tough on my mom after that. She..." He shakes his head.

"Grief changes everything," I say.

His eyes meet mine with a look that says he's grateful for the understanding, the space.

Suddenly, I'm overwhelmed by how attractive he is. It's not just his looks—though, God knows, he's devastatingly handsome—it's this vulnerability. The way he's sharing, carefully but genuinely. The depth behind his eyes. The careful tenderness I've seen in how he talks about Hazel, about Geneva.

Stop it, I tell myself, but the warning sounds weak, even in my own head. *He's your boss, a single dad who's more than a decade older than you. Completely, absolutely OFF. LIMITS.*

But the voice in my head sounds less convincing with

each passing moment. He doesn't feel off-limits right now. He feels achingly, dangerously present.

The way he's looking at me like I'm someone who might actually understand him makes my heart race in a way that has nothing to do with professional respect and everything to do with pure, inconvenient attraction. There's something in his gaze that's different tonight. Something heated. Something that makes me wonder if he's feeling what I'm feeling.

But my body isn't listening to my brain's very rational warnings.

"Dance with me," I say suddenly, standing up.

Grant blinks, clearly surprised. "What?"

I hold out my hand, surprising myself as much as him. "Dance with me. We're celebrating, there's music playing, and I want to dance."

For a moment, I think he'll refuse. The professional distance he's maintained since I moved into the guest house has been carefully and meticulously preserved. But then his hand slides into mine, warm and strong, and he lets me pull him to his feet.

The music shifts—because of course it does—to something slower, more intimate. Suddenly, we're swaying together under the string of lights, and every point of contact feels like a live wire.

His hand rests on my waist, keeping a respectable distance. Always so careful. Always so professional. But tonight, I don't want careful. I don't want professional.

I step closer, eliminating the space between us. His breath catches—a sharp, involuntary intake that sends electricity racing through me. He doesn't pull away.

"Sophia..." The way he says my name is a warning. And a prayer.

I don't know who moves first. Maybe we both do. Suddenly, we're breathing the same air, suspended in a moment that feels both infinite and impossibly fragile. My hand finds his cheek, and my thumb brushes across his skin. His eyes are dark, intense.

Our lips barely brush—the ghost of a kiss, electric and promising. Time suspends, crystallizes. The world narrows to just his fingers threading through my hair, the warmth of his breath against my lips, and the thundering of my heart. For one perfect, infinite moment, everything I've been trying not to want seems within reach.

Then Grant pulls back—not abruptly, but with a deliberate gentleness that somehow hurts more than if he'd jerked away. His hand lingers on my cheek for a heartbeat longer, his thumb brushing across my skin in what feels like an apology.

"We can't," he says. The roughness in his voice betrays how affected he is, and that knowledge sends a complicated ache through my chest. "This isn't—" He stops, collecting himself. "You're young, Sophia. You have your entire career ahead of you. The last thing you need is complications with..." He gestures vaguely between us, and I understand what he's not saying: *With someone older. With your boss. With a single father.*

The space between us feels vast now, though we've barely moved apart. I wrap my arms around myself, trying to hold on to some semblance of composure. He's right. Of course he's right. This would complicate everything. The movie, our working relationship, and my temporary living situation in his guest house.

"We should get some sleep," he says, his voice gentle but firm. Professional. Like we hadn't just been swaying together under string lights. Like my skin isn't still tingling from his touch.

I manage a smile that I hope looks more collected than I feel. "You're right." My voice comes out steadier than expected. "Early meetings tomorrow too."

As I take a step back, the words *I don't regret it* rise to my lips, but I swallow them back. He's set a boundary. The least I can do is respect it.

"Goodnight, Grant," I say instead, proud of how normal I sound.

Something complicated—longing, restraint, regret—flashes across his face. Then, with a tenderness that makes my chest ache, he reaches out and tucks a strand of hair behind my ear.

"Goodnight, Sophia."

The guest house feels cavernous and empty after the charged evening. I lean against the closed door, letting out a long, shaky breath I didn't realize I'd been holding. The ghost of his almost-kiss lingers on my lips. My skin still hums where he touched me.

This is for the best, I tell myself firmly, but in the quiet darkness, the words ring hollow.

I move through my evening routine on autopilot taking my makeup off, throwing pajamas on, and brushing my teeth. Normal, safe things—things that don't involve almost kissing your very attractive, very off-limits boss under string lights.

In bed, I stare at the ceiling, unable to stop my mind from wandering. What if he hadn't pulled away? What if we'd given in to whatever this is between us? I can still feel the phantom pressure of his hand on my waist, the way his heart raced against my palm.

But Grant is right. I'm living in his guest house, working on his movie, and building my career. And he has Hazel to think about—sweet, creative Hazel. The timing is wrong. The situation is wrong. Everything about this is wrong.

So, why does it feel so right?

I roll over and bury my face in the pillow. Tomorrow, I'll be professional and collected, but tonight? I close my eyes, reconstructing the moment. His hand on my cheek, the electricity between us, and the way he looked at me like I was something precious and threatening.

I imagine his lips on mine—not the ghost of a touch we'd shared, but a real kiss. Deep. Consuming. The kind of kiss that would rewrite everything.

Stop, I warn myself, but the fantasy lingers.

One thing I know for sure—working together just became a lot more complicated.

fourteen

. . .

Grant

"WHY IS a reporter asking me if Sophia Ford is staying at your house?" Lucas leans his head around the doorframe of my office, his brow furrowed with a mixture of confusion and concern, maybe even a hint of suspicion.

I'm seated behind my expansive mahogany desk, covered with scattered scripts and budget docs, when he interrupts my morning. The memories of last night flood my mind—Sophia in my arms, her lips brushing across mine. God, I wanted more, but we can't. I can't.

"Because she is," I tell him, my voice deliberately casual.

Lucas has now fully entered my office, and he drops into one of the chairs facing my desk. I can feel his gaze—assessing, probing. He knows me too well.

"Why is she staying at your house?" he asks, one eyebrow raised.

I lean back in my leather chair and run my hands over my face before dragging them up to rest on the top of my head. "Her house flooded. The entire second floor is basically sitting in her kitchen and living room. I offered her the guest house until she can figure out what to do."

"You just offered..." Lucas leaves the sentence hanging, waiting for me to fill in the blanks.

I know exactly what he's implying. That this isn't just about helping a friend, that there's something more simmering beneath the surface.

"Hm," Lucas says, that single sound loaded with meaning.

"Hm. What?"

He rises from the chair, his professional mode switching on. "I'll let the press know what's happening, but I'll ask them not to print anything. Protect Sophia's privacy. She doesn't need random journalists camping outside her place, hoping for some tabloid-worthy story."

"Thanks," I mutter.

"You'll let me know if there's anything else there?" Lucas asks, and we both know he's not talking about the flood damage.

"What do you mean?"

I run my hands across the scruff on my face, a tell I've never been able to hide. I know exactly what he means, but there's no way I'm mentioning last night. That was a fluke, a one-time thing that shouldn't have happened and won't happen again.

"When's the last time you had anyone stay in your guest house?" Lucas probes.

"I've never had anyone stay in there."

"Hm."

"What?"

He stands there, glaring at me with that look—the same

one my mother used to give me when she knew I was lying through my teeth.

"Just let me know if there is anything else going on," Lucas says. "It would not be great if the paparazzi or some nosy reporters fabricated their own version of the truth."

"There's nothing going on," I insist.

"Fine."

He leaves me alone with thoughts of Sophia, and my mind wanders back to her body pressed against mine. I'm getting hard just thinking about it.

I wanted to give in to her, sink into her lips, and run my hands down her body. I wanted to pick her up, carry her into the guest house, and lay her on the bed. I'm drawn to her. She has this magnetic pull over me; it's almost like a trance I fall into.

I shake my head like I'm shaking the thoughts of her off my brain, and as I'm attempting to get back to work, my phone lights up.

WYATT

Jake and I are nearby. Want to grab lunch?

The guilt and shame that wash over me are palpable. Wyatt is Sophia's brother and a really good dude. I also met him at the *Pink Slip* premiere last year when I accompanied Blair as her date. But they ended up disappearing together, and that's how I ended up getting to know Sophia better.

Since then, I've gotten to know Wyatt better, too—and, by extension, his best friend, Jake. Our circles had overlapped before, given the kind of deals Jake brokers for actors and directors, but back then, he was just another name in the industry. Now, after a few shared conversations and crossing paths at all the industry events, he's become a good friend. He's sharp, quick with a comeback, and loyal to a fault.

ME

> Yeah, tell me where and when and I'll meet you there.

It's probably better for me to get out of the office and reset anyway. And I need nothing more than a stark reminder that trying to do anything with Sophia is a bad idea. Between working with her, hanging out with her brother, and the huge age gap, the obstacles are high. Not to mention that whole "I have a daughter" thing. Sophia doesn't even know if she wants kids.

As I cross through the heavy wooden doors of The Smokehouse, I alert the hostess I'm meeting Jake and Wyatt. She walks me through the maze of white tablecloths and past the old-fashioned red leather booths until we're on the other side of the bar, and I spot the two of them seated at the farthest table back, nearest the windows that face the studio lot.

The restaurant is iconic and popular with industry professionals, and there's always a chance you'll see a few celebrities with a basket of cheese bread and a few bottles of wine. I see the guys already have the cheese bread ready to go.

Guilt rushes front and center at the idea that I almost kissed—kinda kissed—Wyatt's baby sister. Does he even know she's staying with me?

"Jake, Wyatt, I trust you both are well?"

I decide right then to lock down any mention of Sophia. If she wants Wyatt to know she's staying with me, then she can tell him. I'll let her handle that conversation.

"Living the dream. Literally," Wyatt says. He's beaming, and I have no doubt it's because of Blair. I can't imagine what it must feel like to have love, lose it, and then find each other again. It sounds painful.

The server arrives and takes our order, and we slip into the small talk. That's better than what's really on my mind.

"Did you settle on a venue yet?" Wyatt and Blair are finally getting married. I'm pretty sure he would have married her the minute they agreed to move in together, but she was focused on opening her new agency, and Wyatt finally left the chains of his father's law firm to work over at Hays and Cole. They both decided to tackle one big life change at a time.

"We're close. All the places we like are either way too big or way too small."

"There's a joke in there somewhere," Jake says as he reaches for another slice of cheese bread.

"What about you?" I ask. "How's wedded bliss?"

A deep sigh escapes Jake before he answers, and I worry it's not going well.

"Fantastic. I love being married. Someone to come home to and share your day with. A hand to hold, a body to love. I love the idea of having someone to share my hopes and dreams with or being able to share the details of a hard day." He trails off as if he's remembering a recent conversation he had with Lauren.

I'll admit, all of that sounds nice.

"Sounds like you're still in that honeymoon phase."

"One year coming up in July."

The server interrupts the love fest at the table and delivers lunch, and I brace myself for Manmorial weekend planning. It's the annual guys' trip to San Diego to play golf. I'm sure it may have been a little wild in previous years, but I have a feeling it's tamed quite a bit. I'm just excited to be included in the fun this year.

However, we don't talk about the trip. Instead, I'm blind-sided by Wyatt's question.

"What about you, Grant? Think you'll ever get married? Would Hazel be ok with a stepmom?"

My immediate reaction is no—at least, no to ever getting married. Would Hazel want a stepmom? Maybe. The way she was instantly drawn to Sophia and led her around our house like she was her best friend did something to my heart. It made it ache with a little concern that maybe I'm depriving her of another woman's influence because I'm so comfortable without it.

"I think that ship has sailed."

"Are you kidding me?" Jake says. "You are in your prime. Most eligible bachelor in town and a single dad. I can't imagine the numbers you must get."

"It's also hard to tell the seriously interested from the seriously deranged."

We all nod in understanding. This town is full of superficial and selfish people. Even if I wanted to date, it would take a serious amount of time to ensure I was dating someone with all the right intentions. There are agents and PR reps setting up love matches for a reason.

"That's how Sophia feels, too. I imagine you both have the same issues. I guess I'm lucky I was just a boring lawyer who worked for his dad."

"You're lucky you knew Blair," Jake says. "Dating is hard. I remember a time when I didn't think I was going to find anyone. It's hard to trust people in this town. But when I met Lauren, she didn't even ask what I did for a living until our third date. It was nice."

I catch a sour look on Wyatt's face and wonder what that is all about. But I want to hear more about Sophia.

"I don't think I've ever seen much about Sophia dating," I say, digging into my salad to appear unattached to this conversation.

"She doesn't date at all now," Wyatt says. "She was burned pretty bad by her co-star in *Code Crusaders*. I'm not exactly sure what happened; it's probably better I don't know."

He fucked her over is what happened. But I don't say that out loud. I remember the headlines when they got together, but there weren't many about the end. That's why I was so surprised when she shared what really happened. From what I saw, the show ended, and they fizzled out. I want to ask Wyatt more questions, but that wouldn't be appropriate since I'm not interested in Sophia in that way. In fact, I shouldn't even be wondering about her love life at all. She's a colleague and friend who needs a place to stay while she sorts out her home catastrophe.

"She's young. She has plenty of time to date," I say casually, but the thought of her dating makes the salad settle like lead in my stomach. The fact that someone else might be on the receiving end of her eager kiss or have those legs wrapped around their waist annoys me.

"Ok, enough about the women. Let's talk golf," Wyatt says as he rubs his hands together like he's an evil genius.

"Let's talk handicap. I'm going to need an advantage for my first Manmorial weekend." I laugh, and for a minute, I wonder what it would be like if I were sitting here with Wyatt and Jake, knowing our women would be getting together the same weekend to celebrate girl time without their men.

For the first time in my life, the idea of someone waiting for me at home doesn't sound so terrifying.

fifteen

. . .

Sophia

I HIDE out in Grant's guest house while I peek through the glass doors—doing my best not to be seen in this fishbowl of a place—waiting for him and Hazel to leave. I saw her reach for the back door like she might be coming to say hello, and my heart stopped for a minute. Then it immediately sped up when I saw Grant come up behind her, lift her, throw her upside down over his shoulder, and set her up at the island in his kitchen for breakfast. I have a front-row seat to the dad show, and it's five stars. Would recommend.

I force myself away from the windows so I can get ready. I should already be at the studio, but I couldn't sleep after that almost kiss. And I just need a little more time this morning to get my head straight. I woke up late and then started second-guessing if I should hurry and leave or wait until Grant was gone. I'm embarrassed that I asked him to dance and then put us in an uncomfortable position. He's been so generous, offering me a place to stay and then offering all this support on this project; why did I have to throw myself at him?

I still when I hear voices, and I slide down on all fours and crawl from the bathroom on my hands and knees over to the couch, where I can hide and also have a clear view of the path from his back door to his driveway. I see Hazel running toward my doors, and I panic, yet I do nothing to move or prepare for the possibility of saying good morning to her.

Just as she reaches for the handle, I hear Grant yell for her, and then I watch as she slumps with a frown on her face like he just ruined her whole day. I let my head drop as I smile with both warm affection that she wanted to say hello and complete understanding at how it feels not to get your way.

I watch as he lifts her into his back seat and buckles her in. Then he looks over at my car and back up toward my windows before he slides into his driver's seat. Is he wondering why I'm still here? Does he know my schedule? Technically, I don't have to be there today.

As they pull down the drive, I stand back up, take a deep breath, and head back into the bathroom to get my big-girl panties on for the day.

Thirty minutes later, I'm in my car and headed over to West LA to see Blair. Yes, I'm avoiding the studio lot, but I need to catch up with my agent, too. Official agent-client business. Ok, I need to talk this whole kiss thing out with someone, and I know Blair knows I have a crush on Grant, even though I deny it every single time. She's been trying to convince me there's a spark there since the first time she brought me with her to have lunch with him.

I pull up into the tiny lot behind Tangerine Talent, and when I walk in the door, I'm thrilled to see everyone here. Stella is carrying over a box of Porto's baked goods to the lounge space, where Jess is already relaxed with her feet kicked up on the coffee table.

"Hey, babe! So glad to see you!" Blair wraps her arms around my neck and pulls me close for a warm hug and kiss on my cheek. "How's the movie?"

"Great! We've already shot all city scenes and are putting the finishing touches on the cabin set this week. We start shooting those scenes next week. Oh, and Grant took me to Honey Pine Farms last week, and yesterday, they approved our location shoot!"

Before Blair can respond, Jess pipes up.

"Speaking of cabins and Grant...a little birdy told me that you are staying in his guest house?"

"What?" Blair's eyes go wide. "Why would you be staying with Grant?"

"Who told you that?"

I swear, Jess knows everything. She probably knows when I need to go to the bathroom even before I do.

"Lucas."

"Lucas? Why would Lucas tell you that?"

"So, it is true? You're staying in Grant's guest house? Why? You know you can stay with us any time. I mean, unless there's a reason you are at Grant's?" Blair is rambling and also has one eyebrow raised in question.

"Lucas did a courtesy call to key press to tamper down the gossip. Guess someone spotted you there and threatened to run with it, but I have a hard time listening to Lucas, so I tuned out the details," Jess says as she picks through the box of goodies from Porto's sitting on the table in front of her. "That man's voice is like nails on a chalkboard. He makes me wish I had more middle fingers." She seems to be talking more to herself now than us.

I wonder if Grant knows that people are already talking about me staying there. The word is out.

"Oh, but I'm sorry to hear about your house. That sucks big time. No bueno."

"What happened to your house?" Stella chimes in as she carries over a tray of coffee, drinks, and water for all of us.

I sigh before I dive into the cluster that is my life and tell her, "I had a flood at the house."

"Oh, gosh, Sophia! Are you ok?" Blair comes up to wrap her arms around me and help me sit down like I'm too fragile to walk.

"I'm fine. I wasn't there when it happened. Can't even imagine what would have happened if I had been there. Basically, my whole second floor is currently hanging out in my kitchen."

I give the girls the scoop on what I know so far, how Grant was with me when I found out and was a hero, swooping in and saving the day.

In typical fashion, Stella swoons over the idea that Grant, Hollywood's hottest bachelor, is playing exactly the type of role she has created for him in her head. Blair has gone into planning and concerned-mother mode. She's going to make a great mom one day, by the way. And Jess is kicked back, clinging to every word and interaction like a hawk. Her journalism is showing.

As for me, I'm keeping my mouth shut.

I like Jess. Really. The more time I spend with her, the more I think we could be really good friends, but right now, because of her job, she's the enemy. I know that sounds harsh, but I'm an Oscar-winning actress who's producing and starring in a movie that's been written by Oscar-winning and fan-favorite movie icon Edie Lang. I'm single, young, and staying in the guest house of this town's favorite hot guy—who's also single. Yeah, my lips are sealed right now.

"How long will you stay there?" Jess asks.

"Just a few more days. Remediation is done, and they are just stabilizing the second floor so they can remodel. I'm hoping they let me in by this weekend."

"There's no way you're getting back into that house anytime soon," Jess says.

"Well, maybe Grant will let her stay longer," Stella sweetly chimes in.

"I'm sure he will." Jess laughs, but she's not trying to be mean. It just puts me a little on edge.

"Oh, there's no way I would impose that long on Grant. If it takes much longer, I'll see if there is room at The Oakwood, or maybe there's an Airbnb near the studio I can find for a temporary stay."

"Soph, stay with us. You know we have room!"

I love Blair. I love Blair with my brother even more. But Grant is right. There is no way I'm staying with them when they are still in the honeymoon period of their relationship. As much as I love them both, there is no need to witness any of that love. I shiver at the thought.

"Let's just see what I find out. The good news is there are lots of options."

We finish off the treats, and everyone scatters off to their day jobs. I follow Blair into her office. After shutting the door behind me, I lean up against it and spit out, "I kissed him."

Blair spins so fast that her hair levitates straight out to the side, spinning as if it were a circular saw blade whacking through the secret I just spilled.

"What?"

"I kissed him. He didn't kiss me back, which was mortifying, and then he gently shut me down." I walk over to the chairs in front of her desk and slip into them, pulling my knees up to my chest. We're talking full fetal position.

"I'm sorry. I thought I just heard you say you made out with Grant."

"Not exactly, but I wish." I bite my bottom lip as I look up at her with guilt all over my face.

"Start from the beginning."

I fill her in on how I offered to make dinner to celebrate the good news about Honey Pine. After Hazel went to bed, we stayed up talking. The wine must have hijacked my brain, causing me to ask him to dance, and with him that close to me, I apparently lost all control. I bring my thumb up to my mouth to nibble on a straggling cuticle and wait for her to say something. Anything.

"Holy shit."

"I can't stay there."

"Does your brother know?"

"What? No! And you can't tell him. I'm swearing you to secrecy. This is a client–agent privileged conversation."

"I'm not sure it works like that."

"Blair!"

"I won't tell him. Sorry. I'm just processing all of this. There's a part of me that wants to jump up and scream, 'I knew it!' But then my agent side is thinking about the movie."

She looks up at me with sympathetic eyes. This is the part where reality enters and the actions of two people could destroy the livelihoods of many—not counting our own.

"I know."

"Have you talked about this? How did it end?"

"He said we can't and said goodnight. He was a perfect gentleman and totally professional."

"That's good, but if I know Grant, he'll likely want to confront it head on, discuss it, and define what it all means or doesn't mean."

"Great. I can't wait to get back to his place."

"He's a good guy, Soph. You know that. He won't make you feel awkward or ashamed or anything. He's a professional, and I would assume he will be complementary and reassuring. He'll want to continue to make this project successful."

"I know you're right." What I can't seem to push down is this feeling of despair, that he'll tell me I'm great but we should just remain friendly co-workers. And that has me feeling like I can't get enough air into my lungs.

At what point did I start to like this guy—like, for real like this guy? When did he become more than just a "hot dad" crush?

sixteen

. . .

Grant

I'M MET with shrill squeals followed by laughter as I enter the house, and I wonder who Hazel has over this late. I missed dinner, hoping to avoid any awkward conversation with Sophia. I need to talk to her, but I'm not ready to say what I should say. I'm not ready to be professional and lock us into the co-working zone—and that right there is more fucked up than I'll allow myself to think about. Right now, I'm going to go find the source of all the commotion I hear and enjoy every second of dad time.

"Hey, what's all this noise—" I nearly give myself whiplash from the abrupt halt I make as I round the corner into the living room. Sophia is down on all fours, crawling under a bridge of sofa cushions, as Hazel stands on a chair across the room, waving a sword at my sister, who is tied up with a jump rope.

The place is a mess, but all I can see is that small, round peach of Sophia's ass bent over at the perfect angle that if I were to drop to my knees, I could grab her hips and slide into her so clean and quickly that it wouldn't take long before we'd have our own mess to contend with.

"Dad! Quick, get on the couch! The carpet is the ocean, and you'll drown!"

I quickly sit on the leather sofa to comply with the orders, but also because I'm dumbstruck and not sure what to say.

"Now, sit back and watch as Sophia walks the plank so she can save Aunt Sarah!" And then the most ridiculous-sounding evil laugh escapes my daughter, and I see Sophia peeking over her shoulder at me with tears of laughter in her eyes, clearly enjoying every minute of this.

"Save me, good sir. The evil pirate is so cruel. I want to save my sister, but she's making me jump into an ocean of piranha!"

"No, Dad, don't listen to her. You're nobody right now."

Ouch.

"Get to walking, missy, or I'll cut your sister's head off."

Jesus. This took a turn.

"Ok, that feels like a good stopping point to me. Join us next week when Pirate Crazy Pants decides the fate of Princess Plank-Walker and her sister."

"Daaaad."

"Haaaaze."

"Fine. But I'm not waiting until next week. Sophia, can you come over tomorrow? Aunt Sarah won't be here, but we don't need her to keep playing."

"Hey, I was an important part of this game today!" my sister whines. "Don't do me like that!"

Hazel runs up to her and places both hands on her face. She looks her right in the eyes and says with the seriousness of a responsible adult, "You are very important. Don't ever forget that." Then she drops her hands and shrugs. "But you won't be here tomorrow, and the show must go on."

Sophia rolls onto her back and slaps a hand over her mouth to hold in her laughter. She's looking at me like she doesn't want to offend Hazel, but it's too hilarious to ignore.

"Untie your aunt, and let's get this place cleaned up."

"I'll help her clean up," Sophia says. "You should go eat. We left you some dinner in the oven."

I still as I take in those words. *We left you dinner. Go eat.* Words that real families use. It feels warm and good, but then the feeling slowly turns into panic, icy tingles, and the need to escape the room.

I turn and walk out toward the kitchen as I hear my sister say, "Someone must be hungry." She's right. I'm starving. But not for food. For Sophia. God, that little taste last night was not enough, and now she's in my house again, on all fours no less, and playing with my daughter? I grab the plate out of the oven and am stunned at what I see. Meatloaf? Who made this?

"Sophia made dinner," my sister says as she walks up next to me to grab a water out of the fridge.

I just grunt. After sliding onto the stool and placing my plate on my kitchen island, I dip my fork in and savor the bite of the most delicious meatloaf I've ever had in my entire life.

"It's Mom's recipe."

I knew it. Now I don't feel so bad saying it was the best, since it's technically my mom's and hers is the best.

"Why does Sophia have Mom's recipe?" I try to ask in the most neutral voice I can muster.

"We were outside swimming when she got home, and she hung out with us for a bit. Hazel mentioned dinner and that she wanted meatloaf, and Sophia offered to make it. When we came inside, Hazel told her that Grammy's meatloaf was your favorite, and Sophia asked if she had the recipe. I couldn't say we don't have it. That would be rude."

"Of course. It's fine."

"She's amazing, you know."

"It's not like that, so don't even start."

She holds my stare for a minute and then clicks her tongue against her cheek.

"Ok."

I roll my eyes and turn back to eat more of this fucking delicious meal. She's gorgeous, funny, and can cook, too? I shake my head. I don't need someone to cook for me. I can hire people to do that. Josie does it sometimes. I do not need to be in a relationship so I can get a home-cooked meal.

I turn back around and can see Sophia and my sister talking and laughing as they help Hazel clean up the mess, and the constraint around my heart tightens. I like how she looks in there, chatting comfortably with my sister, effortlessly brushing her hand over Hazel's hair and helping her pick up her things.

I'm probably making more of this than it is. She's an actress, for Christ's sake. Of course she can play any part she wants.

But something tells me this isn't a role she's playing. She looks genuinely at ease.

I see her bend down and kiss the top of Hazel's head, and

I turn around because I can't watch it anymore. I focus on my favorite food instead.

"Sorry to crash dinner again. I'm headed back to the guest house, so you can enjoy the rest of your evening with your daughter."

"Ok, thanks for dinner."

The words come out clipped and professional. Distant. I'm hyper-aware of maintaining boundaries after last night's mistake.

I don't look up from my plate. I can't look up because, if I do, I might see something in her expression that could crack this carefully constructed wall I'm trying to maintain, brick by methodical brick.

She lingers just for a moment, long enough that I can feel the weight of her uncertainty, her attempt to read the situation. Sophia's smart enough to recognize I'm trying to keep things professional.

"You're welcome. See you tomorrow."

And then she's gone.

The silence feels like a reprieve—and a loss.

After dinner, I finally get Hazel showered, and she convinces me to read her three different books before going to sleep. Then I go up to my room, where I try and fail to work. All I can think about is Sophia, and I'm as hard as a fucking rock.

I feel bad for wanting to get off to memories of her, but there's no way I'm sleeping until I get some relief. I turn on the shower and press my hands against the top of the counter as I brace myself, lean forward, and look at myself in the mirror.

She's too young for you.

You work together.

This would cross every professional line there is.

I run through the entire list of reasons why allowing myself to be with Sophia is a bad idea, and then I stomp over to the shower and slip into the stream of warm water. I place my hand against the wall and fist my cock, pulling on it, hard and angry, like I don't deserve to get off, so I'll punish myself with the grip and pace. Only that has me growing harder as I imagine what it would've felt like last night if I had shifted my hands to grab her hair and bent her over the outdoor table.

I'd have peeled those tiny athletic shorts down, the ones she's always wearing around the lot and here at the house, the ones where I can see the curve of her perfect ass peeking out of the bottom hem. My feet would have kicked her legs apart, and I'd have run my hands over her ass. Then my fingers would have slipped into her silky cunt, dripping wet for me.

My dick throbs at the image as I thrust harder into my hand, and when I imagine my dick slamming into her pussy, imagining her tightness choking me, I immediately see stars and spew all over the shower wall.

Hanging my head, I try to catch my breath.

I'm totally fucked.

seventeen

. . .

Sophia

I LOVE the smell of margaritas and Mexican food. Living in LA, there is no shortage of places to find both, but nothing beats an evening out at Casa Vega, where I can stuff my face with the best carne asada enchilada I've ever had. Plus, the dark dining room is perfect for hiding in the shadows, although the place is usually buzzing with industry folks, so it's a talent-friendly place to go. The Latin music in the background, mixed with the clattering of dishes being delivered to and taken away from tables, completes the laid back vibe.

I spot Brandon toward the back and give the hostess a brief wave and point, indicating my party is already here.

"Hey, beautiful. You are looking lovely this evening," Brandon says. He leans in for a kiss on the cheek. "All this for me?" He's such a flirt.

"Thank you. I had a scene today and took advantage of hair and makeup."

"You could at least pretend you are excited to see me."

Brandon is the kind of guy who turns heads without even

trying—not just because he's built like an action hero, but because he carries himself like he knows exactly who he is. At six feet tall, all lean muscle and effortless confidence, he moves with the controlled ease that comes from years of stunt work. His brown hair is always slightly tousled like he just ran a hand through it after stepping off a motorcycle or out of bed, with both being equally likely. Warm brown eyes gleam with mischief, always ready to catch the punchline before it lands.

I'm here to beg him to help me with some stunt blocking, but I also want him to play a firefighter role we still haven't cast yet.

"Honestly, I'm not sure how I've gone this long without seeing you. I think I'm dying a little on the inside."

"That's more like it. So, come on now. Spill it. Why am I here?"

"You could at least pretend you are excited to see me!" I mimic back to him. His bluntness is one of my favorite things about him. You never have to guess where you stand with him. He is clear about how he feels and what he wants. Just like someone else I know.

"You bring me to my favorite restaurant. You actually scheduled this dinner. You want something. I know you, my love."

Brandon signals to a server and orders us each a margarita on the rocks.

"Aren't you going to ask about my movie?"

I'm trying to stall a bit. I need to set this up first so he sees that this is a great opportunity for him, not a favor or a handout. He can be so prideful about work sometimes.

"Fine. How's the new movie? How's the handsome boss-man? You still living together?"

I bring the cold glass to my lips to stall, savoring the rough pinch of salt on the rim as it mixes with the drink's sweet and sour taste. I ignore his question about living together.

"We're averaging about five pages a day. We're blocking for all interior shots first and then will go on location for the rest of it."

"Nice! Look at you showing everyone how it's done!"

I've loved it so far, but it's been tricky balancing my scenes with my production to-do list. Thankfully, the studio sent over an amazing PA to help me out. And my assistant, Jamie, is my lifeline.

"Honestly, Grant has been a tremendous support. Ever since he showed up on opening day and sat through the table read, everyone has been on their best behavior."

"Speak of the devil..." Brandon's gaze rises over the top of my head, and his professional smile creeps across his face—lips closed, eyes squinty.

I turn to see who he's looking at, and my breath stops. Grant is headed this way, flanked by three other men. One is Lucas. He hasn't noticed us yet, and I take the stolen moment to snake my eyes up and down Grant's body. He's wearing his signature studio executive uniform—dark suit, white shirt, shiny shoes, and those sexy glasses. Who knew guys who wear frames would turn me on so much?

My eyes linger on his hands and follow them as they rise to adjust those foxy lenses, and that is the moment that he catches me staring. Surprise crosses his eyes, and then his gaze flits behind me and lands on Brandon. I can see his mood change immediately. His smile drops, and his hands move to grip and adjust the lapels of his jacket.

"Give me just a minute. I'll be right over," he tells the men with him. "Sophia, good evening." He nods, his eyes glancing between Brandon and me.

"Hi, Grant. Great to see you. What are you doing here?"

"Work dinner. Nothing exciting. What about you?" His eyes land on Brandon again, and he's waiting for an introduction.

"Oh, I'm sorry. How rude. This is Brandon. He's a stunt actor, actually one of the best, and a good friend of mine. I'm here with a proposition for him, but I'm buying him dinner before I make the ask."

"I knew it!" Brandon glares at me before he stands to shake Grant's hand. "Great to meet you. I've heard fantastic things so far. Sophia loves working with you."

Grant looks surprised at the confession, but it's no secret I admire him. I've only told him a million times.

"I wish I could say she's mentioned you, but I feel the same about her. We're lucky to have her at Wonderland Studios."

There's a weird vibe I've not seen from Grant. Maybe this is another layer of his professional executive persona. Maybe it's the people he is dining with; maybe they are super boring, and he's dreading it.

"Well, I better get back to my table. Sophia, Brandon, enjoy your evening."

"You, too, Grant."

"Someone's got a crush on you," Brandon says, snapping me from my internal lust.

"What? No way."

"Yes way. He crushed my hand when he shook it. And the comment he made, 'wish I could say she mentioned you'—boy has it bad."

I search the room for his table, and when I spot him, he's staring at me. I let my eyes linger on his until he breaks contact and joins the conversation at his table.

I snap out of my drool session and steer this conversation in a different direction. The last thing I need is Brandon suspecting I have any real feelings for Grant. He'd latch on and never let it go.

"I think you are reading way too much into that. I mean, he's totally hot, but he's my boss! Plus, there's no way he'd go for someone as young as me. He's a single dad. We're in completely different stages of life."

"And are you still in the 'never going to date anyone' stage of life?"

"Stop it."

"I love you, Soph, but when are you going to move past the Connor thing? We all get hurt. It's like a rite of passage in relationships. You can't say you've ever had one unless you've been destroyed by one."

"Has one destroyed you?"

"At least monthly."

Brandon smirks at me. He loves love, but I'm not sure he's ever been in love. He has no problem finding dates, and I'm always amazed at how well he treats women. The relationship timeline with each one is short, and it's a gift how he maneuvers out of them with no drama.

I look back at Grant, but this time, it's Lucas's eyes that

snag mine. He gives a nod and a smile, and while it's friendly, it feels protective, too, like maybe Brandon and Lucas see something Grant and I haven't quite noticed yet.

"Well, speaking of relationships, how would you feel about having another working one with me?"

"I knew it." Brandon shakes his head and digs into his dinner. "You know I can't say no to you. What is it this time?"

We dive into the rest of dinner while I tell him all about my vision for the stunts and his role. And I force myself to avoid looking over at Grant for the rest of the evening. Thank God I'm a well-trained actress.

eighteen

. . .

Grant

I'M COMPLETELY THROWN by seeing Sophia here. My eyes stay on the producers Lucas and I are dining with, but my focus is shot, hijacked by the scene unfolding just beyond them. My thoughts spiral. Why is she here with Brandon? I've seen them together before—maybe at Blair's agency opening? I think we were introduced. Are they together? An ex? The thought knots in my stomach, tight and unwelcome. It shouldn't matter. I don't have any claim over Sophia.

Still, my attention drifts behind the blonde guy talking—James something?—drawn back to Sophia like a tide I can't fight. She twirls a strand of hair around her finger, her eyes alight as she listens to whatever Brandon is saying, her laughter slipping out, warm and unguarded. It's the kind of laugh that gets under your skin, the kind that lingers in your ears long after it's gone. My jaw tightens when she leans back, completely at ease, like this is exactly where she wants to be. I swallow down something sharp and unfamiliar.

"I think Grant would agree," Lucas says, pulling me out of my momentary tailspin. His expression is expectant, but beneath it, there's a glint of irritation. Pay the fuck attention.

I straighten. "Wholeheartedly. Sounds great."

The dinner meeting is mostly a courtesy—an assessment of what the duo has in their pipeline and whether we might buy, partner, or pass. I haven't worked with them before, but their latest self-funded film performed well on the festival circuit. Maybe they'll be the next Coen brothers. In this business, it never hurts to have the dinner. You've got to eat.

"Hey, man, appreciate the time tonight. We'll send over the clips we spoke about and the numbers and projections for the next five years. We're psyched to take the next step with you," the blonde one says. Jeff? Or maybe he was James?

"Sounds great. You've done impressive work. Looking forward to learning more." Especially when my mind isn't tangled up in the woman behind you.

"Lucas, you have a minute?" I ask as we wait for the duo to depart.

"I knew I should have switched places with you," he says, his voice dry.

"What are you talking about?"

His gaze flicks toward Sophia before he leans in, blocking my line of sight as he opens his laptop. "Any updates to share? Don't blindside me."

"There's nothing to share. I won't blindside you."

But I'm already distracted again. I catch sight of Sophia standing, her small frame lifting above the sea of people. Her gaze seems to skim the room in slow motion before landing on mine. I hold still, waiting for her reaction. Her lips part slightly, and surprise flickers across her face before she schools it into something more neutral. She lifts a hand in a small wave. I give her a single nod before she turns and disappears toward the back of the restaurant.

"I'll be right back," I tell Lucas.

I follow her down the hall and slip into the restroom behind her, locking the door with a quiet click. The moment she turns, her brow furrows.

"What are you doing?"

With every step forward I take, she takes one back until she's pressed against the sink. I plant a hand on the counter behind her, caging her. My pulse hammers in my ears, and my thoughts are a tangled mess.

"I thought you weren't dating anyone."

Her eyes narrow. "What are you talking about?"

"Brandon. Who is he?"

She exhales sharply, and the breath puffs against my collarbone. She doesn't flinch, doesn't try to escape. If anything, she's sizing me up, searching for something in my expression.

"He's one of my best friends," she finally says, her voice even. "We've never dated. Never kissed. He has a new girlfriend every month, so he wouldn't be interested in me anyway. And he's someone I trust completely."

Her words settle between us, but I don't move. I don't trust myself to. I'm still unsettled, still trying to figure out why I followed her back here, why the thought of her with someone else has me feeling like my skin doesn't fit right. I'm so used to uncomplicated indifference to women. But Sophia? She's unraveling me.

Her gaze flicks up at mine, waiting. I can't bring myself to step away, but I also don't know how to close the space between us.

"Oh."

She lets out a quiet laugh and shakes her head. "Goodnight, Grant."

"Enjoy the rest of your evening, Sophia."

I force myself to leave, and the lock clicks open as I step back into the dim hallway. When I return to the table, Lucas is still there, eyeing me with barely concealed amusement.

"You know you are allowed to date. Sometimes, I think you take this whole single-dad thing too far. It's turning into an excuse at this point."

I pull my glasses off and drag a hand over my face. "I know."

"You guys look great together."

He turns his laptop to face me. An email is open featuring images from the Oscars' red carpet, attached to an inquiry from a reporter.

When I saw her in front of me that night, I couldn't stay away. I was drawn to her. She has a way of putting me at ease —such ease that I ended up with my arm around her hips, and our friendly interaction looked more like friends with benefits.

"Will you stop harassing me if I admit she's attractive?"

Lucas leans back with a grunt. "Fine. Some of those journalists, though? They are out for blood. If there is something brewing between you two, I need to know before you take it too far."

"A young Oscar-winning actress producing and starring

in her first movie, one written by Edie Lang no less, should be all the coverage anyone cares about."

"You know as well as I do that doesn't sell papers," Lucas says as he closes his laptop.

"I appreciate it. I promise you'll be the first to know—if you haven't already been tipped off by hell freezing over."

Lucas shakes his head and laughs as he stands. I rise to walk out with him, eager to get home to my actual number one girl.

nineteen

. . .

Sophia

IT'S BEEN a week since Grant trapped me in the bathroom at Casa Vega, demanding to know who Brandon was, and two weeks since the almost maybe kinda kiss where he flat out rejected me. I thought for sure he was going to kiss me in the bathroom or maybe lift me onto the countertop and take me right there. That might also be my wish-fulfillment fantasy. I guess I'm grateful he's staying professional and doing his best not to make it awkward.

Our schedules are hectic, but he pops by the guest house most mornings to leave me a coffee, and I've visited him at his office for production updates and to review script changes. I imagine it's a good example of what it might be like to date him in real life—a whisper of moments here and there.

I will admit that it's been nice not to feel any pressure to give more than this right now. I like how we both understand that our work is important, and I've loved spending time with Hazel and him, getting to know them both better. I tried dating a "normal" guy after Connor, but when I had to leave for a six-week shoot in New York City, he confessed he couldn't do long distance and broke up with me. Six weeks apart was too much for him.

That's why it's so hard to date. People who aren't in the industry don't get it. They don't understand the hustle and sacrifices you make to pursue your passion. They don't understand that you've already sacrificed so much to get to your level, that the relentless pace and focus are just part of your DNA now. It doesn't feel unusual.

But dating within the industry isn't much easier. It's a catch-22. On the one hand, they get the long hours, the last-minute schedule changes, and the way a project can consume you entirely. But on the other, that means you're both always running, always chasing the next opportunity—two people constantly in motion, rarely in the same place at the same time. And if you're not careful, work becomes the only thing you have in common.

I think that's why being around Grant has felt easy. He gets it. And maybe that's all this is. He understands the life, and I'm confusing feelings with his understanding.

I can't shake how similar this feels to what it was like with Connor, though—low pressure, fun, supportive—which, in hindsight, makes sense since everything with him was a complete set-up and arrangement, unbeknownst to me. I'm an actress—a damn good one, too—so nobody knew how much Connor hurt me. Not even him. When our show wrapped and he shook my hand—that's right, shook. My. Hand—and said it was a pleasure working with me and thanks for the relationship, I wanted to melt into any substance that would allow me to disappear within seconds.

We had just cut the cake, and the wrap party had been a hilarious trip down memory lane. His actions caught me so off guard that I was still laughing. Yes, laughing. And then I kept the frozen smile on my face as I processed the confusion, the realization that it had all been a setup. I replayed so many things that started to click and make so much more sense. I hate thinking about it even now.

This is different, I tell myself. This is just a friendship, a connection built on mutual understanding. There's no arrangement, no hidden terms, no expiration date looming overhead. And most importantly, I will not be blindsided by any of it.

"Sophia! Wait up!"

I turn and see Jess Lexington running across the lot toward me, her blonde ponytail bouncing, her blue eyes smiling at me. I like Jess. She's Blair's best friend from college, and over the past year, I've come to enjoy her abrasive and over-the-top directness. I just don't trust her.

She currently hosts *On the Red Carpet*, the go-to podcast for the entertainment industry. She was a reporter for *Deadline*, *Variety*, and *The Hollywood Reporter*—all the places entertainment reporters, well, report. She went out on her own last year, and the pod and subsequent newsletter Substack have taken off.

She's never done me wrong, and honestly, she seems pretty reputable, but I've been in Blair's office when she's unloaded the latest gossip. She knows everything about everyone in this town. It's a little scary. What I'm never sure of is whether she considers something on or off the record.

"Hey, Jess! What brings you to the lot today?"

"Podcast record with the cast of *Pink Slip*."

"Oh, I love that show so much!"

"You're welcome to sit in if you want?"

"I wish. We have a full shoot day here."

Jess follows me into the sound stage and marvels at the set we've built of the main character's home. I'll never tire of the magic of Hollywood. The way our set designers bring things to life, the props that help define the tone and time-frame of the film and bring authenticity to it all. Even the lighting is positioned through the fake windows to represent where the sun might be at that exact time of day for that scene.

"So, Grant's house, yeah?"

And here we go. But again, I'm not sure if this is reporter Jess or friend Jess.

"Yes, he really came in clutch for me. My house is a disaster. I can't believe a leak behind a tub spout could cause that much damage."

I use my media skills to try and divert the conversation to the chaos that is my poor, sweet home. It's coming along. After a few weeks, the crew has finally finished gutting every-thing, and the repair and rebuild is underway.

"I bet. I'm curious how long you'll stay?"

She's relentless; I can see it all over her face. Her eyes are lit up like she's about to open the first present on Christmas. I hate this part. Grant and I are just friends.

"He's been very generous to let me stay as long as I need. I think he feels sorry for me."

"Hm."

Here's where I need to lean in and shut it down. Her skepticism is at an all-time high.

"Oh, come on. Would you want to stay with Blair and Wyatt right now? And I'm not driving from my parents' house in Santa Barbara. Grant has been great and supportive throughout this entire process. And our schedules are so packed, it's like I'm not even there."

"Here's what I know for sure," she says as she lifts her hand and raises her fingers to count down the evidence she thinks she has. "He invited you to his Hamptons party when Blair, who has always been a good friend of his, has never attended—until he invited you. He picked you up for Tangerine Talent opening—"

"He did not pick me up," I tell her, my voice clipped. "We were both here at the lot, and you know it's murder to park down there. We just carpooled."

My interjection does nothing to slow her down.

"He was on set for the table read."

How does she know that?

"He introduced you to Hazel."

"We were at the Oscars," I reply, folding my arms across my chest. "We were walking the red carpet together when she came up to greet him at the end. I don't think he had a choice in that."

She ignores me again.

"He's apparently driving you out to Santa Clarita for hikes in the mountains," Jess says, her eyes narrowing like she's just presented her final piece of evidence in a courtroom.

I roll my eyes and turn to walk toward the staging area behind the set, but she follows.

"And he's offering his guest house to you. As far as I can tell, nobody's even been to Grant's house, much less stayed in his guest house."

I stop. My pulse ticks in my jaw as I slowly turn to face her.

"Jess, I know you're besties with Blair, but that doesn't give you an all-access pass to my life." I cross my arms, and my nails dig lightly into my forearms as I let my words settle between us. "I can appreciate that you're curious, but there's a line, and you're trampling over it."

Jess blinks but doesn't back down.

"Living in Grant's guest house is a practical solution to a problem, not a romantic getaway," I continue, my voice firm. "And honestly? That you think you have the right to pry into my life like this is pretty damn bold."

I ignore the flicker of amusement in her eyes and sort through the stacks on the table, looking for today's shoot schedule. My face remains neutral, but something in my gut twists with satisfaction at the flicker of resignation I spot on Jess's face. It's not that I owe her—or anyone—an explanation. But there's something about the way she's digging, like she knows something I haven't even let myself consider.

My logical brain tells me this thing with Grant can't work. But I've grown up in a world of make-believe, and sometimes, it's easy to imagine a different ending just for a moment, a happily ever after that isn't part of a script. One that's real. But I also know better. Real life doesn't work like that. Not for someone like me.

I force my gaze back to Jess, leveling her with a look. "So, he's nice to me. Did you ever think maybe it's to his benefit to keep me close? I'm a sought-after actress who brings in the box office numbers. Maybe that's all it is."

Jess studies me for a long beat, and for once, she doesn't have a comeback.

"Fair point." She grabs a donut off the opposite table and shoves it in her mouth. "Hey, I'm not after a story here. I'm just nosey. And you and Grant are two of my favorite people. I'd love it if there were some kind of love connection happening."

She licks her fingers before she pulls out her phone—to check for any missed messages, I'm assuming. I guess the interrogation is over.

"Besides, if anything were happening, I would've gotten it out of Lucas already. He's terrible with secrets."

Note to self: tell Grant not to tell Lucas anything.

"Well, thanks. I appreciate that. And I'm happy to share all the love that's happening with this movie. I can't believe how well it's turning out. We're on time and on budget. When does that ever happen?"

I take Jess on a tour, and she visits with some actors already on set. I know she'll mention this as an unofficial visit on her podcast, so I want to make sure I'm pointing out all the elements that will tease her audience without spoiling the plot for everyone.

Just when I think I've shut down and escaped Jess's obsession with Grant and me, we run into him on the way out of the sound stage.

"Hey, Soph. Hey, Jess," he says.

"Hey, Grant! What brings you out to the set today?" Jess asks with way too much glee on her face, and she's probably getting whiplash from the back-and-forth her head is doing as she looks from one of us to the other.

"Oh, I just wanted to connect with Sophia on a few budget items."

"Right. Well, I better head back to the office. I'll leave you two to figure out how you're going to make all the big things fit."

She's shameless, and she giggles at her terrible joke as she walks away.

"What was that about?"

"Nothing," I say and then redirect quickly. "I hope you have good news about the budget."

"Good and bad. You have time now?"

"I don't. I'm about to start shooting. It's a full day. I can swing by after dinner if you don't mind if I interrupt your home life with work stuff?"

"Not at all. Swing by once you get home."

Home. I don't even think he realizes that he's said it—like it's our home and we're living there together.

"Will do."

He pulls his phone out of his pocket and lifts it to his ear, giving me a wave as he walks across the lot back toward his office.

I head back to the set, ready to channel this unrequited crush into my next scene. At least someone will benefit from all of these feelings.

twenty

. . .

Grant

"DAD! Check this out! Aunt Sarah helped me make the planet Mars!"

The kitchen island is covered with Styrofoam crumbs, glue, paintbrushes, and what I think is molding clay, but I can't be sure with all the disaster that surrounds my little STEM genius.

"Hey, G. Sorry about the mess. I'll get it cleaned up before I go."

"Don't worry about it. I can pick it up after Hazel goes to bed." I glance at my wrist, noting the time. "Something must be wrong with my watch because it says that it's PJ o'clock, but I don't see any PJs."

Hazel leans on crossed arms resting on the counter, trying not to smile. "Your watch doesn't say that."

"Are you sure?" I hold it up to my ear. "Uh, yep. It's whisper-singing to me right now. *PJ time, PJ time, Hazel missed her PJ time.*"

She climbs up onto the island, crawls over to me, and reaches for my arm, trying to get a listen.

"I don't hear anything."

"Listen really close."

I wait for her to put her ear on my arm and then grab her and throw her over my shoulder. As she releases all the giggles and screams from her little body, I sing really badly, "PJ time, PJ time!" and bring her upstairs to her room.

"Ok, then. I'm heading out!" my sister yells from the bottom of the stairs.

"Thanks, sis!"

"Bye, Aunt Sarah!"

My sister has been a huge help lately, and I don't know how I'd be surviving without her right now. I love that she moved out to LA for a fresh start. She's a cybersecurity analyst who contracts with companies to ensure that their data is protected. She's a genius, and the shit she sees is fucking scary. Thankfully, it's a job she can do from anywhere so she can accommodate my desperate pleas for help. Josie's been gone for three weeks, and it looks like she'll be staying at least three more. I'm happy she's getting this time with her daughter, but some days, we sure do miss her.

I slide my shoes off and slip onto the edge of Hazel's bed, and she darts from the bathroom right after I settle. She pounces on me, fully dressed in PJs.

"We're on Chapter Thirteen," she tells me as she grabs *The Martian* from the side table. Yes, I know she's six, but she's smart, and I'm not going to baby her with kid books if she wants to read above her level. Although, it does mean she's slightly obsessed with Mars now, and I've yet to convince her that she can't really move there when she grows up.

"Alright. Do you want to try and read, or do you want me to take this one?"

"You take it. I'm tired from creating a whole planet."

She scoots over on her bed, making room for me, and I slide on top of her covers and position myself against the headboard as I stretch my socked feet out on the bed.

"Daddy, do you have dates?"

"What do you mean? I have had dates before."

"When are you going to go on one again?"

"Oh, I'm not sure. I guess I don't really have anyone in mind I'd like to go on a date with. Why are you asking?"

"I heard Aunt Sarah telling her friend she has a date. But she said you never go on dates. That you won't go on them because of me."

Hazel curls up against my body and avoids looking up at me.

"Hey, listen to me." I lean down and tilt her chin up so we're eye to eye. "That is not true at all."

I'm going to kill my sister.

"I date. I just haven't lately because I'd rather spend time with you. Sometimes, dates take up too much time, and other times, they aren't very fun."

"Maybe I could help you find a fun date?" She looks up so innocently that I can't help but think the universe is shoving this idea down my throat tonight.

"I think taking you to the space center is a fun date. What do you think about that?"

"I think that would be a fantastic date! When?"

She's got me there. Bamboozled by a six-year-old.

"I'm sure I can find some time this weekend. Now, can I get back to this book?"

"Yeah. But Dad? I know you date so you can fall in love. And you already love me, so maybe you should find someone you want to love and ask them to date you."

Gut-punched by a kid.

When I reach the end of the chapter, Hazel is already asleep. I guess creating a planet does wear you out. As I head downstairs, my mind drifts to Sophia as I think about what Hazel said about finding someone to love. I'm not sure if love is what I'm after, but I'll admit that being around her isn't a burden at all.

"Knock, knock," Sophia says in her softest voice. The kitchen door is open, and she's leaning inside, hesitant to enter.

"Come on in. I just got Hazel to bed. Perfect timing."

"Oh, bummer, I wanted to say hi."

Something about her disappointment pulls at my heart. I sidestep the comment and bring us back to the reason she's here. "Come on back. I brought home some ideas I want to show you."

The house is quiet except for the gentle clink of Sophia's wine glass against the coffee table. We've been reviewing the script for a few hours, and the bottle between us is nearly empty. Papers are strewn across the couch cushions, covered in her neat handwriting. She's curled up at the other end, her feet tucked under her, wearing an oversized UCLA sweat-shirt that makes her look younger than her twenty-five years.

"I know if we can shoot this scene on the lot, we can find the money for the shot we want at Honey Pine, but this scene still isn't working." She sighs and runs a hand through her hair. "I get why Maya won't leave the house, but we need the audience to understand, too."

I scan the pages again. The scene is simple on the surface. Maya is arguing with her mother about evacuating as mudslides threaten their neighborhood. But there's something deeper there, something about holding on to the past that feels achingly familiar.

"What if..." I pause, choosing my words carefully. "What if it's not really about the house at all? Maybe it's about what leaving means to her. Every memory of her husband is in those walls. Leaving means accepting that life goes on without him, and she's not ready for that."

Sophia looks up sharply. "You sound like you're speaking from experience."

The wine must be hitting me harder than I thought because I find myself saying things I rarely talk about. "My mom was like that after my dad died. Watching her...it was like she died, too, in a way. She stayed in our old house until it practically fell apart around her. Wouldn't even paint the walls a different color because Dad had picked the original shade."

"Grant..." Sophia's voice is soft. She shifts closer, and her knee brushes against mine. "I'm so sorry."

"It was a long time ago." I take a sip of wine, buying time. "But I think that's why this scene matters so much. It's not just about a stubborn woman refusing to evacuate. It's about grief and how, sometimes, we confuse holding on to things with holding on to people."

"Is that why you..." she starts, then stops herself.

"Why I what?"

She bites her lip, considering. "Why you keep everyone at arm's length? I mean, besides your sister and Hazel. And maybe Geneva."

The question hits closer to home than I'd like. "Maybe," I admit. "It's easier to avoid getting too attached than to risk..." I trail off, suddenly aware of how close she's gotten.

"Risk what?" she whispers.

"Losing yourself," I murmur, "when they leave."

"Not everyone leaves."

Her eyes are a darker shade of blue in the low light and fixed on mine with an intensity that makes my heart race. She breaks the moment when she leans back and stretches her arms over her head. Her sweatshirt rides up slightly, revealing a sliver of skin. I shouldn't be looking. But I am.

I clear my throat, dragging my gaze back to the script in front of me. "I think if we make that change—it's stronger. It hits where it needs to."

Sophia turns her head toward me, studying my profile. "Yeah," she says softly. "It really does."

I can feel her looking at me, and it takes everything in me not to turn, not to meet her eyes. If I do, I'm not sure I'll be able to stop what's coming.

But then she does it for me. She shifts closer, and her knee brushes against mine again. Her voice is quieter now. "Grant."

I finally look at her, and the breath leaves my lungs. The way she's watching me—like she's seeing something she can't ignore anymore—sets every nerve in my body on fire.

"Sophia..." My voice comes out rough, a warning I barely believe myself.

She tilts her head, her lips parting slightly, her breath warm as it fans across my skin. "Yes," she whispers.

Something snaps.

My hand slides into her hair, and suddenly, my mouth is on hers. The kiss is hard, desperate, like I've been starving for it and didn't even realize how badly until now.

She makes a small sound when my fingers tighten in her hair, and it sends something electric through me. I pull her closer, with one hand on her waist, anchoring her to me. She fists my shirt, dragging me against her like she's just as wrecked by this as I am.

Her lips are soft, and her taste is something I already know will haunt me. I angle her back against the couch, pressing into her, my hands exploring the curve of her waist beneath her sweatshirt. She arches into me, her breath hitching when my mouth moves to her jaw, then lower, tracing along the delicate line of her throat.

"Grant," she breathes, her voice breaking.

"You're going to be the death of me," I murmur against her skin.

She laughs breathlessly, but it turns into a sharp gasp as I find a sensitive spot just beneath her ear. "What a way to go, though."

I pull back just enough to look at her, and for a moment, neither of us moves. Her hair is a mess from my fingers, her lips swollen, her pupils blown wide. She's the most beautiful thing I've ever seen.

"We should stop," I say, my voice strained.

"We should," she agrees, but her fingers are still in my hair, and I can't bring myself to move away.

Neither of us moves.

It's only when a car alarm blares from somewhere outside that reality slams back into me. I shift, exhaling hard and running a hand through my hair. She pulls her sweatshirt back into place and clears her throat, but neither of us looks at each other right away.

"It's late." I exhale. "We should—"

"Yeah." She straightens, still a little breathless. "We should definitely..."

"Get some sleep."

"Right. Sleep." She laughs shakily. "That's...yeah."

I stand first, extending a hand to help her up. She hesitates for half a second before taking it, her palm warm against mine. As I walk her to the door, every step is thick with something unspoken.

When she reaches for the handle, she pauses, finally looking up at me. My pulse kicks hard in my chest.

"Goodnight, Grant."

I swallow against the ache in my throat. "Goodnight, Sophia."

She steps out, and I stay there, watching her go, knowing nothing between us will be the same after this.

twenty-one

. . .

Sophia

I KICK off my shoes outside the door to the guest house so I don't trail in the sand I picked up on the beach while hanging out with Wyatt and Blair this afternoon. I look at the script on the island and know I should review lines, but I'm so distracted by that kiss with Grant.

I can't stop daydreaming about his body pressed against mine. Why does he have to be so hot? More than that, I can feel things between us shifting. I think he feels it, too. I'm both excited about the idea of it and terrified. In moments like this, where I'm alone, I can actually picture what it might be like to belong to Grant and Hazel. I can imagine this as my home, putting Hazel to bed together, going on family trips, and maybe even having more children.

I'm letting my imagination run away again. I shake it off because the reality is it's unlikely and, more so, unrealistic for there to be anything more between me and Grant. I'm not sure if he would even let it go any further than a kiss. I'm not sure I'd want it to, either.

Our feelings are amplified right now because everything feels easy and convenient. I'm staying at his house. I'm shooting at his studio. But what would it be like six months from now when I have a shoot in another state or country and he's back and forth to whatever project he's running? The "normal guy" I dated after Connor couldn't deal with it, and he was young, single, and had no children. Grant has so many responsibilities as a single parent. I'm also not willing to slow down on my career right now. I know he's supportive of my ambitions, but it's as a colleague or mentor. Would he feel the same as a partner?

The buzzing of my phone snaps me out of my spiral, and I pick it up to see a message from Grant. I can't stop the smile that overtakes my face.

GRANT

You have plans for tonight?

I look up at the pool, trying to decide how to respond. Is he asking because he wants me to come over?

GRANT

I can see you trying to come up with an excuse.

I twist my head to peer out the door and search the wall of windows on the backside of his house, and then I see him standing at the kitchen back door.

ME

I'm not trying to think of an excuse. I'm trying to figure out a nice way to say…It depends…

GRANT

Your favorite show Pink Slip is having a wrap party on Season 3 tonight. It's fairly low-key and on the lot. I have to make an appearance, but I thought maybe you'd join me.

ME

And you think that's a good idea?

GRANT

It wouldn't be weird for another production team to show up. You're filming just a few stages apart from each other. In fact, I'm pretty sure a lot of your crew will be there.

ME

They did mention it to us. Who else will be there?

GRANT

Just cast, crew, and some of the Wonderland team. No press. Also, it's casual dress – nothing fancy.

ME

Time?

GRANT

I thought we could head out at 7pm.

ME

Meet you there?

GRANT

I can drive us. No need for two cars. We can park at my office and walk over.

ME

I'll be ready at 7.

I look up, and he's still standing in the doorway, looking this way with his hands in his pockets. I wonder if he's contemplating the same things I am. We keep pushing the boundaries of whatever this is, and I'm not mad about it.

The studio lot is quiet on our walk over to the wrap party, which seems to inspire Grant to lead us slightly off course.

"This isn't the way to the party," I say, but I don't stop walking.

"Just a quick detour."

We step onto the deserted New York Street set, our own private world bathed in soft amber streetlights. Grant walks beside me, his presence warm and steady. He's dressed like this is his version of a casual weekend—button-down shirt, sleeves rolled to his forearms, top button undone, dress pants just relaxed enough to be comfortable. He looks effortless. Comfortable in his skin. It's disarming.

"This is surreal," I say, trailing my fingers along the edge of a vintage-looking newsstand prop. The texture of the worn wood is oddly grounding. "An entire street just for us."

The set is a marvel—brownstones, fire escapes, perfectly aged storefronts. It looks like a slice of Manhattan transplanted to our studio lot. But right now, it feels like a different kind of space—suspended, timeless.

"Sometimes, the most genuine moments happen in the most artificial places," Grant says. Then he makes a face like he wants to take it back immediately.

I laugh, and it comes easier than I expect. "Deep thoughts from a studio executive?"

He bumps my shoulder lightly, and though brief, the contact is distracting. "I'm not just about balance sheets and greenlighting projects."

We walk slowly; the air between us feels charged with something neither of us wants to name yet. I can still feel his lips on mine. He hasn't touched me tonight. Not really. But there's a moment—when our arms brush, when our steps slow at the same time—when I think he might. When I think we both want to.

"Can I ask you something?" I stop near the old-fashioned ice cream shop, hesitating before meeting his gaze. "Why this project? Why my film?"

Grant exhales and looks down for a moment like he's choosing his words carefully. "Because it reminded me of why I got into this business in the first place. Not the money, not the power, but the stories that actually mean something."

I hold his gaze, trying to see if there's anything more beneath his words.

"I was terrified of making this film," I admit, my voice softer than I intend. "Not because I thought I'd fail, but because I wanted to prove I was more than just an actress. That I could create something. Shape it. Tell a story the way I've always wanted to."

His expression shifts, and his focus sharpens on me in a way that makes my breath catch.

"You already have," he says, his voice low and edged with something protective, something I shouldn't like as much as I do.

We've stopped walking now and are standing beneath the streetlight. It casts a soft glow over us, and for a second, I wonder what we must look like to an outsider. Two people standing too close, caught in something we don't quite want to admit yet.

"You know that, right?" he adds.

I want to believe him. More than that, I want to believe in myself.

"Maybe," I say, forcing a small smile.

His fingers flex like he wants to reach for me but then thinks better of it. I let the moment stretch, let the possibility of it settle between us. Whatever this is, it's shifting, becoming something neither of us planned for, and that both excites and terrifies me.

twenty-two

. . .

Grant

IT WAS PROBABLY careless to invite her to this wrap party and risky for us to arrive together, but apparently, I don't care anymore. I want to spend all my time with her. As I watch her from across the room, I pretend I'm listening to whatever merger talk one of my colleagues is droning on about. Sophia's laugh carries over the noise of the party—the genuine one she rarely uses in public, not her press-ready chuckle. My fingers tighten around my glass of bourbon.

Blaze Winters, an up-and-coming hotshot actor from Everest Studios, has been hovering around her for the past twenty minutes. He's got that look I know too well, the one that says he thinks he's about to land his next big star. He's standing too close, touching her elbow too often. Sophia's being polite and professional, but I catch the slight tension in her shoulders, the way her smile doesn't quite reach her eyes.

It's not your business, I remind myself. We may have given in to a moment, but we're not together. I have no claim on her, and vice versa.

"Don't you think, Grant?" someone says, breaking through my thoughts.

"Sorry. What was that?" I force my attention back to the man standing next to me, but my gaze keeps drifting to Blaze and Sophia with their heads bent together as he shows her something on his phone.

I shouldn't be jealous. I've seen Sophia act, and I've seen her when she's real, and every one of her reactions with Blaze right now is a performance. He touches the small of her back, and something inside me snaps.

"Excuse me," I say to the group I'm standing with, already moving across the room. I don't have a plan, but my feet carry me toward them anyway.

"Sophia," I say, my voice carrying that studio executive authority I've perfected over the years. "Sorry to interrupt, but I need to discuss the reshoot schedule for next week. Blaze, I'm sure you understand. Time-sensitive matters."

Her eyes meet mine, and there's a flash of relief followed by amusement. And my heart is hammering against my ribs like it's trying to escape.

"Of course," Blaze says smoothly, though his smile has an edge. "We'll catch up later, Sophia."

She nods graciously, but she's already turning toward me. "The reshoot schedule?" she asks once Blaze is out of earshot, one eyebrow raised.

"You looked uncomfortable. I was just trying to help." I try to keep my voice light and professional. Anyone watching would see a producer and his star talking shop. They wouldn't see how my hands itch to touch her, how I have to force myself to maintain this careful distance.

"Funny," she says, taking a sip of her champagne. "I didn't know I needed help."

"You don't." The admission comes out rougher than I intended.

Her eyes soften just a fraction, and I see the understanding there. It terrifies me. "Grant—"

"It's fine, Sophia. I'm sorry. I shouldn't have interrupted."

"I'm glad you did. I'd rather be with you."

The party continues around us, but for a moment, we're in our own bubble, teetering on the edge of something neither of us is ready to name. And God help me, but I'm thinking some things might be worth the risk after all.

"Let's go."

The city lights blur past the car window, but I'm not really seeing them. All I can think about is Sophia insinuating that she wants me. My hand grips the steering wheel in an effort to control myself when all I want to do is touch her, put my hand on her leg, run it up her thigh, and see what's waiting for me under that skirt.

I finally break the silence. "You're quiet."

"Just thinking," she says as she turns toward me. "Do you think Blaze bought the reshoot excuse?"

My jaw tightens. "Does it matter?"

"Grant..."

"I know, I know. I shouldn't have..." I sigh, taking one hand off the wheel to run my hands through my hair. "It was unprofessional."

"That's not what I was going to say."

I pull into the driveway, but neither of us moves to get out. The house is dark. Hazel's at Sarah's for the night. The silence stretches between us, heavy with all the things we've been careful not to say.

"What were you going to say?"

"I was going to say..." She takes a deep breath. "When Blaze started flirting with me, all I could think about was how wrong it felt. How I wanted to be anywhere else but there."

"Sophia..." I stop, not sure what I want to say. Before I can respond, she's opening the door to escape the awkward moment. My hands race to unbuckle my seatbelt, and I jump out of the car and rush to meet her. I shut the door behind her, leaving my hand there while raising my other arm to cage her in.

"It felt wrong seeing you near him. I want your attention, your laughs...to touch you."

I bring a hand down to tuck her hair behind her ear, and she brings her arms up and wraps them behind my neck. It's the permission I need to smash my lips against hers. I devour her lips like I'm starving, and when I hear a moan escape from her, I snap.

I bring my hands down to her legs and lift her so they're wrapped around my waist and carry her through the gate and toward the bungalow. She's got her hands in my hair and is kissing down my jawline to my neck, and I'm so hard my pants are strangling my cock.

I reach for the sliding door and wedge it open just enough for us to slide through and stumble over to the bed. She's laid out before me, and as much as I want to take her right now, I slow it down.

"Grant," she whispers, her eyes hungry, her face flushed.

"Lie back."

She does exactly as I ask her to, and I reach for her. I glide my hands over her thighs, pushing up her skirt to reveal a pink lace thong. It barely covers her bare pussy.

"Christ, Sophia. You are so fucking gorgeous."

She twists with need at my praise, lifting her hips toward me.

I move my hands to her shirt and push it up past her bra.

"Can I take this off?"

"Yes." She nods and raises her hands in the air.

I pull off her shirt and pull down her bra so her tits pop out over the top. My mouth finds her breasts, and my tongue dances over and swirls around her tight nipples. I bring my hand up to her other breast, unable to keep my hands off her.

I bring my face back up to hers and press into her lips again, and when I pull back to look at her, she's panting.

"Your body, these lips. I'd love nothing more than to fuck that sweet mouth and take that sweet cunt."

She responds by pulling at my shirt, struggling with the buttons.

"Can I take this off?" she asks.

I push back and pull the shirt off over my head. When her hands touch my skin, it feels like a bolt of electricity crackles through my chest. They are soft and delicate as they roam across my chest and abs. Before she can go any lower, I drop to my knees and pull her to the edge of the bed.

"Can I take your panties off? I want to see that perfect pussy."

"Yes."

My eyes follow her hands as she pushes her panties down her legs, and they fall to the floor. My mouth is almost drooling with need. I want to taste her, explore every inch of her body, and watch her scream with pleasure. She's glistening, slick with need.

"Lay that beautiful body back, pull your knees up, and open them wide, Sophia. I'm going to lick this pussy until you are begging me to let you come. I want to feel your orgasm on my tongue and my head smashed between your knees."

I breathe in her sweet scent and then slide my tongue up her center, swirling my tongue around the bundle of nerves at the top of her slit.

"Oh, yes. More of that, please."

"You like how my mouth feels on your cunt?"

"Yes."

My hands hold her thighs in place as I lick her slowly, exploring every inch of her. She whimpers and grabs my hair, grinding on my face. I'm so turned on that my dick is leaking precum, and I have to thrust against the bed for just a little relief.

"More, Grant. I need more."

I drag my fingers down the inside of her thigh, resting them at her entrance, teasing her.

"Is this what you want, Sophia? You want me to fuck you with my fingers?"

"Yes!"

I circle around her entrance with one of my fingers as I

flick my tongue over her clit. She pulls my head closer to her, almost suffocating me. I thrust a finger inside her, and she instantly clenches around me, calling out my name.

"Grant, I'm going to come," she says, panting.

I slide another finger inside her and press my mouth against her, running my tongue up, down, and around her most sensitive parts.

Her knees tighten around my head, and her body convulses around me.

"That's right, baby. Let it go. Fuck my fingers and take what you need."

She explodes, and I hear her call out my name again as I keep stroking her, carrying her through her orgasm. When her knees release my head and she relaxes, I pull back and crawl on top of her, leaning in to kiss her again.

My dick presses against her, and she wriggles beneath me as she pulls me closer to her, breathless.

"See how hard you make me, Sophia? You make me want more."

"Take more, then."

Our eyes lock for a moment. Those words are filled with so much meaning.

I lean back in to gently kiss down her neck and her breasts again. and then I tell her, "Not tonight. Just you tonight."

My lips trail down the rest of her body, and I give one last kiss to her beautiful pussy. Then I find her panties on the floor and slide them back up her legs. When she sits up, I press my forehead against hers and take a moment. I want her so fucking bad, but this was already way over the line. It's not too late to stop what's happening. We didn't fuck; we could chalk this up to the weird energy of the evening.

Sophia brings her hands to my jaw and pulls back, forcing me to look her in the eyes. She doesn't say anything, just watches me for a minute like she can read my mind and knows the conflict raging inside of me.

"Thank you for tonight," she tells me as she runs her hands through my hair. "Don't overthink it. I wanted you as much as you wanted me."

I reach past her, grab the blanket that's hanging on the arm of the chair beside the bed, and wrap it around her.

"Walk me out?" I grab my shirt off the bed and slide my arms through the sleeves before buttoning just a few buttons to keep it closed.

She nods and follows me to the door. When I turn to say goodbye, she reaches up and covers my lips with hers—softly, sweetly, as if she's confirming everything is ok. We are ok.

"Goodnight, Grant."

"Goodnight, Sophia."

My shoes tap softly as I cross the back patio over to my house, and I realize I never even took them off. I slide through the back door and turn to look back at the guest house, hoping to catch a glimpse of Sophia one last time, but the curtains are already closed, and my heart sinks.

twenty-three

. . .

Sophia

I ADJUST my posture in the small armchair by the window, my script balanced on my lap, but I can't focus—not on the words, not on the scene, not on anything. Every time I close my eyes, I feel Grant's hands on me, the heat of his mouth, the way we finally gave in. We didn't cross every line, but we crossed enough that there's no taking it back now. And I don't want to. I want more.

But what does that even mean? For us? For me? For the cautious behavior we've kept in place since I moved into his guest house?

I shake my head, exhaling sharply. Focus, Sophia. I've read the same line three times now, but it still doesn't feel right. Not yet.

Ugh! Ok, I've got to get out of this tiny room filled with the scents and sounds from last night before I walk over and throw myself at Grant.

I throw on some running shorts, a tank, and a light jacket

since I know it will be cool outside. I'm tying my shoes when I hear the tapping on my glass doors.

I raise my head and see the biggest chocolate chip eyes looking back at me over a big, toothy grin. My heart.

"Morning, Sophia!" Hazel yells through the glass.

I open the sliding door, and Hazel steps in and immediately hugs my legs. My hands move automatically, holding her head against my lower abdomen, and my fingers slip into her soft curls.

"Morning, nugget. Why are you up so early?"

"Dad is dropping me at Aunt Sarah's house. He has an early meeting with some East Coast assholes."

"Hazel!" Grant's voice is a gruff reprimand as he follows just a few steps behind.

"That's what you said, Dad!" She shrugs like she's obligated to repeat it exactly for the record.

I press my lips together to keep from laughing, but my eyes betray me when I glance up at Grant.

"Morning," he says. His eyes roam over my body, igniting tingles in the wake of his perusal.

"Morning." I fight the impulse to close the distance between us. "Sorry about the meeting with the East Coast folks."

"It's just a finance meeting. The investor relations team wants to talk through some numbers so they can spin a story for Wall Street."

"Sounds fun."

He smirks, the kind that says he hates it but thrives on it at the same time. It's one thing I admire about him—his ability to find purpose in all of it, even the mundane, the exhausting, the absolute bullshit of it all. I've spent years in this industry, but his gratitude for the process is something else entirely. Maybe that's why he's so successful. Maybe that's why he's so damn magnetic.

Our eyes catch, and suddenly, it's just us again. My pulse kicks up, and the air between us charges with the memory of his touch, the way he looked at me like he wanted to consume me, the way I wanted to give him everything.

I wonder if he's thinking about it now. If he wants more. If his hands are in his pockets because he's resisting the urge to touch me again. I want him to. God, I want him to.

Hazel, oblivious to the wildfire spreading between us, breaks us out of our trance.

"There's a play, and I think I might want to audition, but I think my friend Hannah is going to audition for the same thing I want to audition for, so I'm not sure. But Sophia, can you help me prepare a hologram?"

I blink, trying to process the whiplash of her words. "Hologram?"

"She means monologue," Grant says, covering his mouth to stifle his laughter.

"That's what I said! Monologue!" Hazel exclaims with her hands on her hips.

I don't hold back my laughter. Her confidence is enviable. I want to say yes immediately, but I glance up at Grant first to make sure he won't mind. I love helping her. I love seeing the world from her six-year-old perspective.

Grant catches my look and gives me the smallest nod, his silent cue that it's fine.

"I'd love to, nugget. When is the audition?"

"Oh, I think it's tomorrow, but I'm not sure."

My head snaps down to her. "Tomorrow?"

I turn to Grant, my eyes wide in a mix of surprise and amusement. He just shakes his head, his lips twitching like he's holding back a smile.

"Ok, then," I say, exhaling. "I guess we better get started as soon as you get home today. I'll be here by four o'clock. You get the snacks ready, and I'll bring some suggestions for you."

Hazel throws herself at me for another hug, making me stumble back with a laugh.

"You're the best, Sophia!"

Grant clears his throat. "Let's go, nugget. I need to get going."

Hazel grabs his hand, and they head down the driveway toward his car. I should turn away, go back inside, and shake off whatever this morning has done to me, but I don't.

I watch as he buckles her into her booster, moving with care and ease. And then, like he knows I'm still watching, he looks back at me. Our eyes meet again, and for a beat too long, neither of us moves.

A shiver runs down my spine, and anticipation curls in my stomach. Then, as if the moment needs a closing note, Grant smirks and says, "Don't be late this afternoon. Hazel's serious about those snacks."

It's so simple, so normal, but the way he says it, the way his voice dips just enough to make it feel like something else entirely, sends heat licking up my spine.

"I wouldn't dare," I say, my lips curving.

He holds my gaze for another second and then slides into the driver's seat before pulling away.

I stand there longer than I should, my fingers gripping the doorframe, my heart racing. I was going to go for a run and burn off some of this restless energy, but now I just want to relive the memory of his lips on me.

Or better yet, do it all over again.

twenty-four

. . .

Grant

"MORNING," I say, deliberately focusing on the contract revisions spread across my desk. "If this is about the Elle production, I already talked to—"

"This isn't about the production." Lucas drops into one of the chairs across from me and crosses one leg over the other. "This is about the wrap party for *Pink Slip* this weekend. The one you attended. The one I didn't know you were attending."

"And that's a problem?"

"I think it's interesting you happened to be on the lot. For a wrap party. On a weekend." Lucas's eyebrow inches higher.

I keep my face carefully neutral.

Lucas shakes his head. "I have a Google alert set up for anything involving you, and you're lucky it didn't blow up. However, I did hear about your appearance from Monica in marketing, who heard it from her friend at *Variety*, who was apparently fascinated by how much time you spent talking to Sophia Ford."

The pen in my hand stills. I'm calculating potential damage—not to myself, but to her. Sophia's first major production. Her first time producing. One wrong move, one misinterpreted interaction, could destroy everything she's worked for. This proves that it's a bad idea for us to go any further than we've already gone.

"It was a party, Lucas. People talk at parties."

"People do talk at parties," he agrees mildly. "They also notice things, like how you swooped in to rescue her from Blaze Winters or how you both were deeply entrenched in conversation for twenty minutes after that."

Shit. I didn't think it would seem unusual. I'd been careful—or thought I had been. But more importantly, I'd been protective. Blaze has a reputation, and Sophia doesn't need that kind of attention.

"Is there a point to this?" I ask, though I know exactly where this is going.

Lucas leans forward and gives me his serious face. "Grant, you know I respect your privacy. Whatever is or isn't happening between you and Sophia is your business, but my job is to protect you and this studio from any PR disasters, and I can't do that if I'm blindsided."

The word "disasters" echoes in my mind. But I'm not thinking about potential damage to me. I'm thinking about Sophia—how vulnerable she is right now, how much this could cost her.

"There's nothing to be blindsided by." The words taste like lies, like protection.

"Really?" He scrolls through his tablet. "Because I have three different people who described your intervention with

Blaze as, and I quote, 'territorial,' 'possessive,' and my personal favorite, 'like watching a lion mark its territory but in Armani.'"

I pinch the bridge of my nose. My first instinct is to pull back, to create distance, to protect her from any potential fall-out. "It wasn't like that. I wasn't even in a suit."

"That's not the point," Lucas says gently. "Perception is reality in this business, and you know that better than anyone. If something is happening—"

"It's not," I say, cutting him off, too sharply. What I really mean is, not if it means risking her career. Not if it means potentially destroying everything she's worked for. I won't let whatever feelings I seem to have ruin what she's worked so hard for.

"Ok." He holds up his hands in surrender. "Then let me rephrase. If something were to happen, hypothetically, with an Oscar-winning actress who's currently starring in our biggest production of the year...I'd appreciate a heads-up so I can do my job. So I can protect you both."

The silence stretches between us. Lucas waits, patient as ever, while I wage an internal war with myself. Finally, I say, "There's nothing to protect. We're professionals. That's all."

Lucas stands, straightening his jacket. "Of course." He heads for the door and then pauses. "Just...remember that I'm on your side, Grant. Always have been."

Lucas is right—he's always had my back—but how can I explain something to him that I can't even explain to myself?

I reach for my phone, and my thumb hovers over Sophia's name in my recent calls.

Before I can follow through, my assistant's voice crackles through the intercom. "Mr. Hall? Geneva is here to see you."

Shit.

The door opens before I can even respond, and there she is—still impossibly tall, still making casual clothes look runway-ready.

"Grant," Geneva says, gliding into my office like it hasn't been three months since we've seen each other in person. "Don't tell me you forgot I was coming."

"Of course not," I lie, standing to give her a quick hug and peck on the cheek. "Just lost track of days. You look great."

"Liar." She drops gracefully onto my office couch and crosses those famous legs. "But I'll take the compliment. How are things?"

I fill her in on all things Hazel and the schedule for the week so we can coordinate drop-off and pick-up.

"I know I said I'd take her full-time from Thursday through Sunday, but I just found out I have this charity thing Thursday night, so any chance we can shift to Friday through Sunday?"

Project Teddy Bear Gala, which I'm supposed to attend. Where Sophia is presenting an award.

"Yeah, about that..." I settle into the chair across from her. "I'll actually be there, too. Studio obligation."

"Any chance your sister might help?" Geneva grins, knowing she will.

"Yeah, she'll be fine to watch her."

"I'll have her every other moment I'm here, I promise. Anything new with her I should know?"

I can't help smiling. "Apparently, she's going to audition for the school play."

"Really?" Geneva's perfectly shaped eyebrows shoot up.

"I guess. She's recruited help for her audition. From Sophia Ford."

"The Sophia Ford?" Geneva leans forward slightly. "Oscar-winner Sophia Ford is helping our six-year-old with her school musical audition?"

"She's producing and starring in one of our new projects," I explain, keeping my voice carefully casual. "Her house flooded the first week of production, so I offered to let her stay in the guest house while she waits for repairs. Hazel asked for her help this morning."

"That's...surprisingly sweet." Geneva tilts her head. "And very convenient for you, having her right there to help."

"It's been productive." I resist the urge to loosen my tie. "She's good with Hazel."

Geneva's smile softens. "You always did know how to pick good people to have around her." She stands and smooths her dress. "Well, I should let you get back to work. I guess I'll see you Thursday night. And Grant?"

"Hmm?"

"You're a good father and person. The way you've managed all this—your career, Hazel, keeping good people around her, being supportive of me—you're doing it right."

Something in my chest tightens. If she only knew how complicated I've made things, how I'm risking everything by falling for Sophia.

"Thanks, Gen." I clear my throat. "Oh, and on Thursday, Sophia will be there, too. Presenting an award."

"Well, then." Geneva grins. "I look forward to meeting the woman who's going to turn our daughter into a star. Think she'd give me some acting tips? I have this perfume campaign coming up..."

I laugh, grateful for how easy this is, how uncomplicated. "I'm sure she'd be happy to help."

She's already heading for the door, phone in hand. "I can't wait to meet her then. Kisses!"

The door closes behind her, and I sink back into my chair. Thursday night. Sophia. Geneva. All in one room.

I reach for my phone again. I should warn Sophia, prepare her, but what would I even say?

Hey, you know how we can't seem to stay away from each other? Well, my extremely perceptive ex is about to spend an entire evening watching us pretend we barely know each other.

Instead, I pull up Lucas's number. Maybe he was right about needing a heads-up for these things because something tells me that Thursday night is going to be interesting.

twenty-five

. . .

Sophia

AFTER A FEW HOURS of trying to focus on memorizing my lines, I finally give up and shower. Then I spend the afternoon scanning some of my favorite princess movies for an age-appropriate monologue and have three solid choices for Hazel. Rapunzel when she stands up to Mother Gothel, Moana's speech to Maui, and of course, Belle taking her father's place with the Beast. It's a role I know quite well. All winners.

"Soooopppphhhhiiiiiaaaa!" Hazel's voice grows louder as she runs up the driveway to the guest house. I slide the door open just as she reaches it.

"Hey, nugget!"

She wraps her arms around my hips again. She gives the best hugs.

"Hey, Sophia! How are you?" Sarah gives me a quick hug and readjusts what appears to be several bags hanging from her shoulders.

"Here, let me help. What is all of this?" I grab a few totes off one arm as she shifts a few others onto the arm I've just emptied so the bags are more evenly distributed on her body.

"Let's see. Costume possibilities, snacks, and possibly a Lego set we didn't need at all."

I love that Grant's sister loves Hazel so much. We're all just a pawn in Hazel's game.

I wrap my empty arm around her and squeeze her in solidarity. "Alright, let's see what we're working with, then, shall we?"

We all head over to the main house, and Sarah unloads the bags as I lay out the printed monologues on the island. Hazel crawls up on a stool and gazes up at me with a look of surprise.

"What's this?"

"Some options for you!" I'm feeling smug and proud that I have some killer choices and can actually really help her with this. I watch as she picks up the papers and reads through them carefully. Her eyebrows scrunch together, and I can't tell if she's confused or something upset her.

"Sophia, I can't do a princess monologue. They are for babies."

My eyes open wide, and I steal a glance at Sarah. I'm relieved to see that she's got the same look.

"Oh?"

"Yeah. I went to the library during lunch, and Ms. Raymond helped me Google some monologues, and I found the perfect one."

"Do tell."

"Yes, do tell," Sarah says. "I'm dying to hear what you found."

Hazel jumps down from the stool and breaks into the "I completely blacked out" monologue from *Chicago*. You know —the musical where the women kill their spouses or significant others because "they had it coming."

"That...well. Oh. Um. That was amazing." It actually was amazing.

I look back at Sarah, and her shoulders are shaking, and moisture is glinting from under her eyes. It's hysterical, silent laughter, and it's contagious. I try to hold back. I don't want Hazel to think we are laughing at her, but in what life does a six-year-old choose that monologue? It feels very on brand for a studio executive's daughter, I suppose, especially one living in La La Land.

"Why are you laughing? Did I mess it up?"

"Oh, no, sweetheart, you were incredible. So good that I'm not sure if you even need my help."

"I definitely need your help. I need to bring the emotion out in the scene."

This causes the sound to escape from Sarah's silent hysterics.

"Stop laughing at me!"

I place my hands on Hazel's face. "We are definitely not laughing at you. It's just a shock to see someone so young perform a part meant for a grown-up."

"Oh." She stops to think about that for a moment. "But it was good, yeah?"

"Fantastic."

Sarah finally regains her composure and reassures Hazel that she did a fantastic interpretation of one of her favorite musicals, but she holds firm on not letting her watch it. The scary part of this whole thing is that Hazel nailed the reading without ever seeing how it's been performed.

We spend the next hour trying on costumes and rehearsing the scene around two dozen more times before we end up ordering takeout and crashing on the couch.

I offer to keep an eye on Hazel so Sarah can head out early, and once she leaves, we decide to watch *Beauty and the Beast* because it really does have a great monologue moment.

Hazel is lying in my lap as my fingers rake through her hair, and I can tell she's just about ready to fall asleep.

"My dad was like Beast. He was kind of cranky and alone and never let anyone come over until you. You've changed him. You made him happy."

I still as I take in what she's just said. I don't know how to respond to that. I'm not sure she's asking me to.

"Maybe he'll build you a library, and you'll live happily ever after."

The sound of the front door opening makes me glance up, and there he is—Grant—stepping inside, looking tired but still entirely too good. Hazel and I are curled up on the couch, with the evidence of our evening of rehearsing scattered across the coffee table, along with a half-empty bowl of popcorn and a couple of juice boxes.

"Dad! You're home!" Hazel scrambles off the couch, practically vibrating with excitement. "Watch this!"

Grant barely has time to set down his keys before Hazel launches into her performance, standing tall, her shoulders back, her voice steady as she recites her monologue. She throws in dramatic pauses like a pro, and her confidence is unwavering. I steal a glance at Grant, who watches her with that mix of pride and amusement I've come to recognize. His attention flicks to me for just a second, and something in his expression makes my stomach dip.

When Hazel finishes, she throws her arms out with a flourish. "What do you think?"

Grant claps and lets out a low whistle. "That was incredible, nugget. You're going to crush that audition."

I stretch my arms over my head and smile. "Nailed it."

Hazel beams as she hops back onto the couch beside me. "Sophia helped me so much. She's the best."

Laughing, I brush a strand of hair behind my ear. "You did all the work, Hazel."

Grant's eyes meet mine, and for a second, I can't breathe. "Thank you," he says, his voice low.

I stand and smooth out my sweater, trying to steady myself. "I should get going," I say, but I don't move right away. Neither does he.

Grant nods, but his jaw tightens just slightly. "I'll walk you out."

Hazel groans. "Do you have to go?"

I lean down and press a quick kiss to the top of her head. "You need to get some rest for tomorrow. Big day."

She sighs but hugs me tight before bouncing to the stairs and up to her room.

Grant follows me to the back door, and when I turn to face him, he steps closer, backing me against the door, his body almost touching mine.

The silence stretches, thick with the weight of everything we aren't saying. My pulse pounds as his gaze drops—to my mouth, to my throat, then lower. His fingers lift to trace a line up my arm, and for a second, I think he's going to close the distance between us. My breath catches as he exhales, and the faintest hint of restraint flickers over his features.

I should go, break whatever spell we've fallen under, but I don't. Instead, my hand shifts slightly, brushing against his waist. The contact is barely there, a whisper, but it's enough. A spark ignites, slow and smoldering, curling low in my stomach.

His fingers skim my jawline, and then he sweeps his thumb over my bottom lip. My heartbeat stumbles, and my panties are soaked.

"This fucking mouth. I dream of it."

His jaw tightens like he's battling the same war inside himself that I am. His other hand lifts—just slightly, just enough that I wonder if he's about to touch me.

"Ready, Dad!" Hazel shouts from upstairs, breaking the moment between us.

He grabs my hand, which is resting on his waist, and lifts it to his lips before dropping it and backing away.

"Goodnight, Sophia."

"Goodnight, Grant." My voice is soft, and my fingers tighten slightly around the strap of my bag like I need something to ground me. "See you tomorrow."

He nods. "Yeah. Tomorrow."

I force myself to walk away, but my body protests every step. I feel the weight of his gaze on me. When I hear the door close behind me, I let out a breath I didn't realize I was holding, but it does nothing to cool the fire still smoldering between us.

twenty-six

. . .

Grant

I LEAN against my office doorframe, still processing the evening. When I put Hazel to bed just now, she couldn't stop talking about how Sophia helped her with her audition piece. The way Sophia is patiently working with Hazel for her audition, you'd think she belonged here.

The memory of our moment at the back door makes my pulse quicken. Sophia looking up at me with those ice-blue eyes, my fingers tracing up her body, her hand on my waist, both of us breathing harder just from standing close. If Hazel hadn't called out... I shake the thought from my mind and head to my desk. There's still work to do, even if my mind keeps drifting to the way Sophia's lips parted when I leaned in.

Movement outside catches my eye. Through the wall of windows in my home office, I spot a flash of blue disappearing beneath the surface of the pool. Sophia. My pulse races as I watch her glide underwater with graceful strokes, her dark hair streaming behind her like silk ribbons in the moonlight.

She breaks the surface and pushes her hair back from her face. Water droplets cascade down her shoulders, gleaming silver in the pool lights. The tiny blue bikini she's wearing leaves nothing to the imagination. The top barely contains her small round breasts, and her hard nipples poke against the material. The bottoms ride high on her hips, showing off the curve of her ass as she stands up out of the water. Wet fabric clings to every curve like a second skin, and my mouth goes dry at the sight of water trailing down between her breasts. The sight of her like this is a threat to my self-control.

I should look away. Get back to work.

This is exactly what I was afraid of when I offered her the guest house. The temptation. I told myself it was a practical solution. She needed a place to stay while her house underwent repairs and the guest house was sitting empty. But now, watching her through the window like some pervert, I'm forced to admit that maybe I had other motivations.

After reading the same email three times without absorbing a word, I admit defeat. Maybe a swim would clear my head. I close my laptop with more force than necessary and head to my bedroom, trying to ignore the way my heart is already racing at the thought of joining her. I change quickly into board shorts, my dick already growing hard at the thought of her wet body against mine.

The warm night air hits my skin as I step outside. Sophia's doing lazy backstroke laps, but she stops when she hears the door close behind me. Water streams down her face as she rights herself, and I can't help but stare at the way her practically transparent bikini clings to her tits, with the outline of her nipples visible in the pool lights.

"Hey." Her face lights up with that smile that never fails to make my stomach flip. She moves to the edge of the pool and rests her arms on the concrete. "Your pool was calling my name. I couldn't resist."

"It does have that effect on people." I hesitate at the pool's edge, suddenly self-conscious. This feels too intimate. Maybe I didn't think this through.

She must sense my hesitation because she pushes away from the wall, giving me space. "Water's perfect. Join me?" Her voice carries a hint of challenge that makes my pulse jump.

What the hell? I dive in, and the cool water is a shock to my system. When I surface, I don't hesitate before reaching for her and pulling her close—close enough I can see the water droplets on her collarbone and the glare off the water reflecting in her blue eyes.

"You lied. This water is not warm."

Her breath catches as our bodies align, and her soft curves press against my chest.

"I said it was perfect, not warm."

The water makes her skin silky smooth against mine, and I have to bite back a groan when I feel her thighs wrap around my waist and she presses her center against my now steel-hard cock.

"Grant," she whispers, and it's full of want. Her hands slide up my chest to my shoulders, leaving trails of fire despite the cool water.

My grip tightens around her waist, and my fingers tangle

in her hair, pulling her lips to mine. Her lips are cool from the water but quickly warm under mine, and when she parts them with a soft moan, I'm lost. She tastes like chlorine and something sweet. Her fingers thread through my wet hair, pulling me closer as the kiss deepens. I let my hands roam down her back, feeling every inch of exposed skin.

Her legs grip me harder, drawing her impossibly close as she moves her hips. I bring my hands down underneath her beautiful round ass and guide her thrusts so we're both grinding against each other. If we keep going, I'm going to come right here in this pool, in my swim trunks.

The splash of water from the pool filter startles our lips apart, and we both freeze, listening for any sound from the house. Reality crashes back in when we realize we're outside where anyone can see—where Hazel could look out her window at any moment. Sophia's flushed cheeks and swollen lips test every bit of willpower I possess not to pull her back to me.

"We should probably..." She gestures toward our respective houses. The want in her voice is clear, but so is the understanding that we can't—not here and not now, not with Hazel upstairs.

Her legs drop, and the warmth instantly disappears as she pulls away from my embrace. I can't help but notice it's a good metaphor for how I feel every time she's not around me.

"Yeah," I agree, though everything in me rebels against the idea.

We climb out of the pool, and as I hand her a towel, our fingers brush—deliberately this time. The tension between us is a living thing now, impossible to ignore.

"Good night again, Grant," she says, wrapping the towel around herself. The way she says my name makes me want to forget all the reasons this is complicated.

"Good night, Sophia." I watch her walk to the guest house, with water still dripping down her legs, before forcing myself to turn away.

Back in my house, I head upstairs and check on Hazel out of habit. Her quiet snores reassure me that she's still sound asleep, completely unaware of the way her father's world is tilting on its axis.

In my bathroom, I turn the shower on hot, hoping it will clear my head. All I can think about is Sophia. The feel of her skin under my hands, the way she tasted when I kissed her, and the way she looked at me like she wanted more. There's no way I'll sleep until I release some pressure. I'm still hard from that kiss.

I run through the entire list of reasons why allowing myself to be with Sophia is a bad idea.

She works for me.

I have Hazel to think about.

Office relationships never end well.

The potential fallout could be catastrophic.

Then I stomp over to the shower and slam the stream of water off.

"Motherfucker."

I walk out of the bathroom and across my room to the hall, checking once more that Hazel is still asleep. Before I can talk myself out of it, I walk through the kitchen and out the back door and march across the pool deck patio to the guest house.

Her door isn't locked, like she was waiting for me. I find Sophia curled up in bed, watching TV in a thin tank top and shorts that might actually just be panties.

"Grant?" Her voice is breathy and uncertain, but her eyes are filled with want.

"Take off your clothes, Sophia." My voice is rough. "Tonight is my turn."

The way she scrambles to comply makes my dick turn to steel.

"Good girl," I tell her, and her responding shiver tells me everything I need to know about where this night is headed.

twenty-seven

. . .

Sophia

I'M NOT sure what is happening, but I am here for it. His eyes are dark with promise, burning into me with an intensity that steals my breath. He's gripping the door handle like it's the only thing keeping him anchored to reality, and his knuckles are white with restraint. His chest rises and falls with deep, controlled breaths that tell me just how close he is to losing that iron control he's famous for. When his eyes rake over me, there's something primal there, something that makes my heart race and my skin tingle with anticipation. He's going to devour me. The thought sends a shiver down my spine.

His command to strip comes out as a growl, rough and unhinged, so different from his usual measured tones. It bypasses all thought, shooting straight to my core, and suddenly, I'm putty in his hands, my body lighting up from the inside with need. Every cell in me yearns to obey, to please him. I can't strip fast enough, and my fingers tremble with urgency.

I pull my shorts and panties off, and as I'm reaching for my tank top, he's there, grabbing my legs and pulling me to the edge of the bed with a possessiveness that makes me dizzy with want. When he lifts my foot in his hand, the tender press of his lips against my ankle is an exquisite contrast to his earlier intensity. Each kiss as he moves up to my calf, then knee, then thigh, sends waves of sensation through me. My skin erupts in goosebumps; each touch is both soothing and electric, making me arch toward him, seeking more.

"I should've asked if you were ok with this—"

"Yes. More than ok. Keep going. Enthusiastic consent all the way." I cut him off before he can change his mind or question what he's doing to me. I need to see where this is going. I like demanding Grant.

His hand traces the curve of my hip, and when he speaks, his voice fills the quiet pool house, low and intense. "Turn over," he commands, each word deliberate and weighted with promise. "Get on your hands and knees." The authority in his tone makes my breath catch, and heat floods my cheeks. His fingers trail along my skin, raising goosebumps in their wake, before delivering a gentle pat that makes my pulse jump.

I flip over for him, suddenly hyper-aware of how exposed I am in this position. It's both thrilling and vulnerable. I've never felt more awkward yet more desperately wanted. The silence in the pool house makes everything feel amplified— my rapid breathing, the rustle of sheets, his appreciative hum. The cool air against my skin reminds me just how bare I am to his gaze, but the way his breath catches tells me he likes what he sees.

Before I can have another thought, I feel his tongue swipe through my heat, and it takes my breath away.

"You taste so fucking delicious, Sophia. I've thought about this sweet cunt all day long."

His mouth is so dirty—and I like it. He feels so good. He's got the tongue of a superhero.

He pulls back, slides his hand through my wetness, finds that magic button, and rubs against it, making my head drop, and a moan escapes from me.

"You like that, Sophia?"

"I do. I like it a lot."

He slides his fingers down my center and inserts one inside me. I groan again and lean back into it.

"Look at you grinding against my fingers. You want more?"

"Yes, give me more." I'm already close. He makes me feel like he's got the map of my body. I've had sex before, but not like this. This feels incredible, and I don't want him to stop; I want more.

He inserts another finger and slides his hand from my hip across my bottom, squeezing and rubbing it like it will bring him good luck.

"This ass almost killed me tonight. When I saw you in that bikini, I wanted to spank you for torturing me like that."

Oh. That just caused a little rush of hot liquid through me. I wonder if he could tell.

"You're clenching around me. You like the idea of being spanked?"

"Maybe."

"Ok, Sophia. But first, I want you to come for me."

His lips replace his hands on my ass, and they take a slow trail up my spine. He's gently kissing over my body as he's curling his fingers inside of me, and I feel a build-up I've never felt before. His hand glides up my side, and he places his warm palm over my chest, rubs my breasts, and pinches my nipples. It sets off a trail of sparks that erupt down my spine and into my belly, twisting the grip I have on his fingers until I'm clenching so hard I'm afraid I'm going to break them.

"Oh, Grant, don't stop. I'm going to come. Please keep touching me. Keep fucking me with your fingers. Don't. Stop." And that does it. The minute the expletive comes out of my mouth, so do I.

I rarely cuss, but I've never had an orgasm like that, either.

Before I have time to recover, I hear the tear of a condom wrapper, and I'm flat on my back.

"I want to worship every inch of this body, but I need my dick in your pussy right now. If you don't want this, you need to tell me now. We don't have to do this. I don't want you to feel pressure just because I'm crazy for you."

His body hovers over me, bracing on one arm as his hand grips his cock, stroking it from base to tip.

"Fuck me, Grant."

He teases me by running his tip through my center, spreading my wetness over him. His eyes are glued to where we are joined, and then his eyes connect with mine, his desire written all over his face.

"I want you to watch as I slide into you."

My head moves to see where he's ready to enter, and we both groan as he slips in before stopping to let me adjust. His eyes glaze over with pleasure, and my legs lift around his hips to try to pull him in for more.

"We're going slow, Sophia. I'm going to take my time with you."

He slides in another inch, and instantly, I understand. I knew he was big, but I didn't realize how big. It's a pressure that also feels incredible when I move against him. The way he's stretching and filling me has me groaning for more.

Grant throws his head back; the tension from holding back is visible on his face.

"I need more, Grant." I lift my hips, hoping to pull him further into me, and then he brings his eyes to mine and crashes his lips down on mine while thrusting all the way inside me.

The nerves inside tingle as I feel him moving back and forth, and his breath against my lips, his groans, have me on the brink of another orgasm already.

"God, your pussy is magic. It's grabbing my dick so tight. You feel so fucking good."

I nod my head against his, unable to talk. His body is draped over mine as he presses into me over and over, and it feels like pure heaven.

He sits up on his knees and pulls me up so I'm balanced over him, almost like I'm sitting in his lap. His hands slide under my bottom as he braces and balances me, but it's also his leverage as he slams up into me. I look down between us, and his cock looks incredible sliding in and out of me. I have to look up, or I'm going to come again right this second, and I don't want this to end.

"Look at me, Sophia."

I look at Grant, and his lips crash against mine as one of his hands moves to hold and guide my head so he can kiss me within an inch of my life while the other holds on to my hip so he can fuck me within an inch of my life.

I've never had lips that were so talented pressed against mine. His tongue licks inside my mouth like he's painting a masterpiece. I smile against his lips, and he pulls back for the briefest moment and gives me a smile I've never seen from him—his real smile. He's happy in this moment. Really happy.

He lays me back down on the bed and lifts my knee so it's resting on his hip, giving him a better angle, and he uses his other hand to play with my clit. I bat it away because I'm already close and it will be too intense with the extra help.

"Come for me, Sophia. I want to feel you come all over my cock."

And that's all it takes.

I'm releasing sounds I've never heard come from my mouth, and he's grunting profanities, and it's pure bliss. He stills after we've both finished and looks down at me as I catch my breath and stare back at him. It's just for a moment, but it's full of meaning and understanding. It's not like this with other people. He knows it, and I know it.

Now I just have no idea what we're going to do about it.

He pulls out of me and heads to the bathroom—I assume to take care of the condom and get sorted—and I sit up in bed, looking around in shock but unable to get this goofy grin off my face.

"Holy shit," I whisper to myself.

Grant walks back out with a washcloth in his hand and

offers it to me. I grab it but run into the bathroom to clean up in a less-public space. Besides, I need to pee.

I splash cool water on my face and can't help but grin at my reflection. My hair is a disaster, my lips are swollen, and marks are blooming along my collarbone that will require strategic wardrobe choices tomorrow. But my eyes are bright and alive with satisfaction and lingering pleasure. My muscles have that delicious ache that only comes from really good sex.

Grant in bed is exactly what I'd imagined—commanding, intense, thorough. And while part of me wants to bask in the afterglow and imagine what this could mean, I know better. It's fine. I won't mistake great sex for something more, no matter how electric it felt when he touched me and no matter how my body lit up every time he growled my name. Grant's made it crystal clear he doesn't do relationships. He's all about his daughter and work. I respect that kind of honesty.

I run my fingers through my tangled hair, making it some-what presentable, and reach for my robe. When I open the bathroom door, I'm already rehearsing casual ways to say goodnight, assuming he's dressed and halfway out the door.

But he's still here, sprawled across my bed like he owns it, with the sheet draped low across his hips, scrolling through his phone. The sight stops me in my tracks. Now this...this, I wasn't expecting.

"Hey."

"Hey."

"I know you have to get back to Hazel."

"I do. She's a heavy sleeper, but I don't like to leave her alone." He pats the bed beside him. "Come here."

I crawl onto the bed, and he groans and leans his head back against the headboard.

"Jesus, Sophia, you're killing me."

I look down at his lap and see what he's talking about. He's already growing again. I'm stunned and thrilled when he turns to kiss me. This is way more than I bargained for. He's being sweet and attentive after all that action. I know I shouldn't be surprised, but I admit that it's more than I expected.

"I didn't plan to come over here tonight and fuck your brains out, but here we are."

"Here we are." I nod and smile back at him.

"We should talk."

His smile drops, and his expression becomes serious. He brushes my hair back from my forehead, and he places a gentle kiss on my forehead. It's sweet. I think that's what drives me to say what I say next. Nothing to lose.

"I like what we just did, Grant, and I know you don't do relationships. I'm not ready for one right now, either, but I think it's obvious there's an attraction here."

He's quiet. His eyes are shifting back and forth between mine, waiting for me to continue.

"My house should be ready in a few more weeks. About the same amount of time we have left to shoot *Survivor*. While I'm here, we do whatever this was. No expectations."

"Are you sure?"

"I'm sure. I just have one rule. While we're doing what-ever this is, we don't sleep with other people."

"Of course," Grant says. "I may not date, but if I'm sleeping with someone, it's only them."

"We should keep this between us."

"And no sleepovers. I don't want Hazel to get confused or too attached."

"I agree."

He pulls me on top of him, with my legs straddling his hips, and then he reaches over to the nightstand, pulls out another condom, and slides it on, already hard and ready to go again.

He guides my hips so I'm lifted over him, and when I slide down, I feel the buzz of exhilaration spiral up my spine, down my legs, and through my arms as I wrap them around his neck.

"You're mine for the next month, Sophia."

"You're mine for the next month, Grant."

Then he drives into me until we're both gasping, twisting, and moaning with pure joy.

Afterward, he heads back to his house, leaving me to pass out with a smile pasted across my lips for the rest of the night.

twenty-eight

· · ·

Grant

I'M ON MILE FIVE, and this pent-up desire for Sophia still hasn't subsided. It's been two days since we gave in to each other, and I haven't been able to see her between her production schedule, my insane calendar, and spending time with Hazel.

I slam the stop button on the treadmill and click the off button on the remote, turning off the TV hanging above me in my home gym. I know this is casual, but maybe I should schedule a date night or something. We could do it here or in the guest house.

"Dad, I'm leaving for school. Bye! I love you!" Hazel yells out as she runs past.

"Wait!" I step out and follow her to the kitchen. "Don't I get a hug and kiss?"

"No way. You're sweating. I'm all ready for school, and you're going to mess up my outfit if you touch me."

I pull my arms up to imitate an ogre and make a funny

face with my tongue hanging out of my mouth as I take heavy, exaggerated steps toward her.

"Must hug Hazel."

The scream she belts out has my shoulders crawling up to my ears as they ring. But the giggles that escape after are the sound of pure joy and life. I'll never tire of hearing her laugh. It creates a deep sense of peace and happiness within me.

When I found out Geneva was pregnant, I'll admit that I went through some dark days. I never wanted kids. I never wanted to get married. And I still don't. But when they placed Hazel in my arms, life changed. Yeah, I know everyone says that, but what they don't say is that once you see this reflection of flesh that has pieces like a puzzle of your exact features, an instinct kicks in. You know right then that you can't imagine ever having lived life without this child. Seeing eyes that look like mine and a nose that looks so much like my mother's was—still is—surreal. The lips and face shape—that's all her mother, and no doubt she'll be a knockout just like her.

Geneva and I discussed how we wanted to parent when she shared she had a once-in-a-lifetime career opportunity. I didn't hesitate to accept full custody. We have an agreement in place, but we don't need it. The greatest thing about Geneva is that she's a lot like me. She didn't want to get married, and I'm pretty sure she didn't want kids—at least at that moment. We work well together as co-parents. She calls and visits Hazel as often as she can, and we've never missed a chance to share how much we love her and our role as co-captains of Team Hazel.

"Dad, no, no, Dad, stop," Hazel sputters as she tries to catch her breath while laughing.

"Ok, you two," Sarah says. "We gotta go, or you'll be late for school." She's been a lifesaver since Josie decided to take a leave of absence to stay for a few more months with her daughter in Nashville. We miss her but we're learning to survive on our own too. Kind of.

"Ok, nugget, I love you so much. Have the best day ever!" I smack Hazel on the cheek with an over-exaggerated kiss and run my hands over her hair before I add another kiss to the top of her head. "Love you, too, sis."

She and Sarah head out the garage door, and I run upstairs to get ready for the day—and maybe to relieve a little of this tension that's backing up.

"Sophia's still in the guest house?" Lucas says as he walks into the small conference room across from my office.

"She is. Why?"

"Oh, you know. Just trying to keep straight all the information you've hired me to manage."

I release an annoyed breath and look back down at the stack of folders in front of me. He's right. I need to fill him in on the latest decision that Sophia will stay in my guest house until her house is ready. What I'm not ready for is the question that's going to follow.

"She'll be there for at least another month. Until her house is ready."

"Hm. Ok. Can I ask why she's staying with you when she

could get a hotel, rent another house, stay with her brother, or a dozen other scenarios out there?"

"Lucas."

"Grant, I just need to know what to say."

We're both quiet for the longest minute in history.

"It's a matter of convenience."

"You want me to tell the press it's convenient for her to stay with you."

I run my hand down my face. He knows why she's there. I don't have to say it. I just need to figure out a way for us to spin it.

"My house is close to the studio. Her brother lives all the way in Santa Monica. You know that drive is a nightmare."

"So, it's a logistical solution."

"Yes. Practical. Logistics. Oh, and maybe safe, too. Staying with me eliminates the need for additional security that could be needed at a hotel or rental house."

"Ok, I can work with this. But we're going to have to do some proactive press drops of normal shit happening in your lives—separately—to help deflect and defuse any drama around this."

"Thank you."

"It's what you pay me the big bucks for."

We discuss a few ideas that Lucas can share with friendly reporters to make it seem like business as usual in my life, even with the extra mouth to feed, before the room fills with my marketing and finance teams for another long day of promoting our next blockbuster.

An hour later, I'm headed back to my office when I spot a tiny brunette from the corner of my eye.

"Sophia?"

"Hey!"

Lucas walks past me, giving me a knowing look that I ignore.

"What are you doing here?"

She looks back at the receptionist and then back at me.

"Um, I had an update about our production schedule I wanted to walk you through if you have a minute?"

I look at her, totally confused. "Sure. Come on back." I lead the way back to my office, and once we're in the doorway, I stand aside so she can enter ahead of me, and then I shut the door behind us. As soon as she hears the click, she spins to face me.

"Hey."

She walks over to me. My dick perks up, and I mentally flip through all the reasons why I shouldn't take her right here on my desk.

"Hey."

She stops just short of pressing up against me.

"Um, how are you?"

"I'm good. How are you?"

"I'm good."

"So, you wanted to walk me through production schedules?"

I watch as she glances around the room and brings her hands together, twisting her fingers.

"No. That was just something to say so nobody up front would think it's weird for me to follow you to your office."

"I don't think anyone is going to think it's weird that one of my producers wants to meet with me."

I step a little closer to her.

"If you aren't here for production schedules, then why are you here, Sophia?"

She looks up at me, and her eyes hold mine, causing a bolt of electricity to run through my spine.

"Don't you watch the dailies at three?"

I glance up at the clock on my wall, which reads 2:55 p.m.

"I do."

"I thought I might join you today if you want. You know. No expectations?"

And that's all it takes for my will to snap. I grab her hand and lead her through the door connected to my office, which takes us down the hallway to the private theater. I lock the door behind us, turn on the screen, and scroll to play today's recordings from the shared drive. I don't even care which ones. I just need some sound to drown out all the moans I plan to steal from this gorgeous woman beside me.

As soon as the first clip plays, I turn back to Sophia.

"Strip."

And then she does.

twenty-nine

. . .

Sophia

THE FOUR SEASONS' presidential suite is chaos in the best way—makeup artists weaving between racks of designer gowns, champagne glasses perched precariously on every surface, and the kind of laughter I didn't realize I'd been missing until right now.

"Girl, you have got to tell me everything about this movie," Stella says, perched on the edge of a chaise while someone works on her hair. She's still in her robe, but I can see her emerald gown hanging nearby, ready to make every other dress in the room look casual in comparison.

Brandon lounges on the suite's plush sofa, allegedly here to kill time before meeting his date at eight, though he showed up suspiciously early with Stella's favorite cold brew and those little French macarons she loves. For a stuntman who spends his days coordinating death-defying scenes, he cleans up surprisingly well, already dressed in a perfectly tailored suit that makes him look more James Bond than an action double.

"We are still on set for another week, and then we head up to Honey Pine for location scenes. It's amazing how realistic they've made everything!"

"I heard that," she says, nodding toward Brandon, who's got his face in his phone, pretending not to listen while clearly hanging on every word. These two have been practically inseparable lately.

"We also were able to schedule a local class of second-graders for some dramatic moments once we're on location. It's going to be incredible."

"Oh, I heard that, too!"

I tilt my head, looking unimpressed. Stella, at least, has the grace to look sheepish as she catches Brandon's eye in the mirror; their shared smile speaks volumes.

"Did you hear who agreed to play the title soundtrack?"

Stella bites her lip, admitting nothing, but the look on her face tells me Brandon has filled her in on everything. "Then you have the scoop!" I take a sip of champagne, careful not to smudge my freshly applied lipstick. "I don't want to jinx it, but I'll share that it's been spectacular working with Edie. She is fantastic!"

"I knew you two would be a great pair," Blair says as she crosses the room to check out the dress options. "Two fucking phenomenal women, ready to take over the box office. I can't wait to see opening weekend numbers."

"At least tell us what it's like working with Grant Hall." Stella wiggles her eyebrows suggestively.

"He's professional," I say, maybe a bit too quickly. "And before you ask, yes, I'm still staying in his guest house. Probably until production is finished."

Brandon's head snaps up from his phone. "Isn't your house ready, though?"

Oh, now he hears what we're saying.

I fill them in on the latest remodeling details. Close to finished. Another few weeks, and then I can move back in.

Everyone's quiet.

"It made sense logistically," I explain, ignoring the knowing look Brandon exchanges with Stella. He's known me too long. He can probably see right through my casual tone. "It's so close to the studio lot."

"So, I guess staying there is working out, then?" Jess asks, her reporter's instinct clearly piqued.

"It's fine. I'm actually helping him, too. His daughter auditioned for a role in her school play and got it. I may have helped her rehearse."

"Oh, I adore Hazel," Blair chimes in from where she's being zipped into her gown. "Wyatt mentioned you helped with a monologue. So sweet."

I feel a rush of gratitude for my future sister-in-law's casual tone and how she makes it sound so normal.

"Speaking of sweet," Jess says with that glint in her eye that means she's got gossip, "guess who's going to be at Project Teddy Bear tonight? Geneva. Just flew in from Paris."

My stomach drops, but I keep my expression neutral. "Oh?"

"Mm-hmm. Word is she's in town for a few days to see Hazel. She's so gorgeous. Did you see that *Vogue* cover last month? I questioned my sexuality after that. Good God. But she and Grant have the most civilized co-parenting situation I've ever seen in this town."

They do. I've seen it firsthand, heard Grant's easy laughter during FaceTime calls with Geneva, and watched how seamlessly they coordinated Hazel's schedule for this visit. So, why didn't he mention she'd be at the gala?

"Remember that charity auction where you bid against her for that Chanel bag?" Stella laughs. "Before any of us knew who she was?"

"God, don't remind me," Jess groans. I'm grateful for the change of subject. "I still can't believe I tried to outbid the face of Chanel."

"Speaking of fashion disasters," Stella continues, "wait until you hear what happened at the *Vanity Fair* shoot last week."

The conversation flows on, and I let myself sink into it. This is what I've missed, the easy banter and inside jokes. How easy it is to just pick up right where we left off. But there's a hollow space in my chest where all the things I can't say live.

"Earth to Sophia." Blair waves a hand in front of my face. "Lost you there for a minute. Everything ok?"

"Just nervous about my speech," I lie. "You know how I get about live events."

"Please," Brandon scoffs as he stands to leave. "You could do this in your sleep. Text me all the gossip later? I should head out. Can't keep Victoria waiting."

He straightens his already impeccable suit. "Ladies, you're all going to be the talk of the gala. Sophia, that blue is absolutely your color. Stella..." He pauses, and their eyes meet again in the mirror. "That dress is going to stop traffic."

"Bye, Brandon," we chorus, and for a moment, everything feels simple again.

But as I slip into my gown, I can't stop thinking about Geneva being there tonight. About Grant not mentioning it. About secrets I'm keeping from the people in this room.

"Your hair is perfect," Stella declares, coming up behind me in the mirror. "Grant Hall won't know what hit him."

"I'm not..." I start to protest, but she just winks.

"Sure, I know."

I check my phone one last time before we head out. No messages from Grant. Whatever happens tonight, I'll have to handle it the way I handle everything else in this industry— with a smile and an Oscar-worthy performance from someone who isn't falling for someone she isn't supposed to.

thirty

. . .

Grant

"*VANITY FAIR'S* HERE, along with *The Hollywood Reporter* and *Variety*," Lucas murmurs, somehow scanning the room while appearing completely focused on our conversation. "*Deadline* is still asking about the reshoot schedule from your little stunt at the wrap party."

The annual Teddy Bear Gala has transformed this industrial warehouse into a whimsical dreamland that walks the line between childlike wonder and black-tie sophistication. Oversized paper lanterns float beneath the exposed beams like luminous clouds while strings of twinkling lights weave between towering sculptures made entirely of teddy bears.

The wait staff glides through the growing crowd with champagne flutes garnished with cotton candy wisps. Wyatt and Jake maneuver around them to join us.

"Gentlemen." I adjust my bowtie as they grab glasses from the tray. "How's the planning going for the Manmorial Weekend?"

"Jake's set us up at this incredible villa," Wyatt says, clapping his friend on the shoulder. "Private beach, personal chef, the works."

"The chef's wasted on you," Jake snorts, nodding to Wyatt as he throws back his glass of champagne. "Last time we went anywhere, you survived on protein bars and spite."

"Some of us appreciate the finer things," I say, thinking of how much I've enjoyed cooking with Sophia lately. A smile tugs at my lips before I can school my expression.

Jake's eyebrow ticks up with keen interest, but he keeps his observations to himself. Wyatt's too busy watching the entrance for Blair to notice my comment.

"Speaking of food," Jake says, "Lauren's been obsessing over this caterer for weeks. He's some hotshot that was featured on *Real Housewives of Beverly Hills*. Says they better not screw up the salmon the wives rave about, or heads will roll."

I catch Wyatt rolling his eyes as Jake diverts his attention to the entrance—I suspect to watch for the aforementioned Lauren.

Lucas takes a sip of his drink and then pulls me aside. "When Geneva arrives, introduce her to Sophia immediately. It'll look weird if you don't, given she's staying at your place and helping with Hazel. Keeping things natural is our best..."

The words fade into background noise as Sophia enters the room in a midnight blue dress that seems to have been poured over her body. Her skin shimmers like moonlight against a dark sky. Her hair is down tonight in loose, natural curls that cascade like a seductive waterfall. It's swept dramatically to one side and held in place by a delicate diamond pin that catches the light with every subtle movement.

I can't look away. It's impossible.

She's mesmerizing—not just beautiful, but alive. Her eyes spark with an infectious joy, taking in the room with a curiosity that makes her more radiant than any perfectly poised socialite. When she smiles, it's genuine—reaching her eyes, lighting up her entire face. She's turning heads without even trying, completely unaware of the effect she's having on everyone around her.

I force myself to look away, to remember where we are. Who we are. But God, it's the hardest thing I've done all year.

"Grant?" Lucas is watching me too carefully. "Did you hear what I said about introducing Sophia and Geneva?"

"Yeah, of course." I haven't heard a word because Sophia's making her way toward us and I have to remember how to act like I don't get to see her naked, like I don't know exactly how she looks underneath me, how my name sounds on her lips.

"Mr. Hall," she says formally, making my dick twitch. "Lucas. Beautiful event."

"Ms. Ford," I manage to reply with what I hope is an appropriately professional smile. "We're all looking forward to your speech tonight."

There's so much I want to say—about how stunning she looks, about how much I've missed her today, about Geneva. But we're surrounded by people, the press, and the pressure to maintain appearances.

"Grant!"

Geneva's voice carries across the room, and heads turn. They always do. She's wearing something silver and flowing, and the flashbulbs start immediately as she makes her way to us.

"There's my favorite ex," she says, pulling me into a hug. "And you must be Sophia! I've heard so much about you from Hazel."

I watch Sophia's face carefully as Geneva pulls her into a hug and see the slight tension in her smile as more cameras turn our way.

"Is this a Grant-Geneva reunion?" Lauren calls out. "Give us a pose, just like old times!"

I might understand Wyatt's disdain for Lauren a little more. Of all the things to say.

Geneva laughs it off easily. "Please, we're much better as friends. Besides"—she turns to Sophia—"I hear you're the new star in Grant's life. Professionally speaking, of course. However, Hazel won't stop talking about your acting lessons. It's all 'Sophia says' this and 'Sophia showed me' that."

"She's a natural," Sophia says smoothly, but I can see the uncertainty in her eyes. I step closer, not touching her but hopefully close enough that she can feel what I can't say.

"It's so refreshing," Geneva continues, placing her hand on Sophia's arm—a genuine gesture. "Finding someone in this industry who's real. Grant's always been particular about who he lets into Hazel's life, so the fact that you're staying at the house, helping with rehearsals? It really speaks volumes."

I see Lucas stiffen. The press members scribble frantically.

"Speaking of rehearsals," I cut in, "Sophia's presenting soon. We should probably—"

"Oh, of course!" Geneva beams. "We'll catch up later. I want to hear all about this project you two are working on."

Lucas smoothly steps in to redirect the press, but what's done is done. Something about the way they're watching us—I can almost see the way their heads are working on the angles they can spin.

I walk her toward the stage near the front of the room and try to apologize, but she stops me.

"I need to get ready. Can we talk after?"

I can't tell if she's upset or nerves have her, so I just nod. I watch her step behind the makeshift platform before I head back over to the bar.

From my spot at the back of the ballroom, I watch Sophia take the stage. The lights soften around her as she approaches the microphone, and even from here, I can see how the audience leans forward, drawn in by her invisible magnetism.

"The children at Project Teddy Bear," she begins, her voice clear and strong, "have become my greatest teachers." She pauses, and a gentle smile touches her lips. "In Hollywood, we love to talk about bravery. About diving into challenging roles and tackling difficult subjects. But true courage? I see it every day in those hospital rooms. I see it in these incredible kids who've faced battles no child should have to fight yet somehow wake up each morning with hearts wide open, ready to love and trust and hope again."

She glances down at her notes but doesn't need them. The words flow from somewhere deeper. "What amazes me most is their pure, unshakeable belief in possibility. They don't let fear of falling stop them from reaching for the stars. They don't let past hurts keep them from opening their hearts to new joy. While we adults spend so much time building walls to protect ourselves, these children remind us what it means to live with real courage, to chase your dreams with your whole heart, no matter the odds."

Her eyes find mine in the crowd—just for a moment, but it's enough to stop my breath.

"These children show us that sometimes the bravest thing we can do is simply believe. Believe in magic. Believe in miracles. Believe that some things are worth the risk of any pain that could follow. Because, in the end, isn't that what makes life beautiful? Not the chances we calculated perfectly, but the leaps of faith we took when our hearts knew it was right."

The applause is thunderous, but I barely hear it. My mind is racing as pieces fall into place. Lucas was right. We need to get ahead of the press narrative. But more than that, Sophia's words echo in my head. Some things are worth the risk despite the pain that could follow.

I've spent so long protecting myself, protecting Hazel, calculating every risk, but maybe it's time to be brave. I pull out my phone.

ME

We need to talk tomorrow. About Sophia. About getting ahead of things.

LUCAS

Finally. I'll be in your office at 9am.

Twenty minutes later, I find Sophia in a quiet alcove off the main ballroom, looking out at the LA skyline. The sounds of the gala feel distant here. I step up behind her, and I'm surprised when she speaks.

"Why didn't you tell me she'd be here?" she asks quietly, not looking at me.

I wrap my arms around her and relax when she leans into me. "I don't know," I admit. "I thought about it. Kept picking up my phone to text you. Maybe..." I trail off, not sure how to finish that sentence.

"Maybe what?" Her voice is soft and vulnerable in a way she rarely allows herself to be.

"Maybe I was afraid for my two worlds to collide," I whisper.

She turns in my arms and brings her hands up to my face to trace my jaw before pulling me closer and eventually pressing her lips to mine. The kiss is delicate but quickly turns eager. Her fingers twist in my hair, and my hands slide down her hips and around the swell of her ass as my dick turns to steel.

"Grant," she moans.

I search my memory for any place we can escape to undetected, but there's just too much risk someone will see us. We're already taking a chance by making out like teenagers in a dark corner.

I break the kiss and place my forehead on hers.

"God, Sophia, everything about you is perfect. I'll never get enough of you. I can't stay away."

"I'm staying at the Four Seasons tonight. With the girls."

"Oh." My chest feels tight. One night shouldn't feel like this much of a loss.

"I promised them a girl's night."

I nod. "It's ok. We can survive one night apart," I joke.

She leans her head into my chest as she groans like she's not sure she will survive, and that makes my heart skip a beat.

"We should get back out there, or people are going to figure out we're both missing, and that's how rumors start," she says, straightening her dress.

I laugh as I follow her down the hallway, but she's not wrong.

"Grant?" She turns slightly toward me. "Geneva seems lovely. I can see why you're such good friends."

"Sophia..." I catch her hand, just for a moment, hidden in the shadows of the alcove. "Before I forget to tell you, you look beautiful tonight."

She squeezes my fingers once before letting go.

I watch her walk away, elegant and poised, everything a leading lady should be—and everything I'm falling for.

thirty-one

. . .

Sophia

THE MORNING LIGHT streams through floor-to-ceiling windows. Everything is cream and gold, from the plush carpet under my bare feet to the silk throw pillows scattered across what might be the deepest, softest couch I've ever sunk into. But even surrounded by all this luxury, my mind keeps drifting back to Grant's house, with its lived-in comfort and the way morning the sun hits the kitchen counter just right.

I curl deeper into the oversized armchair with my legs tucked under me and wrap both hands around my coffee mug. The warmth seeps into my palms as I let myself have this moment—this moment where I'm happy, maybe even a little in love.

Somewhere down the hall, I can hear Stella humming in the shower and the soft click of someone's heels on marble, probably a housekeeper.

"There you are." Blair's voice is soft as she pads into the living area in hotel slippers, her dark hair pulled into a messy bun. She looks impossibly fresh for someone who was dancing until two o'clock in the morning. "I thought I heard someone out here."

"Just got up," I admit as she settles onto the couch across from me, sinking into its cloud-like depths. The Los Angeles skyline stretches out behind her, already hazy with morning light.

As Blair studies me over the rim of her coffee cup, a knowing smile tugs at her lips. "You disappeared with Grant last night."

I take a slow sip of coffee. "You're going to think I'm crazy."

She tilts her head. "Try me."

I exhale and set my cup down on the glass table. "I keep telling myself this thing with Grant is casual, that I want it that way. But last night, I..." I shake my head, swallowing against the lump forming in my throat. "I said those things in my speech, and it felt like I wasn't just saying them to a room full of people. It felt like I was talking to him. And to myself."

Blair doesn't rush me, doesn't fill the silence like most people would. She just waits.

I press my fingertips against my temple. "It's so easy with him. I don't have to try. I don't have to be anything other than who I am, and he still...he just..." I let out a short, breathless laugh. "He looks at me like I matter. Like he sees something in me that I haven't even let myself see yet."

Blair leans forward, and the morning sun catches the diamond on her left hand—the promise of a future that is already so certain for her. "Maybe it's time to take your own advice from the speech, then?"

"I'm scared." The confession falls from my lips before I can stop it.

Blair's expression softens. "It's fucking terrifying."

I nod, staring down at my hands. "It's not just the idea of falling for him. It's everything that comes with it. His daughter. Geneva. His whole world that already exists and works without me in it. What if I walk into it and ruin it? What if I can't fit?" I look up at her, my chest tight with the weight of it. "What if I let myself hope, and it all falls apart?"

Blair shakes her head. "Or what if it doesn't?"

A simple question. But it cracks something open in me.

Hope.

It's such an exciting and terrifying thing when you think about it. But at the end of the day, it's what we all live for.

Exhaling, I push off the couch to lean in and wrap my arms around Blair. "Thank you. I'm so lucky to have you in my life."

"Damn right, you are." She squeezes me tight before pulling back with a smirk. "Now, drink your coffee and start figuring out what you're gonna do about this man before I have to make spreadsheets and intervention plans."

I roll my eyes, but a laugh escapes me. For the first time in a long time, the fear feels a bit smaller.

"Alright. I need to get to the lot." I rise out of the chair and head down the hall to get ready for the day.

"Take the risk, Sophia!" Blair calls after me as she heads down the hall to her room.

The studio lot is unusually quiet, which is why I notice Jess immediately. She's coming from the direction of the PR building, looking entirely too pleased with herself.

"Just the woman I was hoping to see," she says, falling into step beside me.

"Let me guess...terrorizing Lucas?"

"Me? Never." Her grin is wicked. "Though it does make my day to see him get flustered when challenged. But better than that...the press from last night? Overwhelmingly positive. Everyone loves the idea of America's sweetheart mentoring Hollywood's favorite mini-me."

I stop walking. "Jess..."

"Friend hat on, reporter hat off," she says quickly, raising her hands. "I promise. And as your friend..." She glances around before moving closer to me. "What's really going on with you and Grant?"

Maybe it's Blair's words from this morning, or maybe I'm just tired of holding it all in, but suddenly, I'm telling her everything. The longstanding crush, that first kiss, the currently entangled emotions of something we promised to have no expectations about.

"I knew it." Jess's eyes are wide.

"It's not... I mean, we're not..."

"Stop." She takes my hands in hers. "We all know that man has been gone for you since Blair first brought you to lunch at The Ivy. Why do you think he invited you to the Hamptons last summer? He never invites new people to those parties."

"He was just being friendly."

But even as I say it, memories start shifting into new focus when I remember the way he lingered near me all night, or how we slipped into a dance or conversation so easily.

"You deserve this. And frankly, so does he." She squeezes my hands. "This industry makes it hard to trust genuine connections. But what you two have? I know it's real. And Lucas and I can handle any press fallout."

Her response shocks and calms me at the same time. I think of the women I just spent the last twenty-four hours with and how they've become such an important part of my life. Jess, who's become my unexpected champion. Blair, who saw something in me before I saw it in myself when she supported my dreams to stretch beyond acting. Stella, whom I adore and continue to grow closer to, embracing me as if we've known each other our entire lives. And Edie, too, the industry icon I still can't believe agreed to work with me and who wants to know me beyond who I am as an actress.

For years, I'd resigned myself to a certain kind of loneliness. Fame is funny that way—everyone knows you, but almost no one really knows you. I'd become an expert at keeping people at arm's length, protecting myself from the endless parade of people who wanted something from me. A photo. An introduction. A piece of my life to sell or exploit.

But these women—they're different. They see me. Not the actress. Not the headlines. Me.

They're slowly teaching me that not everyone has an angle. That some connections are real.

It amplifies that feeling of hope—not just about Grant, the film, or my career, but about myself. About what's possible when you're brave enough to let people in.

thirty-two

. . .

Grant

I DRUM my fingers against the desk, staring at the entertainment headlines splashed across my tablet. The photos from last night's gala are in all the trades—me and Sophia laughing together at our table, Geneva chatting animatedly with both of us. Geneva's quotes about what a "perfect match" we'd make and how "Sophia's been such a wonderful influence on Hazel" were being picked up everywhere.

I should be worried. This is exactly the kind of press we've been trying to avoid. But seeing us together in those photos—the way Sophia's head is thrown back in genuine laughter—I like how natural it looks.

A knock at the door pulls me from my thoughts. "Come in."

Lucas strides in, tablet in hand. "So, I'm guessing you've seen the coverage?"

"Hard to miss it." I lean back in my chair. "Give it to me straight—how bad is it?"

To my surprise, Lucas grins. "Actually? It's perfect. Most outlets are playing up the 'power friendship' angle—Hollywood's most eligible bachelor and America's sweetheart, a perfect match. The few that are hinting at romance are overwhelmingly positive, but it's not the main narrative."

"And Geneva's comments?" I ask.

"Coming across exactly as intended—a supportive ex singing your praises. Makes you both look good." His expression grows serious. "But Grant, we need to talk strategy here. This friendly collaboration narrative is working for now, but..."

"But?" I prompt.

"But I've known you for five years. The way you look at her isn't how you look at a collaborator." He holds up his hand as I start to protest. "I'm not saying we need to change anything. Just...be careful. Figure out what this really is before the press does it for you."

I rub my temples. The problem isn't that Lucas is wrong —it's that he's terrifyingly right. This thing with Sophia has grown roots I never saw coming, threading through every careful wall I built. And for the first time in my life, I want those walls to come down.

A soft knock at my door interrupts my thoughts.

"Come in," I call out, already knowing who it is by the gentle rap of knuckles.

Sophia steps into the room wearing worn jeans and her favorite faded UCLA sweatshirt, her hair twisted up in a messy bun. The sight of her like this—casual, unguarded in the morning light—hits me harder than any evening gown could. She looks soft, touchable, and so perfectly at home in my space that it takes real effort to remember we're at work. She stops short when she spots Lucas across the room.

"I'm sorry. I didn't mean to interrupt."

"Actually, perfect timing. I was just heading out." Lucas gives me a pointed look. "Remember what I said, Grant." He closes the door behind him, leaving us in weighted silence.

Sophia breaks it first. "I saw the coverage." She perches on the edge of my desk, and I catch the faint scent of her perfume. "Seems like we're not doing a very good job of keeping this casual."

I can't help but rise from my chair, drawn to her like gravity. "Maybe we were kidding ourselves by thinking we could."

"My contractor called," she says, but her voice wavers slightly. "They said I could move back in if I wanted. The items left can easily be completed with me there." She twists her hands together.

"Stay," I say, my hand catching hers. "The guest house. At least until the renovation is complete."

I move closer, unable to keep distance between us. "I want..." I pause, careful about what I want to say. "I want to see where this goes."

"That's a big statement," she says, but there's hope in her voice. "What about Hazel? I know how protective you are."

"She adores you," I say simply. "And the way you are with her...you see her. Not just as my daughter, but as her own person."

"I like spending time with her," Sophia says. "With you both." She pauses. "I don't want to push anything."

"I know," I tell her. And I do know. She's been careful and respectful of boundaries I didn't even know I needed someone to respect. "And we can be careful until we're ready to tell her more."

Sophia looks up with a mix of vulnerability and caution in her eyes.

Her hand finds mine. "You sure you want me to stay?"

"I do," I confirm.

"Me, too," she whispers, and then she's kissing me, slow and deep and full of promise. I pull her closer, my hands spanning her waist as she wraps her arms around my neck. She leads me back to my chair, sits me down, and then slowly kneels in front of me.

I hit the window shades as she reaches for the button on my pants, my cock already leaking for her.

"Sophia, don't start something you can't finish."

Her warm breath teases what's coming as she grips the base of my dick, licks her lips, and starts to kiss around the head. Her tongue moves from the base up the shaft until she's tickling just underneath my tip. Already, my balls start to tighten, and I know this isn't going to take long.

She licks all around my cock, getting it wet before she takes me inside her mouth. Her tongue feels like velvet as it rubs me back and forth.

"Take off your shirt," I pant.

She pulls back, a puzzled look on her face.

"I'm going to fuck those tits and then cum all over them."

I love the flush across her cheeks like I've shocked her, but I know it turns her on, too. She likes it when I take control. I lean back in my chair, my dark gaze on her as my hands grip the armrests. She takes her shirt off, and her lace bra barely covers those perfect breasts. I lean forward to tweak one of her nipples before I reach behind her and pop the clasp, causing the flimsy fabric to fall down her arms and onto the floor.

She brings her bare chest closer, and I rub my cock across her nipples, circling them until her little nubs are as hard as glass.

"Take me in your mouth as deep as you can. Get me nice and wet."

I watch as I disappear into her mouth, loving how she looks on her knees, with her cheeks hollow with suction, flushed and pink and perfect. Her lips feel like silk as they glide up and down me, and her eyes are glazed with desire like she wants and needs to please me.

I tangle my hands in her hair, trying not to control the pace, but she feels so good sucking me down, and I want to feel her throat close around me.

I bring my eyes down to watch, and when she lifts her eyes to mine, I know I'm not going to last much longer. I pop out of her mouth, place my hands on the sides of her breasts, and nestle in the channel between them.

"Move closer to me; let me fuck those tits," I slide up and down, and she spits on the head of my cock, and I groan at the gesture, knowing I'm about to blow. Her hands move over mine as she presses her breasts closer together, squeezing me tight until the friction is almost too much to bear. She interlaces her fingers so I don't slip from in between her, and in a few more thrusts, my release spills out across her chest.

"Fuck, Sophia. God, you feel so good." I lean back in my chair to catch my breath and admire the mess I've made. "I was not expecting that."

She rises from the floor, but before she can head into the bathroom, I grab her and pull her close to my chest, spreading my mess across my shirt.

"Grant! What—you're ruining your shirt!"

"I don't give a fuck about my shirt, Sophia. I have another one in the closet. I just wanted to kiss you."

And that's the truth.

I drag my thumb across the curve of her cheek, reveling in the way she leans into my touch as if it's instinct. As if she trusts it.

And maybe that's what undoes me the most.

Because she isn't just something temporary. She isn't just a distraction.

Everything about her feels worth the mess.

thirty-three

. . .

Sophia

A QUIET HUM of contentment settles into my bones. I feel...steady. Rooted. Like maybe, just maybe, I belong exactly where I am.

I glance around the guest house as the morning light filters through the sheer curtains, and it's funny how much this place is starting to feel like home. My coffee sits half-finished on the side table, and the faintest trace of Grant's cologne lingers in the air from when he kissed me goodbye earlier.

He doesn't spend the night—not all night, anyway. But every evening, after Hazel is in bed and the house is quiet, he slips in through the sliding doors. We talk, we touch, and we fall into each other in ways that feel both inevitable and impossible to untangle. When it gets late, he presses one last kiss to my lips and heads back to the main house before there's any trace he's been gone.

I haven't asked him to stay, and he doesn't offer.

I tell myself it doesn't matter, that this is enough, that it's only been a few days since we admitted we wanted to see where this could go. But some small part of me wonders what it might feel like to spend an entire night together. If that will happen. If he's ready for that. If I'm ready for that.

I shake my head, exhaling sharply. Focus, Sophia.

Taking a deep breath, I look back at the script in my hands and read my line aloud again, this time drawing out the emotion Edie encouraged me to find during our last rehearsal. She is brilliant—the kind of director who can pull a performance out of you that you didn't even know you had.

"It's not about the fight," I murmur, my voice low but steady. "It's about what you're fighting for."

The words linger in the quiet of the guest house, and I can almost hear Edie's approving nod. Perfect.

Still, I let myself smile. The final scenes before we shoot on location are coming together, and for the first time since we started filming, I can see the story taking shape. The late nights, the endless takes, the self-doubt that creeps in when the exhaustion sets in—it's all been worth it. And knowing I'm giving everything to this role, that I've poured every ounce of myself into it, fills me with a sense of pride I haven't felt in a long time.

I close the script and lean back, rubbing the tension from my neck. I turn to my camera on the table. It's my outlet, a way to distract me from the stress. Through it, I can capture raw, unpolished moments—the kind that don't need a lighting crew or a script supervisor. I have a favorite shot I once captured of an elderly couple dancing on a nearly empty Santa Monica boardwalk at sunset. Those moments, the ones no one stages or expects, are my favorite.

I pick up the camera and scroll through the shots I've taken over the last few weeks. Most are of flowers, sunsets, and the occasional selfie, but as I swipe, a candid shot of Hazel and Grant appears on the screen. They're sitting on the patio, with Hazel's head thrown back in laughter while Grant grins at her with an expression so warm it nearly steals my breath. I snapped it when neither of them noticed, and now, looking at it, I feel a lump form in my throat. There's something about their dynamic—the easy, unfiltered love between them—that feels like sunlight on my skin.

A soft knock pulls me from my thoughts, and before I can answer, Hazel pops her head through the door. "What're you doing?"

I smile. "Just looking at some photos. Wanna see?"

Hazel skips inside and climbs onto the armrest beside me. I hand her the camera and then show her how to navigate through the images. She giggles at the silly ones and points excitedly at her own photo.

"That's me!" she says, her voice bright.

"That's you," I confirm, smiling. "You have a great laugh, you know that?"

"That's what Dad says, too," Hazel replies, her tone matter-of-fact. She turns the camera back to me. "Can I take some pictures?"

I hand Hazel the strap and help her loop it around her neck. "Here, hold it like this." I show her the basics of framing and focus. Hazel snaps a picture of the couch and then one of the lamp, giggling at her newfound skill.

"You're a natural," I say, ruffling her hair.

Hazel tilts her head. "Hey, can we watch *Code Crusaders?*"

I freeze for a moment, my smile faltering. I haven't watched that show in years. But Hazel's eager expression makes it impossible to say no.

We settle onto the couch, with Hazel snuggled under my arm. As the familiar theme song plays, my stomach twists. I remember the late nights on set and the hours spent learning lines while other kids were at sleepovers or soccer practice. And then there was the fake relationship with my co-star.

Hazel laughs as the characters bicker on the screen, oblivious to the memories stirring in my chest. Watching myself as that bright-eyed teenager is like stepping into a time capsule —a version of me so filled with dreams yet so unaware of the harsh realities waiting around the corner.

The laughter on screen brings back the camaraderie I once felt with the cast, but now it's tainted by the sting of betrayal. It's nostalgic, yes, but also a painful reminder of how far I've had to build myself back up. That girl is so different from the woman I am now, yet somehow, the ache still lingers.

"You were really good," Hazel says, her eyes wide with admiration. "Why don't you do shows like that anymore?"

I hesitate, unsure how to explain the complexities of Hollywood to a six-year-old. "I guess I just wanted to try different things," I say carefully. "Like the movie I'm working on now."

Hazel nods as if this makes perfect sense. Then, after a pause, she looks up at me with a hopeful expression. "Are you gonna stay here forever?"

The question catches me off guard. I open my mouth, but no words come out. Forever. The idea tugs at something deep inside me, a part of me that wants to believe it could be possible. But am I even ready for something like that? I've been so careful to guard myself, to avoid the risks that come with letting someone in. And yet, being here—with Hazel, with Grant—makes me wonder if I am ready for more.

"I don't know," I say finally, brushing a strand of hair behind Hazel's ear. "What do you think?"

Hazel grins. "I think you should. Dad's happier when you're here."

My heart squeezes. "He is, huh?"

"Yeah," Hazel says, her tone so matter-of-fact it's almost funny. "And so am I."

I pull Hazel closer and press a kiss to the top of her head. "Well, I'm pretty happy being here, too."

For now, all I can do is stay in the moment and let myself wonder—just for a little while—what it might be like to believe in forever.

thirty-four

. . .

Grant

I WATCH Hazel elbow her way through the small crowd of children to get a closer look at the Gemini 11 capsule. It's part of the Humans in Space exhibit, and she seems determined to get there one day, so here we are. I stay a few steps back, giving her the chance to explore and connect with kids her age. Her world is full of possibilities right now, and I hope she never feels any differently.

It's a school holiday, so I took some time away from the studio for some father-daughter bonding. I've been working a lot lately and, admittedly, have been sharing my free time with Sophia, too. I don't think Hazel has noticed. We've been careful.

"Dad, come look. You can see where the astronauts sleep, and there's a picture of his family!"

Hazel grabs my hand and pulls me closer to the exhibit. Sure enough, there's a photo of what appears to be the astronaut with a woman and two small children.

"Pretty cool, nugget. Looks kind of small in there, though."

"Do you think the astronauts miss their families when they are up in space?"

"I'm sure they do. But I also think they are doing very important work, so sometimes, it can be worth leaving the ones you love for an exciting adventure."

She seems deep in thought as she stares into the glass-covered capsule.

"Yeah. I guess. It's sad when people are alone, though."

Ouch. Where did that come from? Does she feel lonely? I know it's just me and her at the house, but I try to make sure she's involved in activities, and God knows I pay enough for the private school and all the extracurriculars they offer. Maybe she's missing her mom. I make a mental note to send Geneva a text later this evening so she can reach out when she has a free minute this weekend.

"I'm sure it does get lonely, but he has pictures to remind him of what's waiting for him when he gets back home. Plus, I bet they get to bring great books to read!"

She nods but makes her way over to the telescopes so she can peep at some of the planets they have set up to view.

"Do you think you would ever go to space?"

"Hm. It sounds like an exciting adventure, but I think I would have to pass. Too risky for me."

"Yeah, but isn't that the whole point? You could discover something amazing that would change your whole world!"

She's looking up at me, waiting for my response. This kid is so incredibly smart and insightful. Some days, I have no idea if I'm doing anything right, but it's moments like this when I feel like I'm raising an incredible human and maybe, just maybe, I'm doing something right.

"Yeah, I guess you're right, nugget."

"I am. It's like when we are at school and my friend Hannah gets too scared to slide down the big slide. I have to hold her hand, and then, when we get to the bottom, she's always laughing, and she's not scared anymore."

"You're a smart and good friend."

"I know."

I muffle the laugh that wants to escape because I never want to steal that confidence away from her and I hope she never loses it. I watch in awe as she navigates between exhibits, as if she's been here a million times when, in fact, it's only been a handful. She has no fear, and at the same time, she is completely vulnerable. I miss the pure, open honesty I had as a child, and I wonder at what point it disappears. At what point do we shut off a part of ourselves we were so happy to let everyone see?

I know a lot of my walls come from my father passing away unexpectedly. The grief is still harsh, even though it's been close to twenty-five years now. Some nights, just the thought of it sends me into a panic that I might die before Hazel grows up.

I shake my head. I can't go down that rabbit hole here. In fact, it's a dark place I try to avoid at all costs, and I'm not sure why I've even allowed myself to go there today.

We swing by the gift shop, and I'm easily suckered into buying her a space station Lego set. I rationalize that it's an educational toy, so I'm not spoiling her. Yeah, I know. You try to say no to this kid.

We walk out into the warm evening air and head over to the parking garage while Hazel swings my arm back and forth as we walk hand in hand.

"Did you have a good time?" I ask her. I can tell she did, but I love hearing her talk about the things she loves. I hope I never get tired of learning all there is to know about this incredible little human.

"I did. I can't wait to tell Sophia all about it."

"Sophia?"

"Yeah. I asked her if she could come with us today, but she said that sometimes, it's hard for her to go to crowded places."

She asked Sophia to join us today? Why would she do that? When did she do that?

"Yeah. I think a lot of people might recognize her, and sometimes, it's better to keep the attention focused on the museum exhibits."

"I think Sophia would go to space. She loves adventure, and taking risks, and trying new things."

I help Hazel into the car and buckle her into her booster, but my mind is still turning over what she said. It's true that great risk equals great reward.

I've always avoided risk and calculated every move. Relationships, love—I've treated them the way I treat everything else. Measured. Controlled. Safe. And I assumed Sophia was the same. That she'd want something steady, predictable. That she'd never be the type to take a leap without knowing exactly where she'd land.

But Hazel is right. Sophia does take risks. She's throwing herself into this film, into new challenges, into something she can't control but believes in anyway. She's willing to fail if it means chasing something that matters.

And I'm the one who assumed she wouldn't.

Because I wouldn't.

Because I told myself love—real love, the kind that takes over your life—wasn't worth the fall.

But now I'm wondering...what if I'm wrong?

When we pull up to the house, I see Sophia's car in the driveway, and my heart skips a beat. I've spent almost every evening with her, and it still doesn't feel like enough.

"I'm going to show Sophia my space station!"

Hazel has her seatbelt unbuckled before I turn the car off.

"Hang on a minute. We don't know if she has plans. It's not polite to bother her if she's busy."

"She's never busy when I visit her."

"When do you visit her?"

"Dad, I see Sophia every day! She's our guest. It would be rude to ignore her."

My mind is reeling at this new information. A sense of panic creeps in at the idea that Hazel is getting too attached to Sophia. What if it doesn't work out between us? The last thing I'd want is to hurt Hazel.

"I didn't realize you went to visit her so much."

"Oh, yeah. Most days, she's here when I get home from school, and we have a snack together, and sometimes, I come over in the mornings to bring her a Pop-Tart. She loves them."

"And you see her every day?"

"Almost. Don't you?"

And just like that, I'm irritated. I'm irritated my daughter might be getting attached to a person I'm just sleeping with.

My mind has tripped into an irrational space, and now I'm questioning if Sophia is trying to get closer to me by getting closer to my daughter. Is she giving Hazel the wrong idea about us?

I follow Hazel over to Sophia's door and watch as Sophia's face lights up when she sees Hazel outside. She steps outside to greet us.

"Hey, nugget! How are you today? Did you have fun at the science museum?"

My jaw tenses at Sophia's use of my nickname for Hazel. That's my name for her. I know I'm being ridiculous right now, but something has me on edge, with irritation and distrust firing through my veins.

"Oh, yeah. We saw a space capsule where the astronauts live when they are working on the space station, and look what my dad got me!"

She lifts the Lego kit up, and the look of pure elation makes it hard to stay in my anger for a moment.

"Amazing! I can't wait to see what it looks like after you put it together!"

"Can you come eat with us, and I'll tell you all about it?"

"Hazel, I'm sure Sophia already has plans for dinner."

It comes out harsher than I mean, and I can tell it's confused Sophia when her eyebrows dip in confusion. Thankfully, she seems to understand that I'm hoping for a private dinner with Hazel tonight.

"Oh, darn. I have to go back up to the studio, so I can't join you for dinner, but maybe you can tell me all about it tomorrow?"

Sophia looks up at me to see if I'll object to the mention of spending time with her tomorrow. When I don't respond, she continues. "Besides, it sounds like it's been an adventurous daddy-daughter day, and I don't want to ruin the vibe."

"Oh, you won't. But that's ok. I'll tell you all about it tomorrow."

Guilt rushes over me as I turn toward the house, but before we leave, I glance back and catch a flash of hurt or maybe confusion sliding across her face. Well, I'm confused too, so join the club.

We agreed to be careful around Hazel. I know I said I wanted to see where this was going, but it's only been a few days. I'm irritated that she seems to be moving ahead like we're already a couple. The last thing I need is for my daughter to get attached to someone who might not be here for the long term.

thirty-five

· · ·

Sophia

"MAMA! I'm not leaving without you! We're going to fight this storm, and we're going to win. We've survived worse. We're survivors, Mama!"

"And cut!"

Edie's voice echoes throughout the soundstage as the cast and crew come out of the scene. It was an emotional segment, so it's taking a minute for everyone to get back into regular form. I shake off the character and the emotional anger she was holding on to and take a deep breath to release those feelings and get back to core Sophia.

"You're doing amazing on camera," Edie says. "Actually, you're doing amazing off-camera, too. You're knocking it out of the park for your first go at producing."

She gestures for me to sit on the couch as the other actors exit the living room set and head back to trailers, costumes, or whatever is next on their daily schedule.

"Thanks. It's been a learning experience for sure, but is it weird that I love it? All the pressure and obstacles and fighting for what we want—it makes me feel alive in a weird way."

"I totally get it. It's why I'm here with you and not on the set of whatever sequel was next in my sci-fi franchise."

"Do you miss it? The blockbuster set, the blockbuster budget?"

"The budget? Yes. The set? No. I was tired of telling those stories. They lost the heart and humanity in the plot. The deeper the continuation, the harder it is to find a connection with the ongoing saga. This? This, I love. There's no sequel to this. All the emotion that exists can be poured into this story, and that allows it to connect universally with so many people. This, my friend, is going to be a hit. And I'm not just saying that to pat myself on the back."

"I agree, Edie. I can feel it. So many scenes are clicking. You can feel the deep connection to the characters. I'm so thankful you agreed to do this with me."

Before launching her own talent agency, Blair worked at the prestigious TWA. During her time there, she discovered Edie's script—a departure from the blockbuster sci-fi films that defined Edie's career despite her earlier work in different genres. Though Blair saw the script's potential, TWA's layoffs cut short her plans to champion it. Six months later, with her own agency established, Blair signed both Edie and me. Her first major success? Packaging us together for Grant and Wonderland Studios.

That Grant would take on such an unknown factor in me was a shock, but now I'm guessing he saw the potential. Although I admit that some days, I worry his interest in me helped drive some of his decision making.

And now we've crossed all sorts of lines, some I'm not even aware of based on how he was acting last night. I'm still irritated by how he shut me down for dinner. I might have readily accepted, but I saw the trepidation and irritation on Grant's face. A high-powered studio exec, he may be, but an actor, he is not.

I knew when I wasn't wanted, so instead, I made up the excuse of needing to head up here for some work. Then I ended up driving out to Blair and Wyatt's house for a pity dinner. If I'm being honest, I'm growing attached to Hazel. She's such a great kid, and it's hard to tell her no when she's asking you to hang out.

"We have two more days for this set; then we wrap up in Santa Clarita for location scenes. I'm still impressed that Grant was able to help secure some controlled disaster scenes at Honey Pine. I wanted to make sure you are feeling good about it all and ready for that to start next Monday."

"I'm ready. I can't wait—"

"She's living with the guy, and you're telling me there's no special favors for her?" A male voice drifts from behind the interior living room wall frame.

"I'm sure lots of special favors are being exchanged all around," another voice replies, laced with amusement.

My stomach tightens.

"There's no way she's running her own production a year or two removed from being a star on a kid's network without some kind of special favor," the first guy adds, his tone smug.

"What're you gonna do? It's how this industry is. All who you know. Or blow, I guess, in her case."

Laughter. Casual, thoughtless.

They have no idea I'm sitting here, mortified, listening to their assessment of my credibility—not based on my talent, not on my experience, but on the fact that I'm a woman.

A woman who happens to be sleeping with the man financing the film.

A woman who, apparently, couldn't possibly have earned this on her own.

I open my mouth, but before I can speak, a sharp voice slices through the air like a blade.

"Excuse me?"

The laughter cuts off instantly.

Edie steps forward, her expression cold enough to freeze them in place. "You think this is some boys' club where you get to run your mouths about my lead? About a producer on this project?" She takes another step, and her voice lowers to something even more dangerous. "On my set?"

One of them stammers, "We were just—"

"Just being misogynistic, sexist assholes?" she finishes for him. "Let me make this real simple. If I hear either of you say anything like that again anywhere near this set, you're gone. I don't care how long you've been in the industry. I don't care who you've worked with. You do not get to discredit a woman's work because it makes you feel better about your own lack of relevance."

Their faces are flushed now with anger, shame, and embarrassment at being caught.

Edie folds her arms. "So, unless you'd rather be looking for a new job, I suggest you get back to work. And keep your mouths shut unless it's about the scene blocking."

They mumble something—an apology, maybe, or just a

pitiful excuse—before grabbing their gear and hurrying off, suddenly very invested in their work.

I exhale; the tension is coiled so tightly in my chest that it almost hurts to release.

"You ok?" Edie asks, her voice softer now.

I force a nod, but I can still feel the words clinging to my skin like something sticky and foul.

"I'll be fine." I lift my chin, looking toward where the guys disappeared. "You and I both know this isn't the first or last time I'll hear things like that."

Edie's jaw tightens. "No, but that doesn't mean we let it slide."

She's right.

If I were a man, I wouldn't have to deal with this bullshit.

"You're right. Thank you for speaking up. I truly appreciate this opportunity and everything you are doing for this film."

"Anytime, Sophia." I give her a hug, but before I can pull away, she steadies me by my shoulders. "All this. You did this. It's not because of some man. You're talented, and Grant saw that. Whatever else happened after is your business, but do not let it diminish all the hard work you've put into this. You deserve this."

I hug Edie again, blinking away the tears that have formed. She's right. I did earn this. I'm used to critics, and hearing what the crew thinks is nothing new. I just can't buy into it.

I head over to the back corner of the sound stage to my makeshift office. After I stare at the wall for fifteen minutes, I realize I'm not going to get anything done until I talk to

Grant. In fact, I haven't heard from him all day. I'm not sure what's going on. Maybe he's changed his mind about us. Maybe there's another actress he's got his eye on.

Ok, I've got to get out of my head. Besides, we need to talk because, apparently, I'm gossip fodder for the crew here, and the last thing either of us needs are headlines that insinuate what these guys are thinking. I'm with Edie. We've got something really special going with this film. It would be a shame to have it overshadowed by a scandal about the studio exec and his lead actress in the sheets together.

I pull out my phone.

ME

Are you around this evening? Hoping we could talk.

His reply is instant, like he's been waiting for my text.

GRANT

Yes. I was actually hoping to talk with you, too.

ME

Great. I'll be home around 7:30. Come by anytime after.

GRANT

I'll swing by once Hazel is asleep.

My heart both sinks and speeds up. I feel the disappointment of not being invited to join them for dinner again. It's not like I was eating with them all the time, but I guess I got used to hanging out when I was around and able to. I also feel the excitement of what happens after Hazel is asleep. He didn't come by last night, and while we don't spend every minute together, I'd be lying if I didn't admit I missed being with him.

Focus, Sophia.

We need to talk. I need to know what shut him down last night and see if he's changed his mind about us—even though I don't like how it feels when I think those words.

thirty-six

. . .

Grant

I BREATHE a sigh of relief when I see that Sophia's car isn't in the driveway. I know she said she'd be home at 7:30, but knowing it will be after our dinner time makes everything easier with Hazel. I'm still in my head about how much time they've been spending together. I know Sophia would never be deceitful, but I can't help but wonder what her angle is.

I throw my keys on the counter, loosen my tie, and reach for a glass out of the cabinet. I need a drink.

"That kind of day, huh?" my sister says.

"Hey, yeah. Thanks for picking up Hazel again. I appreciate it. You can leave now."

"Wow. What a welcome. Please. Stop. The excitement is too much."

"Sorry. I didn't mean it that way. It has been that kind of day."

I spread my fingers and thumb across my forehead, attempting to relieve the tension. If anyone would understand my hesitation about Sophia, it's Sarah.

She pulls out a chair and sits down at the table. "So, spill it."

"Did you know Hazel has been hanging out with Sophia?"

I twist my glass on the surface and take a sip of my bourbon, trying to keep my reaction neutral so I don't lead the witness. I want to see her honest reaction.

"I did."

"And?"

"And?"

"It's weird, right?"

She doesn't respond. She's staring at me now. I hate it when she does this. She plays the quiet game when she thinks I'm being an idiot and that I need a minute to digest what I've just said.

"What? Just say it."

She looks down as she brings her hands up to rest on her cheeks like she's taking a moment to consider exactly what she wants to say to me.

"You are an amazing father. When Geneva became pregnant, I admit I wasn't sure how you would respond. You've resisted anything serious when it comes to love and relationships for as long as I can remember." She pauses for a minute. "Actually, ever since Dad died."

"Ok, Sarah, we're not going there."

The last thing I want to do is hash out my father's death and the aftermath of the heartache he left behind. Having your father pass away when you are young is one thing. Watching your mother basically check out of life because of it is another.

"Why not, Grant? You never go there, and I think that is your biggest problem."

"Ok, my biggest problem is not wanting to rehash something that happened over twenty years ago?"

"No, your biggest problem is letting something that happened when you were eleven years old and processed with an eleven-year-old brain make decisions for a grownup, thirty-six-year-old man who lives a completely different life than his mother did."

The punch lands. Watching the woman who is supposed to take care of you check out of her role as a mother fucks with a kid. I understood her grief; I missed my dad, too. He was a great dad. What I couldn't understand was how the grief stole her from me.

She was a vibrant lady before. She showed up to every school activity and bake sale and fed the neighborhood kids when we were hungry. She cared for me when I was sick. She made our house a home with decorations to celebrate every holiday and planned the best summer vacations. She did everything you'd expect a mom to do. And all of it, everything, just disappeared when he did.

My sister picked up a lot of the slack since she was older. We wouldn't have even had a Christmas tree that first year if Sarah hadn't pulled all the decorations down and set it all up herself. I watched what love did to my mother, and I swore I would never fall in love. I wouldn't—I won't lose myself because of love.

Sarah doesn't understand the logic, but she's stronger than Mom. She loves in spite of hurt. Hell, she just got out of a ten-year relationship with her partner that should have destroyed her, but instead, she moved out here to start fresh and is already dating again. I wish I were like that, but I know I'm just like my mother.

"What does that even have to do with Sophia going behind my back to spend time with Hazel?"

"Cut the shit, Grant. She didn't go behind your back. You're mad because you have feelings. You're mad because you don't know what to do with those feelings, but you do know how to push people away."

Another sucker punch. That one hurt.

"You never let yourself get close to anyone. In fact, I bet you have some system you follow where it's a max of five dates or five weeks, whichever is longer, and then you politely bow out of any more interaction."

It's six weeks or twelve dates, whichever is longer. I do have an emergency ripcord if the woman gets too clingy, but I don't tell her that.

"You make me sound like a terrible person. I have a daughter to consider, too."

"You didn't even try to make it work with Geneva."

"She didn't want to try."

"Maybe. But we'll never know because it wasn't even in the realm of possibility. What I can't understand, though, is the disconnect between your resistance to an intimate, romantic relationship for you and the deep love and devotion you have for your daughter."

My eyes snap up to hers as a look of confusion crosses my face. "It's totally different. She's my blood. She has my DNA."

There is no alternative with Hazel. It was never an option

not to love her with everything I have. It just was and always will be love.

"It's the same. You let yourself open to the possibility. You could lose Hazel the same way you could lose a partner, but somewhere in your head, you've let yourself take the risk with Hazel. The reward is worth it."

My mind is spinning. She doesn't understand that I didn't have a choice with Hazel. And I'm glad I didn't. I love Hazel with everything I have. It's just not the same as loving someone else, someone romantically. It's different. Right?

"Look. I love you. I don't want to fight with you. You're different with Sophia. You've broken so many of your little rules because of your desire to be around her. You're happy. Go with it. Take the chance. If anyone is worth the risk, I'd say it's her."

I rise out of my chair and go to rinse my glass out in the sink. I hear the chair scrape the floor, indicating my sister is leaving the table, too. When I turn around, I'm alone, and I guess our conversation is over. But the damage is done. She landed the knockout punch.

I admit that Sophia has gotten further into my heart than anyone else I've ever dated or been with, but that doesn't make it love.

The chimes coming from the front living room announce the arrival of pizza, and I silently thank my sister for having the foresight to order in. I don't think I could do a sit-down dinner after that intervention.

Pizza and salad boxes cover the coffee table, and I settle in on the couch, ready to zone out to another viewing of *Wall-E*. We've seen it a million times now, so zoning out won't be an issue. I'll be able to laugh and respond on autopilot if needed, and it means no more talking with my sister.

I spend the next hour in my head about Sophia and wondering what it might be like if she were here eating with us tonight. What if she were part of our family routine?

The credits roll, and after another brutal negotiation to read three books before bed, Hazel is finally out, and I'm eager to talk to Sophia. I walk Sarah to the door, and she has that look on her face that she's worn since we were kids—the one that says she's about to drop some big-sister wisdom whether or not I want it.

"You know," she says softly, "Mom lost herself in grief because Dad was her whole world. But you, Grant? You've built this beautiful life, this career, this relationship with Hazel. You're already doing things differently."

She turns to leave but pauses at the threshold. "Life's going to hurt sometimes, little brother. That's a given. The question is whether you want to experience all the beautiful parts, too."

In the kitchen, I pour another drink. The bourbon burns as it slides down my throat, but it doesn't wash away Sarah's truth. Through the window, I spot Sophia in the pool, and I slip outside so we can finally talk.

It doesn't register that she's swimming until she's pulling herself up out of the pool and my eyes are drawn to her tiny bikini. Water is dripping over every bare piece of skin, and I jump when she speaks.

"Hey! How was your day?"

The smile that lights up her face takes my breath away.

She's genuinely happy to see me, even though I was a total dick to her last night and have been avoiding her.

"Good. Same as always."

"Good."

"Yours was good?"

She walks over to the lounge chairs and motions for me to follow her before gesturing for me to take a seat beside her. I walk closer, but I don't think it's a good idea for me to get comfortable. I see a flash of hurt cross over her eyes, but she's a great actress and recovers easily. In fact, I may have been imagining the hurt. It's really hard to say.

"That's kind of what I wanted to talk to you about. There was a little incident on set today."

I rush over to sit next to her, worried that she is hurt or something worse.

"Are you ok? Are you hurt?"

"No, I'm fine. It's nothing physical. I actually overheard some gossip. Unfortunately, it was gossip about you and me."

I swallow my nerves. I'm not sure where she's going with this, but I'm hoping it's nothing serious.

"You and me?"

"Seems the only reason I'm producing and starring in this movie is because of some special favors I'm offering you."

"You're fucking kidding me. Who said that? I'll fire them tonight."

"It's just some gaffers. Really, it's not a big deal. People talk. And people love to talk about women even more. God forbid we might be smart and talented."

She laughs the insult off, and I'm in awe of her resilience. This woman is so talented and has managed to navigate and overcome the bullshit underbelly this business can harbor. She's only twenty-five years old. Jesus. She's so young. I think her maturity and ambition make me forget she's still a baby in this industry.

It feels wrong to try to make something with her work. She's got so much of her career and life ahead of her that she shouldn't even consider settling down. And she definitely doesn't need to step into a parenting role, especially one that isn't for her own child.

"You're handling it way better than I would. Than I am."

"I guess I just wanted to make sure we're being careful. I know there are some headlines. I know Lucas is probably aware there's something going on, and I appreciate his discretion, but I think maybe we need a plan."

She's laying the path I need to slow down whatever this is. I take advantage of the request.

"I agree. You'll be working up in Santa Clarita next week, so it shouldn't be a problem to tone it down a bit." I clear my throat and stand back up, pacing back and forth. I'm looking for the courage to say what I want to say to her. "Actually, it might be better if we tone it down anyway. I know we talked about seeing where this might go, but I worry that Hazel is getting too attached to you."

She stands; anger sparks in her eyes.

"What?"

"I didn't realize the two of you were spending so much time together."

She's mad. She pushes her hair behind her ears and crosses her arms in front of her.

"I can't help if she's outside when I get home or she pops

by to share with me stories from her day. What am I supposed to do, Grant? Ignore her? Tell her to go away because her father doesn't want her to get any ideas about the two of us?"

She scoffs, grabs the towel off the chair, and wraps it around her body.

"You're right. I appreciate that you are so good to her. She adores you. It's just—"

"It's fine, Grant. Message received."

"It's just—Hazel is my whole life."

I watch as her shoulders relax and her head falls forward. "I know."

She walks toward the bungalow, and I can't stop myself from following her, wanting to touch her, to hold her next to me. I'm overwhelmed with a need to comfort her. Instead, I brush my fingers down her arm to get her attention.

"I really do appreciate everything you do for Hazel. I know she adores you."

Sophia turns to face me. Her eyes hold mine for a minute, like she wants to say so much more to me. "I adore her, too."

She breaks her gaze, walks inside and over to the couch, and folds up the blanket draped over the arm. "I'm pretty tired, and I know you are busy. I've got an early day tomorrow, too."

"Right. Ok. Yes. I better get back to the house, too. Hazel. Sleep."

That's such a bullshit thing to say when she knows I've been over here almost every night since she started staying here.

She locks the bungalow behind me, making it obvious

that nothing will happen between us tonight. I didn't come over here thinking anything was going to happen. In fact, I was pretty adamant that cooling off on being with her was the best thing for us right now. But nothing has felt worse than walking away from her, knowing she won't be in my arms tonight.

thirty-seven

. . .

Sophia

BLAIR'S OFFICE at Tangerine Talent still has that new-paint smell, but she's already made it feel like home. Over-sized photos of her biggest clients line the orange-colored walls, and there's a bar cart in the corner that I suspect sees more action than her actual office.

"He said you should 'cool off'?" Jess air quotes, settling deeper into the plush armchair by Blair's desk. "What does that even mean?"

I shrug, trying to appear more casual about it than I feel. "Apparently, since I'll be shooting at Honey Pine next week, it's a good time to..." I make air quotes. "'Create some space.'"

"Men," Blair mutters, pouring herself a glass of wine. "They get scared the minute things start feeling real."

"I'm not sure that's what this is," I say, but even I can hear the doubt in my voice. "He's just being practical. Hazel has after-school rehearsals, too. Our schedules will be crazy."

"Oh, how are rehearsals going?" Stella asks.

The mention of Hazel makes my chest tight. "She's amazing. Sure to be the star of the show." I pause, swallowing hard. "She asked me last week if I was going to live with them forever."

"Oh, honey." Blair sets down her glass.

"And that's exactly why he's pulling back," I say as the realization hits me fresh. "It's not just about us anymore. Hazel's getting attached, and that terrifies him."

"But isn't that a good thing?" Jess asks. "The three of you seem so natural together."

"Maybe that's what scares him most." I stand, needing to move. "He seemed irritated the other night after they spent the day at the science museum. Hazel kept inviting me to things, and he kept cutting her off, uninviting me. Maybe he doesn't think I'm good enough for her."

"I'm gonna stop you right there," Jess says. "Fuck him. If he's going to be a scared little bitch, then he doesn't deserve you. All of us see how you treat Hazel and how much she adores you. He's blind if he doesn't see how lucky he is."

"Men," Blair says again, but softer this time.

My phone buzzes, and my heart does that stupid little jump it always does when I see Grant's name. "Speak of the devil."

I answer, trying to keep my voice neutral. "Grant?" The girls all lean forward, not even pretending not to listen.

"Sophia, I'm sorry to ask this..." He sounds stressed. "There's been an emergency with one of our studios in Atlanta. I'm stuck in meetings, Sarah is also stuck at work, and Hazel's school just called. She's not feeling well."

"I can get her," I say immediately, already reaching for my bag.

There's a pause, heavy with all the things we're not saying. "Thank you. I really appreciate this, Sophia. I'll wrap up here as soon as I can."

"No problem. Tell her I'm on my way."

I end the call and find three pairs of eyes watching me intently. "He needs me to pick up Hazel."

"Honey," Blair starts, but I cut her off.

"Don't. I know what you're thinking, but she's not feeling well and needs someone to get her."

"And you're just going to drop everything and run?" Jess asks gently.

"Of course she is!" Stella says. "She loves Hazel! Even if Grant is being all weird about everything."

"Exactly that," I say simply. "Because she's six, and she doesn't deserve to get caught in whatever's happening between me and Grant." I grab my jacket. "Besides, maybe a little space isn't the worst thing. Give us both time to figure out what we really want."

The drive to Hazel's school gives me too much time to think. About how close I've gotten to Grant and how comfortable I feel with him. About how easy it was for him to pull back, like flipping a switch. All the little moments we shared now feel like they're slipping through my fingers.

Hazel's face lights up when she sees me walk into the nurse's office, and just like that, all my complicated feelings about Grant fade into the background. She's pale but perks up immediately, her whole body seeming to bounce despite her supposed illness.

"Sophia! Did Daddy send you?"

"He did, sweetheart. Not feeling so hot?"

She shakes her head and then immediately brightens. "Can we work on my song for the play when we get home? I practiced the new part!"

I sign her out and lead her to my car, trying not to think about how natural it feels. How it's a routine I wouldn't mind and could really get used to. How normal it is the way she automatically heads for "her" side of the car, and how she knows exactly where I keep the emergency snacks in the console. "Let's see how you're feeling first, ok? Maybe some soup and rest?"

At the house, Hazel insists she feels well enough to show me her progress on her song, but I negotiate her down to lying on the couch while she sings. I sit on the floor beside her, letting her teach me the hand motions that go with each verse.

"Sophia?" she asks during a break between verses, playing with the edge of her blanket. "When did you know you wanted to be famous?"

I can't help but smile at that. "Oh, sweetie, it wasn't about being famous. I just loved pretending, becoming different characters. When I was about your age, I used to put on shows in my backyard. I'd make my stuffed animals be the audience."

"Really?" She grins and then looks serious. "I like performing, too, but I can't do it forever. I have to focus on my astronaut training."

"Oh?" I bite back a laugh at her grave expression.

"NASA needs someone brave enough to live on Mars," she explains as if this is common knowledge. "And Daddy says if you want something, you have to be dedicated." She pronounces 'dedicated' carefully, clearly proud of using such a grown-up word.

"That's very true. But you know, I bet Mars could use some entertainment. Those astronauts might get bored up there."

Her eyes go wide with possibility. "Maybe I could do shows for them! In my space suit!" She sits up straighter. "Do you think we could practice taking pictures in space? For when I need to document my Mars discoveries?"

"Once you feel better, we can talk about it."

"Promise?" Hazel snuggles deeper into the couch, and I shift us back to the play, afraid to make any promises I can't keep.

"Here, try this verse again, but remember what we talked about with the breathing. Mars has a very thin atmosphere—you'll need strong lungs up there."

She giggles but takes a deep breath, ready to start again. Looking at her, I realize I'm in dangerous territory because it's not just Grant I'm going to miss if he decides we need permanent space. It's this. I'm in way too deep.

I don't hear the front door open and don't realize Grant is home until I glance up and catch him standing in the doorway, watching us. The look on his face makes my heart stop—there's something raw and vulnerable there before he masks it.

But in that moment, I see everything he's afraid of, everything he wants but won't let himself have.

"Daddy!" Hazel spots him and sits up. "Sophia's been helping me with my breathing for the song. Want to hear?"

"Maybe later, princess. How are you feeling?"

As Grant moves into dad mode, checking Hazel's temperature and asking about her day, I gather my things. This is the part where I step back and create the space he wants.

"Alright, nugget, let's get you upstairs. Time for bed." He turns back to me. "Thank you for getting her," he says quietly as I head for the door.

"Wait!" Hazel yells. "I want Sophia to put me to bed."

I hesitate, waiting for Grant to give me the green light to join them for the bedtime routine.

"Ok, but no tricking her into more than one book tonight."

The way my heart skips at his invitation to join them for the bedtime routine betrays my instinct to protect it.

thirty-eight

. . .

Grant

THE HOUSE IS quiet when I step inside, and I can see the glow from the television from the kitchen. It's quiet, so I gently place my keys on the counter and slide off my jacket. It's later than I intended.

As I walk toward the living room, my mind is stuck on the last conversation I had with Sophia. I can't explain why it bothered me, knowing Hazel had been spending so much time with her—more than I realized and certainly more than I'd intended for them to. My instincts said to push back. Set boundaries. No expectations equals temporary.

But since then, I've been questioning everything. Sophia was able to pick up Hazel, no questions asked, and now my excuses feel flimsy, like a low-budget set on the verge of collapse. When I see them now, it's like the whole production is going off-script, and I'm not sure I want to stop it.

Sophia is on the floor, with Hazel stretched across the couch like it's the most comfortable place on earth. It probably is. Sophia's fingers trail absently through Hazel's hair, and a small smile tugs at her lips as she listens to my daughter sing. There's something peaceful about the scene, like they're perfectly at ease with each other.

I don't move. I just stand there, caught in the doorway, watching. I should say something, let them know I'm here, but I can't.

Sophia's touch is so natural, like she was always meant to be here. Hazel is so trusting and unguarded. When Sophia looks down at her with a tenderness, something in me aches.

All of it—the sight of them together, the quiet warmth of it—makes me want something I've spent years convincing myself I couldn't have.

Hazel spots me and calls out. Sophia's head turns, and as her eyes catch mine, her lips part in a small, surprised smile. "Hey." Her voice is careful, as if she doesn't want to intrude on the family dynamic between Hazel and me.

"Hey," I manage, stepping further into the room. My voice feels rough like I haven't spoken in hours. Maybe I haven't—not like this, not to someone who makes me forget what I was supposed to say next.

For a moment, we just stand there as the silence stretches between us. I should say something—thank her, apologize for being an ass the last few days—but all I can think about is how wrong I was. About her. About this.

The idea that we would cross so many lines and spend so much time together yet suggest there were no expectations feels laughable now.

I told myself I was mad because I didn't want Hazel to get attached and didn't want either of us to be hurt when this ended. But now I wonder if I wasn't just trying to keep myself from feeling this connection.

And God, I feel it.

"Thank you," I say finally, my voice low. But when I walk Sophia to the door, Hazel pops up off the couch and demands that Sophia put her to bed, too. I can see Sophia waiting for my approval, and it crushes me that she's hesitating. There's nothing I want more than for her to be a part of our lives.

Sophia follows me upstairs to Hazel's room, and as she promised, Hazel goes right to sleep after one book. We put her to bed together, moving in quiet synchronicity that feels intimate. Sophia adjusts the blankets while I tuck Hazel's stuffed spaceship under her arm. She presses a kiss to Hazel's forehead, and something about the gesture makes my chest tighten.

When we step back into the hallway, I close the door behind us. The house is quiet, but my heart is pounding loudly as I step closer to her.

"Thank you," I say, reaching for her hand. "For tonight. For...everything."

Sophia shrugs, but there's a vulnerability in her expression that I don't miss. "She's easy to love." Her voice is quiet and tentative like she's admitting something she shouldn't.

"You know I didn't expect..." I say, my voice strained. "Us, you and Hazel...this."

Sophia nods, and her eyes search mine. "I know."

"But it's more, isn't it? Whether we intended it or not."

She bites her bottom lip, and I hate how much I want to taste the same spot. "Yeah," she admits. "It is."

My pulse thunders in my ears. I want to blame her for making me fall for her.

"Stay," I say, and the word hangs heavy between us. "Here. With me."

I bring my hand up to her face and dust my thumb over her bottom lip. I've missed feeling her mouth on me. I lean in slowly, trying not to spook her or break the moment, and rest my lips on hers.

"I've missed this. I've missed you," I whisper over her lips.

She presses her lips to mine, and I wrap my arms around her waist and lift her up, moving my hands to help wrap her legs around my waist. She grips me so tightly that I can feel her center rub against my already hard cock. I keep one hand gripping her ass while I reach the other hand up to the back of her head. I tangle my fingers in her hair and grip it tightly so I can tilt her head back, giving me full access to slide my tongue down her neck.

She's wearing another pair of shorty shorts, and my hand easily slides underneath the hem, where I discover the barely there thong she's wearing. The pressure on my dick is painful, so I turn and walk down the hall to my bedroom.

I spread her across the bed and take a moment to appreciate her beauty.

"You have no idea how stunning you are. You take my breath away."

I watch as she blushes, loving how she can be one of the most famous and beloved actresses in the country and still act as if she doesn't believe it's true.

I peel her shorts and panties off and raise her shirt over her head, groaning when I see she isn't wearing a bra. My hands instantly reach for her breasts, and I mold my fingers around them as my thumbs brush over her pebbled nipples. I lean down to taste one, running my tongue around her peak, taking it into my mouth, pulling and sucking on her.

She brings her hands up to my head and runs her fingers through my hair as she whispers, "I've missed you."

"Tell me what you want."

"Touch me. More. All over."

I pull my mouth back and run my hands down over her waist and to her hips and rest them on her lower abdomen, right above her pussy. I let my thumbs graze over the top of her lips and watch her twist, eager for more.

I move my hands to her thighs, and I push them apart, spreading her wide for me.

"Fuck, Sophia, you're glistening. Is all that for me?"

I look up at her, catching the blush on her cheeks again as I watch her bring her hands to caress her own breasts.

The grin pasted across my lips must look predatory, but I can't worry about that right now because I have a feast before me, waiting to be eaten.

I use my thumbs to pull her apart, and I lick from her opening to the tight bundle of nerves at the top of her slit. I swirl my tongue around, listening to her gasp and moan, and move back down, lapping up every bit of her.

Being with her feels so damn natural like we've been doing this for years. It's not just the way we're together physically—it's everything else. We should be too busy for this, too busy to make it work, but somehow, it's easy. It's not about finding time—it's like the time finds us, and it fits like it's always been there waiting. I told myself I didn't want this, but I do.

"Grant, Grant, Grant..." She's chanting my name as if she's pacing it to sync up with her climax.

I dip two fingers into her heat and curl them to reach that place inside her that I know drives her wild. I can already feel her clenching around me.

"Grant, I'm going to come."

Her release is almost immediate, and I can feel pre-cum leaking from me. I'm so fucking hard for her. She sits up almost immediately and pushes me back.

"I want to taste you, please."

She crawls off the bed, places her hands on my shirt, and unbuttons me as I pop the button on my pants and slide them down. I step out of my slacks as she slides her hands across my chest and down my arms, causing my shirt to fall to the ground. Her hands glide down my torso, and when she reaches the waistband of my underwear, she slides in her hand and wraps it around my cock. Her grip jolts me forward, pulling a moan from me. Her soft hands grip me so tightly that I feel like I could explode immediately. It's only been a few days since we've been together, but I've missed this; I've missed her so much.

One hand grips her loose hair firmly but gently while my other hand moves to gently grip her around her neck, controlling her movements, showing her that she is mine and I am hers. The kiss grows more urgent. My tongue demands entry and licks inside her as I guide her back to the bed, with her hand stroking me the entire time.

When the back of her legs hit the mattress, she slides my

underwear off and then turns me around, pressing against me, forcing me to sit and then lie back across the bed. She crawls on top of me, and I can't help but reach for her breasts. They are begging to be touched, cared for, and licked by me. She settles between my thighs and grips me tight again, and I have to relive the cuts of dailies I saw today to hold off my orgasm. Her touch drives me crazy with need.

I bring my hand up to her hair and pull it back so I can see her face better.

"I've been dreaming about those lips wrapped around my cock for two days now."

"Only two days?"

I growl; she knows I dream about those lips constantly.

"Suck on it, Sophia. I want to see you choke on my dick. I want to see those eyes water."

I rub the tip of my head across her lips and wrap one of my hands around hers, helping to guide me into her mouth. She surprises me when she opens and takes all of me until I feel the back of her throat.

"Jesus, fuck. You're going to make me come so fast."

Sophia pulls back until I'm almost all the way out and then slides back down; the pressure and wet warmth feel like goddamn heaven.

She pops off and licks around me like she's cleaning me off and then slams back over my dick, bobbing up and down, sucking so tight my balls are clenching up.

I can't take it anymore and pop her off me, pulling her up from under her arms.

"Grant, what—"

"I want to come in that pussy, right now."

She crawls up and straddles me, rubbing her slit up and down over my erection, and the friction is almost too much to manage.

"Hang on. I need to get a condom."

"I'm on birth control, and I'm clean. I haven't been with anyone in a really long time before you."

I haven't been with anyone in a while, either. "I'm clean. And I've never been with anyone without a condom."

"We can use one," she whispers. "I don't want to pressure you."

I pause, feeling the weight of this moment. For some reason, I trust her. I'm not worried about a condom. Hell, Geneva got pregnant even though we used them, so it's not like they are failure-proof. More than that, I want to feel all of her.

"You're not. Are you sure it's what you want?"

She nods as she rises, grips my dick, and guides it to her entrance. She notches me in and starts to slide down, and the feeling of her bare is incredible. She's warm and wet and gripping me so fucking tight that my head leans back and I shut my eyes.

This. This is it.

I don't want this to end.

She slides herself down slowly, letting her body adjust to me.

"Fuck, that feels incredible."

My eyes fly open at her curse, and I can't help the laugh that sneaks past. "That good, huh?"

She smiles at me, and it takes my breath away.

Then she leans forward a bit to get the friction just right

on her clit, and I reach up to grip her tits as she rides me up and down. I can see her getting lost in the feeling, and if she doesn't slow down, I'm going to blow. I grab her hips and flip her over onto her back without breaking us apart.

"Grant!"

"Sorry, babe. You are fucking me too good, and there's no way I'm coming before you do."

I pull one of her legs up to rest on my shoulder so I can push myself deep inside her, and I rut against her as I bring my thumb up and massage her clit.

"Right there. Don't stop. Keep touching me and fucking me right there."

I can feel her grip on me tightening, and I keep the pace, almost punishing her pussy. I watch as she grips the sheets and twists her head from side to side, and then she whispers my name as she locks her eyes with mine and gives in to her orgasm.

My spine tingles as I feel her clench around me, and I know I can't hold back. My thrusts become erratic, and I follow her into ecstasy.

In this moment of bliss, it's like every piece of my life finally makes sense.

thirty-nine

. . .

Sophia

TIME HAS a funny way of slipping through your fingers when you're not paying attention. One minute, I was carefully navigating the delicate rules of a casual arrangement, and the next, I was helping Hazel practice her lines for the school play while making breakfast in Grant's kitchen. Our kitchen? The thought still makes my stomach flutter.

The guest house sits empty now. I haven't slept there in weeks since I picked Hazel up from school when she was sick. My own house is ready, but somehow, I keep finding reasons not to move back just yet. A late-night script review turns into breakfast, which turns into a whole day, which turns into another night. The transition has been so gradual that I barely noticed it happening until Hazel asked if we could turn the guest house into an art studio "since you stay in Daddy's room now anyway."

"Five minutes to curtain!" The drama teacher's voice echoes through the school auditorium, pulling me from my thoughts. I adjust my position in the auditorium chair, careful not to draw attention. So far, no one's recognized me—the benefits of an elementary school crowd more focused on their own kids than celebrity-spotting.

Grant squeezes my hand, a gesture that's become as natural as breathing. "You ok?" he asks.

"Perfect." And I am, really, even with the flutter of cameras I spotted outside the school. It's the first time we've been photographed together since the gala and with Hazel.

Geneva arrives just before the lights dim, and she slides into the seat next to Grant's with an apologetic smile and a whispered explanation about traffic. Watching them interact gives me that familiar twist in my gut—not jealousy exactly, more like awareness. They move with the easy choreography of people who share a child. Sometimes, I wonder if I'm crazy to think I can fit into this carefully balanced equation, but I'm grateful for the openness and kindness Geneva has shown me.

The show is adorable in that earnest, elementary school way, with Hazel stealing every scene as one of the classmates beamed up into space. During the finale, I catch Grant wiping his eyes, and my heart squeezes painfully in my chest. This man, whom the world sees as an untouchable studio executive, is crying at his daughter's school musical. This is the Grant so few people get to see.

"Mom! Dad! Sophia!" Hazel's voice carries across the crowd afterward, riding the high of performance. She launches herself at us, still wearing half her costume makeup. "Did you see when I did the spin? I didn't drop anything!"

"You were amazing, sweetheart," Geneva says, beaming as she smooths Hazel's hair. "Definitely ready for Broadway."

"Oh, my God, is that Sophia Ford?"

"Look, it's Geneva!"

The whispers start rippling through the crowd, followed by the distinctive clicking of phone cameras.

"Celebratory dinner?" Grant suggests quickly, his hand finding the small of my back. "I can have Emma make us reservations at Firefly."

He escorts us out of the auditorium swiftly, managing to dodge most of the cameras waiting outside.

We arrive at the restaurant and settle in the relative privacy of our curtained cabana on the patio. As Hazel regales us with backstage stories while demolishing a plate of pasta, Geneva shares updates about her latest runway show, and Grant and I pretend we're not getting calls from Lucas about growing press interest.

"Sophia?" Geneva catches me in the hallway outside the restroom. "Can we talk for a minute?"

My heart skips, but her smile is genuine. "I just... I wanted to say thank you. For how you are with Hazel. And with Grant." She touches my arm lightly. "I haven't seen him this happy in years."

"I'm not trying to replace—"

"I know. That's part of why this works. You're not trying to be anything except yourself." Her expression grows serious. "But the press is starting to notice. They're going to try to make this messy, create drama where there isn't any. Don't let them."

My phone buzzes in my purse, followed immediately by Geneva's. The synchronized alerts make my stomach drop.

HOLLYWOOD'S MOST COMPLICATED FAMILY? *Studio exec Grant Hall spotted at school event with ex-partner Geneva AND rumored girlfriend Sophia Ford. Sources say the trio has been spending increasing time together, raising questions about the nature of their relation-ship. Swipe for exclusive photos...*

The headline glares up at me, accompanied by slightly blurry photos from outside the school. In one, Grant's hand is on my back. In another, he has an arm around Geneva. The story practically writes itself.

"Well," Geneva says dryly, "it seems I've jinxed us."

I look through the doorway to where Grant and Hazel are sharing a dessert, their heads conspiratorially bent together. A few months ago, I was so sure I knew what I wanted—success, independence, and control over my own narrative. Now, watching them, I realize that what I want has changed entirely.

My phone lights up with a text from Jess.

"So much for staying under the radar. You ready for this?"

I take a deep breath. The question isn't whether I'm ready for the press attention, the speculation, or the inevitable drama. The question is whether Grant, Hazel, and this complicated, beautiful life we're building are worth it.

Looking at them, I already know the answer.

forty

. . .

Grant

I'VE SPENT MORE than a decade in Hollywood, learning to ignore the press. I've weathered flops, public criticism, and endless speculation about my relationships with the calculated indifference that's become second nature. But nothing in all those years prepared me for the sight of three photographers tracking Hazel's walk from the car to her elementary school entrance.

They are camped out to see who is dropping off and picking up in an attempt to pit Geneva and Sophia against one another—or rather, to urge the public to choose sides when there is no side to pick. Can't they see what this is doing to my little girl?

"Daddy, they're back again," Hazel says quietly, clutching her backpack strap. She's started wearing hoodies to school and keeping her head down. My confident, bright-eyed girl, trying to make herself smaller—the sight makes my chest ache.

"I'll handle it," I tell her, keeping my voice steady.

Back at the studio, I barely make it through two meetings before my phone buzzes. The school principal's voice is apologetic but firm. "Mr. Hall, we've received complaints from several parents about the increased media presence. While we understand this is beyond your control—"

"I'll take care of it," I say, cutting her off.

All of this chaos is turning into another full-time job. I'm pacing my office, halfway through arranging security details for the school, when Geneva calls. Her timing has always been impeccable.

"Before you go nuclear," she says in that knowing way of hers, "maybe we should talk strategy."

"They're following our daughter to school, Gen."

"I know." Her voice softens. "And it's infuriating. Maybe we should stick to only you or Sarah for drop-off and pick-up. I can plan to pick up Hazel at your house this week. It's only one more week, and then school is out for the summer."

I recognize her tone—it's the same one she used when I wanted to pull Hazel from her first sleepover after having a panic attack about being too far away if something happened. "You think I'm overreacting."

"I think you're scared," she says gently. "And I think, before you react, remember that Hazel has two parents who love her, an amazing support system, plus a bonus adult in Sophia, who would move heaven and earth to protect her. That's three more people than you had at her age."

Her words sting, mostly because they're true. But before I can respond, my assistant buzzes through to let me know Hazel's teacher is on the other line.

"You're right. I'll have Sarah pick her up today, and you

can meet them at the house. The school is on the other line, probably wanting to know my solution to keep the paparazzi away. I'll catch up with you later. And thanks, Geneva."

I switch from my cell phone to my desk phone, hoping for some good news.

"Mr. Hall," her teacher says, her voice careful like she's trying not to overstep. "I wanted to let you know Hazel was a little off today. Some of the kids...well, they weren't being so kind. I thought you should be aware."

The words hang heavy in the air long after the call ends. I cancel my afternoon meetings and head home early, my mind racing with worst-case scenarios.

When I finally make it to the house, I find Hazel in her room with her face buried in her pillow, still wearing her school clothes. My heart cracks at the sight.

"Hey, nugget." I sit on the edge of her bed and reach out to stroke her hair like I used to when she was little. "Want to talk about it?"

She turns her tear-streaked face toward me, and I have to fight the urge to bundle her up and run far away from all of this.

"Hannah said...she said I only got a part in the play because of Sophia." Her voice cracks. "And Charlie said his mom says we're attention seekers." She hiccups slightly, and more tears fall. "I don't like school anymore."

The weight of her pain settles in my chest like lead. This is exactly the kind of pain I was trying to protect her from.

"Is Sophia coming over tonight?" Hazel asks, wiping her eyes.

The question hits me like a physical blow.

Since the play, I've been making excuses to avoid Sophia, telling myself that it's in both of our interests to take a beat until the press frenzy blows over. She finally opted to stay at her house tonight. Some gave some excuse about meeting the new housekeeper early, but I think she feels me pulling back.

"Actually your mom is on her way," I tell her. "She wanted to spend time with you tonight."

Hazel nods. "Ok, maybe tomorrow."

My phone buzzes for what feels like the hundredth time today. Sophia's name lights up the screen, and I let it go to voicemail, just like I have with her previous calls and texts. With each ignored message, I'm doing what needs to be done —what any father would do. It's as simple as that. Except it's not simple at all because my finger keeps finding its way back to her name, and the tightness in my chest won't go away.

But then I see Hazel's backpack by the door, the one she didn't want to take to school this morning. Six years old is too young for this. She's too young to understand why her classmates are suddenly so interested in her father's personal life and too young to process why some kids are treating her differently. The simple joy of first grade shouldn't come with this kind of baggage. God, I'm being a coward, letting Sophia face this alone while I hide behind my daughter as an excuse. But isn't that what parents do? Make the hard choices, be the bad guy, sacrifice what they want for what their kid needs?

I'm not being fair to Sophia, shutting her out without a word, but I know that if I hear her voice, if I try to explain, my resolve will crumble, and I can't afford to question this—not when Hazel needs me.

Later, after getting Hazel settled in bed with her favorite

stuffed animal and three bedtime stories, I flip through the photos on my phone from the past couple of months. Shots of Sophia and Hazel baking cookies, all three of us at the beach, and other candid moments of happiness I'd started to take for granted. My finger hovers over Sophia's last text.

SOPHIA

Haven't heard from you all day. Everything ok? I'm worried about you both.

The words blur as I remember Hazel's tears, the photographers' cameras, the way my daughter is learning to hide. I let myself forget the most important lesson my father's death taught me: the more you love, the more you have to lose. I can't lose anything else. I won't let Hazel lose anything else.

I set my phone down without responding and turn away from the photos. The happiness they capture feels like a threat now, like a promise I can't keep.

forty-one

. . .

Sophia

THE WORST PART isn't the silence. It's the perfectly reasonable excuses that come with it. First, they were work-related. Budget meetings all day. Early morning calls with the streaming team. Then he was out of town with my brother, Wyatt, on their Manmorial weekend trip, which was extended into a week-long trip.

I stare at the string of texts from Grant, each one polite, professional, and completely hollow. I moved the last of my things out of his house while he was out of town, and he hasn't said a word since he's been back, not about the empty drawers in his closet or my favorite coffee mug missing from the kitchen cabinet. I've managed to slowly erase myself from his life one box at a time, hoping the gradual shift would spark something in him.

The distance has been growing since the night of the play, the night the press started wanting more from us. I understood he was upset, so I wanted to give him space. That's when I noticed how many pieces of myself I'd scattered throughout his house—my spare phone charger by his bed, my favorite sweater draped over his office chair, the fancy face wash I'd started keeping in his bathroom.

We never talked about me moving in with him. I just sort of adjusted into a routine with him. Moving back into my house was always the plan, but now it feels like it also signifies the end of whatever we just started.

My phone buzzes—Blair, not Grant.

BLAIR

Lunch?

An hour later, I slide into the booth at Olive's Bistro, a restaurant inside a Burbank hotel, perfect for private conversations. Blair's expression is carefully neutral, which is never a good sign.

"Just tell me," I say, pushing the menu aside.

"I had drinks with Marcus last night," she says, naming one of Grant's fellow executives. "There's..." She tilts her head from side to side. "Concern at the studio about perception."

"Perception," I repeat flatly.

"Some people are now questioning whether your relationship with Grant influenced the studio's decision to buy *Survivor*. There's talk about whether a first-time producer with a personal connection to—"

"Stop." The word comes out sharper than I intend. "The film is already shot. We're in post. It's done."

"I know. And the first cuts look amazing. But Soph..." Blair leans forward. "This is about future projects, too. You don't want to be labeled as a 'conflict of interest' hire."

I'm not sure what she's suggesting, exactly. If it's to

break off whatever this is with Grant, I'm not sure that's going to be an issue anymore. The irony of this whole thing makes me laugh. I spent months, maybe even a year, fighting my feelings for Grant because I didn't want our relationship to affect my career. But it looks like it's going to anyway.

"We've had some interesting inquiries," Blair continues carefully. "That period piece shooting in London. The Netflix series filming in Vancouver. Both solid projects, both far from LA."

My throat tightens. "You think I should leave?" That's not what I was expecting at all.

"I think you should consider your options." Her voice softens. "Have you talked to Grant about any of this?"

The laugh that escapes me is hollow. "Grant's barely talked to me in two weeks. Besides..." I twist my napkin, remembering the way he talked about those paparazzi outside Hazel's school like they were a physical threat he needed to eliminate. "He's got enough to deal with."

"Sophia—"

"Start looking into the other projects." The words feel like giving up, but maybe that's what I need to do. "Quietly. We don't need to make any decisions yet, but...let's see what's out there."

Last night, I made one last attempt to return to some sense of normalcy between us. I invited him and Hazel to dinner tonight. My house is finally ready—new floors, fresh paint, and a kitchen that doesn't smell like flood damage. Maybe he will see that we can still work. I spent this morning arranging Hazel's favorite mac and cheese ingredients on the counter, setting out the art supplies I bought her last week. A pathetic attempt at normalcy, maybe, but I had to try one last time.

My phone lights up with a text from Grant.

GRANT

Rain check on dinner? Some of the board members want to meet.

The words blur as I stare at them. I type and delete three responses before settling on a simple reply

ME

No problem.

Professional. Polite. Empty.

My finger scrolls up to the carefully composed invitation I sent last night.

ME

House is finally fixed. Thought Hazel might want to help break in the new kitchen? Dinner at 6?

Such casual words, each one agonized over, trying to sound breezy while extending an olive branch. Now the mac and cheese ingredients will only mock me from their perfect arrangement on the counter, and the art supplies will sit unopened, waiting for a six-year-old's imagination that won't be exploring them tonight.

The truth settles like cement in my stomach. Grant isn't just creating distance—he's erasing us completely. The realization should probably hurt more than it does, but after two weeks of polite deflections and closed doors, maybe I'm running out of ways to be hurt. Or maybe I just finally understand that I've been refusing to see that whatever we were becoming, whatever I thought we might be, clearly meant something very different to him than it did to me.

Outside the restaurant, cameras start flashing before I've taken two steps. The questions come rapid-fire.

"Sophia! Is it true you're leaving LA?"

How do they even know this stuff? I just talked about it with Blair.

"Are you and Grant splitting up?"

"How does Geneva feel about your relationship with her daughter?"

"Is the studio pushing you out?"

I keep my head down as I rush to my car, but one question cuts through the chaos.

"Are you in love with Grant, Sophia?"

The question follows me home, echoing in my head as I walk through my beautiful, empty house—the house I originally bought while imagining cozy movie nights, Sunday brunches, family dinners, and lazy mornings. Now it just feels empty and lonely.

My gaze catches on a picture Hazel made for me, the one I hung this morning so she would see it. It pulls me back to what it might feel like to have a family—how real it felt, how possible.

But maybe that's the problem. Maybe I let myself believe in something that was never meant to last.

I pick up my phone one last time, and my thumb hovers

over Grant's name. There are a dozen things I could say, a hundred ways to fight for this. Instead, I set the phone down and go to bed.

Sometimes, the kindest thing you can do for someone is to let them go before they have to ask you to leave.

forty-two

. . .

Grant

MY OFFICE FEELS COLDER than usual. Or maybe that's just me.

I watch Sophia settle into the chair across from me, noting the careful way she arranges herself—professional, composed, distant. Gone is the woman who'd curl up in my office chair with her feet tucked under her while we discussed production scenes for *Survivor*.

"Vancouver?" I keep my voice neutral, though the word feels like gravel in my throat.

"Eight-episode limited series." She smooths her already-perfect hair—a tell, I've learned, that means she's nervous. "It's with Netflix. Good script, talented team."

"When do you leave?"

"Monday. Blair's finalizing the details." Her eyes finally meet mine for the first time since she walked in. "I think we both know this is for the best."

The rational part of me agrees—the part that remembers Hazel's tears, sees the strain around Sophia's eyes from the constant camera flashes, and hears the whispers in board meetings. But the other part—the part that wakes up reaching for her in the night—that part is screaming.

"It was never supposed to be complicated," I say instead.

A ghost of a smile touches her lips. "I don't regret our time together, Grant."

That stings. I want to reach for her hand, to pull her close and promise we'll figure it out. Instead, I straighten the papers on the table, a habit from a thousand other meetings where I've needed to maintain control.

"The post-production schedule—"

"I've arranged everything," she says. "The team knows what they're doing. I'll be available remotely for any major decisions."

Professional. Practical. Perfect.

"Lucas will handle the press if needed," I say. "We can keep it simple—amicable parting, focus on respective careers. He'll make sure everyone knows your producer credit was earned."

"Grant." Something in her voice makes me look up. "I don't need you to protect me."

"I know."

And I do. She's the strongest person I've ever met.

A knock at the door saves me from saying anything more. Lucas steps in, and his expression shifts as he reads the room. "Sorry to interrupt. The streaming team is waiting for us."

"It's fine," Sophia says. "We're done here."

Her words are like a punch to my stomach.

She picks her bag off the floor as she stands, and then she

walks toward Lucas. "Thank you so much for everything you did for us. I know we didn't make your job easy."

"I've really enjoyed getting to know you better, Sophia."

She pauses at the door, not quite looking back. "Take care of yourself, Grant. Hazel, too."

"You, too, Sophia."

After she leaves, Lucas lingers, watching me with knowing eyes. "Want me to start drafting statements?"

"Only if you have to." My voice sounds foreign to my ears. "Protect her career. Make sure everyone knows she's brilliant."

"And you?"

"I'm fine." The lie comes easily. "It was never meant to be permanent."

The words echo in the room, and I let them fuel the careful wall I'm building in my mind. This is exactly why I've never wanted anything serious. Relationships mean complications, vulnerability, risk. I'm angry with myself because I knew better.

I've built my life around certainties. The studio. My reputation. Hazel. Especially Hazel. She needs stability, a father who isn't distracted by romantic entanglements that could implode at any moment. The past three months have been a departure from everything I believe in, everything I've promised myself—temporary insanity born of attraction and convenience.

This is better. Cleaner. A return to the way things should be.

I repeat it like a mantra, ignoring the voice in my head

that sounds suspiciously like Geneva asking if I'm protecting Hazel or hiding behind her.

Later that night, I find Hazel in the living room, curled up on the couch and watching *Beauty and the Beast.*

"Dad?" Hazel's voice is careful. "Is Sophia coming over tonight?"

I rehearsed this moment, but the words still stick. "Actually, sweetheart, Sophia took a job in Vancouver. She'll be away for a while. She wanted me to tell you goodbye and she's sorry she wasn't able to come see you before she left."

"Oh." Hazel is quiet for a long moment. "When is she coming back?"

"I'm not sure. I think she'll be up there all summer."

"Did you tell her you love her before she left?"

The question hits like a physical blow. "It's complicated, nugget."

"That's what grown-ups always say when they're scared." She turns off the TV and looks at me with eyes that are much too wise for a six-year-old. "Mom says, sometimes, people only get one big love. What if Sophia was yours?"

I stand there, speechless, as she gathers her things and heads upstairs. Through the window, I can see the spot where Sophia's car used to park, now empty in the growing darkness.

What if Hazel's right?

What if I just let my one chance at love walk away because I was too afraid to fight for it?

The house feels impossibly quiet, filled with the echoes of everything I didn't say.

forty-three

. . .

Sophia

Two months later.

"AND THAT'S A WRAP ON ADR." The sound engineer's voice crackles through the booth speaker. "You're officially done with *Survivor*, Ms. Ford."

Removing my headphones, I let satisfaction warm my chest. I just finished re-recording audio segments that were either poor quality or replacing places where the script needed a little tweaking. It's always hard to get back into character after you wrap filming, but it felt good to be Maya again—even if it brought a whole host of other memories with it.

My time in Vancouver wasn't just an escape—it reminded me who I was beyond tabloid headlines and complicated relationships—beyond Grant.

Vancouver was exactly what I needed. I traded my usual gritty survival roles for something completely different—a romantic comedy, of all things—spending my days in designer sundresses, fumbling through meet-cutes, and learning how to make my character's coffee shop disasters look endearing instead of tragic.

Even my temporary apartment felt like stepping into another life, with its view of mountains instead of city lights. I threw myself into the role, into cast dinners, into becoming someone whose biggest worry was choosing between two perfect men, not lying awake at night wondering why the real one stopped calling.

"The dailies coming in from Vancouver look incredible," Blair says as we gather our things in the hallway.

Walking through the familiar corridors of Wonderland Studios' post-production building makes my stomach flutter, but I push the feeling aside. It's ridiculous to be nervous. The executive offices are in an entirely different building, and Grant is probably buried in meetings, anyway. He always is... was.

"It was good to focus on work." I check my phone, a habit I can't seem to break, though I've stopped expecting Grant's name to appear weeks ago. The ache is still there, sharp and constant as a bruise. Throwing myself into a lighthearted role helped during the day, but nights were different. Nights meant remembering all the little moments that felt like we were building something real until they just...stopped.

But life goes on. And now, gathering my purse and script pages, I feel steadier than I have in months. I haven't healed—not even close—but I'm surviving. Working. Moving forward, even if part of me is still stuck in the silence of those last few texts, waiting for an explanation that never came.

The elevator dings at the end of the hall, and I freeze

mid-reach. The sound booth suddenly feels very small, very exposed. This is ridiculous. This whole building is full of actors doing post-production work. The chances of Grant walking through the doors are impossible.

Relief and sadness wash over me as Wyatt strides in. His face lights up at the sight of Blair. "There you are. I was hoping to catch you before my next meeting."

I watch the casual way Blair melts into Wyatt's side, the soft kiss he drops on her temple, and the wordless communication in their shared glance. The sight hits me like a physical ache, and I have to look away. I'm mad at myself for thinking I could have that. I knew better.

"Lunch tomorrow?" Wyatt asks me as his hand absently plays with Blair's hair.

"Can't. Meeting with Edie. But dinner?"

"Perfect."

I haven't even been home for two days, and already, the studio lot feels like a minefield of memories I've been trying to bury. Every corner holds an echo of Grant and the stolen moments between takes.

"Earth to Sophia?" Blair's voice pulls me back.

"Sorry. Just...thinking."

She nods with a knowing look.

We head back down the elevator with Wyatt and say goodbye before he heads off to his next meeting. When we turn to make our way across the lot toward the parking structure, a familiar voice cuts through the afternoon quiet. "Sophia!"

My heart lurches before my brain can catch up. I turn

just in time to brace myself as Hazel crashes into me, all gangly limbs and endless energy. "You're back!"

"Hey, nugget." My heart squeezes as I hug her tight, breathing in the familiar scent of her strawberry shampoo. "Look at you—did you grow?"

"A whole inch! And I started taking guitar lessons because I'm definitely going to audition for the play in second grade, and..." Hazel barely pauses for breath. "Are you coming back to the house? Dad's been weird since you left. He pretends he's fine, but he keeps making too much coffee in the morning like he forgets your not there."

Her casual observation feels like a knife between my ribs. "I've been pretty busy with work..."

"But you're done with Vancouver now, right? And *Survivor* is almost finished?" Hope shines in her eyes. "Maybe you could come over for dinner? Like old times?"

I catch Blair's sympathetic glance. "I don't know if that's..."

"Please? Dad's really lonely. He doesn't say it, but I can tell. He sits in his office, looking at old pictures, when he thinks I'm not paying attention."

"Hazel..." I kneel to meet her eyes, trying to ignore how much they remind me of Grant's. "It's complicated."

"That's what Dad always says." Hazel's expression turns serious. "But it's not, really. You miss us, and we miss you. The rest is just grown-up stuff you're both being stupid about."

A startled laugh escapes me. "When did you get so wise?"

"Mom says I get it from her." Hazel hugs me again. "Promise you'll think about it?"

"I promise to find time to see you soon." It's the safest thing I can offer. "Maybe we can get ice cream or something."

"Ok." Hazel's smile dims slightly. "But think about dinner, too? Dad's cooking got really bad again after you left."

As I watch Hazel skip back to the building, Blair touches my arm. "You ok?"

"No," I admit, surprised by my own honesty. "But I will be."

I just wasn't sure when.

forty-four

. . .

Grant

I STAY HIDDEN behind the corner of the studio building, watching Hazel hug Sophia goodbye. I don't mean to eavesdrop, but the sight of them together has me frozen in place. Sophia kneels to Hazel's level—like she always does—making my daughter feel heard and important.

Her hair is shorter now, falling just past her shoulders instead of down her back. The same golden brown catches the afternoon sun, but everything else about her seems muted somehow. The spark in her eyes has dimmed, and her smile seems more careful, professional. It's the kind she uses for press junkets and red carpets, not the real one that used to light up my kitchen in the morning.

A familiar ache tightens in my chest when Hazel mentions my morning coffee habit. I've tried to hide how much Sophia's absence has affected me, but Hazel notices everything. She always does.

I should have told her. I should have explained about the kids at school, about the panic that gripped me every time I saw another photographer. Instead, I let distance and silence do the work for me, watching her slowly withdraw until she was gone. The coward's way out. Now, seeing the shadows under her eyes and the way her shoulders tense slightly when Hazel mentions my name—I did that. I put that wariness there, that hint of hurt she's trying so hard to hide.

I press my back against the cool concrete of the building, staying hidden. It's safer here, watching from a distance. These past weeks, I've gotten good at burying myself in work, in meetings, in anything that keeps me from admitting I might have broken something irreplaceable—that in trying to protect Hazel, I may have cost her someone who loved her almost as much as I do.

On the drive home, Hazel chatters non-stop.

"Sophia's hair is shorter now," she says, leaning her head to the window. "And she said maybe we could get ice cream soon. Did you know she was back? Why didn't you tell me?"

I focus on the road, grateful for an excuse not to meet her gaze. "I didn't know."

"She looks pretty," Hazel continues. "But kind of sad—like you do sometimes when you think I'm not looking."

My grip tightens on the steering wheel as the memories wash over me. The weeks of burying myself in work until I'm too exhausted to think. Picking up my phone to call her a hundred times before setting it down. Scanning every article about her Vancouver project just to see her face.

I kept telling myself she was probably better off without me, but that didn't stop me from driving by her house some nights, just in case she was back. All I saw were dark windows and an empty driveway.

The worst moments come when something reminds me of her. When Hazel puts on a movie we once watched together, the smell of coconut shampoo in the grocery store aisle, or how my office chair feels too big and empty without Sophia curled up in it. More than once, I've turned to share a joke with her before remembering she's not there.

When we step into the house, the smell of Sarah's home-made lasagna fills the air. She's been coming by more often, probably sensing Hazel and I need the company.

"And Sophia said she'd try to make time to see me," Hazel announces, dumping her backpack by the stairs. "I'm going upstairs to change. Be right back!"

Sarah waits until Hazel disappears upstairs. "Sophia's back?"

"Apparently," I say, sinking into a kitchen chair. "We ran into her at the studio."

"And?"

"And nothing. I'm sure she was wrapping up post-production on *Survivor*. Hazel saw her while I hid in the shadows." I rub my face. "It doesn't change anything."

Sarah sets her spoon down with careful deliberation. "Mom called this morning."

I tense. "How is she?"

"She's good. We talked about Dad," Sarah says softly, "and about you."

I swallow hard. "Sarah—"

"She told me something that stuck with me. If she had the chance to do it all over, even knowing how it would end and how much it would hurt, she'd still choose Dad every time."

I shake my head. "That's different."

"Is it?" Sarah leans against the counter. "You're so focused on keeping yourself—and Hazel—safe that you're guaranteeing you'll both miss out on real happiness."

"I saw what losing Dad did to Mom."

"Yes," Sarah says, resting a hand on my shoulder, "and she still says it was worth it. The only thing worse than losing love is never letting yourself have it at all."

I roll my eyes at the cliché comment. I'm saved from the conversation when Hazel thunders back down the stairs, her sneakers squeaking on the hardwood. "Can we have garlic bread, too?"

Sarah glances up from her seat at the kitchen counter, her lips curving into a soft smile. "Already in the oven."

I lean against the doorway, watching them both, pretending this moment doesn't ache as much as it does. They're my family, my whole world, but there's another silence here that feels heavier now, emptier.

It wasn't like this when Sophia was here. She was the spark that made this house come alive. She knew how to make Hazel laugh so hard she'd snort and how to get Sarah to relax and stay for another glass of wine instead of rushing back to her to-do list. With Sophia, it all felt...*right*.

I swallow hard as the knot in my throat tightens. I thought letting her go was the right thing. Safer. For Hazel. For me. For her. I told myself it would hurt less in the long run, that we'd be fine without her, and that I couldn't risk letting her in only to lose her the way my mom lost my dad.

But I was wrong. Without her, it's like the light's been switched off in this house. I miss her.

I run a hand over my jaw, exhaling slowly. I told myself I could live without her, that I'd be protecting Hazel, saving us all from a pain we didn't need to feel. But this—*this*—is worse. The ache of knowing she's out there, thinking I didn't want her, that she didn't matter when the truth is...I'm in love with her.

"I think I made a mistake," I say quietly, the words slipping out before I can stop them.

Hazel pauses mid-spin, and she turns to look at me with wide, curious eyes. "About what?"

My chest tightens. I glance at Sarah, but she's watching me, waiting. There's no turning back now.

"Sophia," I say, forcing the name past my lips.

Hazel blinks, and then her face lights up. "Finally!" She grins, and her gap-toothed smile makes my chest ache all over again. "I miss her, Daddy. You're gonna fix it, right?"

I clear my throat, nodding once. "Yeah. I'm gonna fix it."

"Good," Hazel says with the certainty only a six-year-old can muster before skipping back to the counter.

Sarah leans back in her chair, crossing her arms. "Well, if you're serious about fixing it, you'd better be ready to go all in. Sophia won't settle for halfway."

I meet her gaze, my jaw tightening with determination. "I know. And this time, neither will I."

Sarah grins. "Well, little brother, you've come to the right people. Let's make a plan."

"You should tell everyone you love her!" Hazel bounces on her toes, flooding the kitchen with her excitement. "Get a megaphone on top of a building or one of those planes that write in the sky, or go on TV and—"

I freeze as her words ignite an idea. "Hazel...you're brilliant."

"I am?" Her face lights up.

I pull out my phone and dial Lucas while I pace. Sarah and Hazel exchange curious looks.

"Hey, Grant. What's up?" Lucas answers.

"I need to make a statement," I say, running a hand through my hair. "About Sophia. Or maybe you can get someone to write an article. Something that lets me set the record straight and share how I feel about Sophia."

"Um."

There's a pause, and then another voice cuts in. "Oh, thank God. You finally got your head out of your ass."

"Jess?"

"You're on speaker," Lucas explains.

"Grant," Jess says, using that brisk, no-nonsense tone she reserves for situations that need immediate fixing, "I have a slot open for next week's podcast. I'll make a deal with you. You go on the record about the rumors around the streaming service sale, and I'll give you air time for whatever public declaration you are after. No pre-recorded questions, no script—just you talking honestly."

"Hang on," Lucas cuts in. "Let's think about this."

"What? Why? The press will eat it up," Jess says. "Exclusive interview, industry titan Grant Hall showing his vulnerable side..."

"Maybe, but it can't look totally self-serving. And what if it backfires?" Lucas asks.

"It won't backfire. You act like I'm not a professional who does this every day."

"I like the idea of this," I tell them both.

"More importantly," Jess interjects, "Sophia tunes in every week. She even listened from Vancouver."

I glance at Hazel, who's practically vibrating with excitement, and at Sarah, who nods her approval.

"One condition," I say. "I want Hazel involved. If we're doing this, we go all in."

"Dad!" Hazel throws her arms around me. "Can I tell the story about how you keep making too much coffee?"

I hug her back, feeling something settle in my chest for the first time in weeks. "Yeah, sweetheart. You can tell that story."

"I'll get some talking points prepared," Lucas offers, "something about setting the record straight—"

"No." My voice is firm. "Jess is right. No PR spin. Just the truth. I love her, I was scared, and I want her back."

A beat of silence follows before Jess speaks again, a smile in her voice. "Well, well. Look who finally learned to use his words."

Sarah squeezes my shoulder. "Mom's going to be so proud. Dad would be, too."

"Thursday at two," Jess says. "Don't be late. And Grant? Show up to win her back."

I hang up, turning to my sister and my daughter—my team. "Any advice?"

"Tell her about the pictures," Hazel says.

I frown. "What pictures?"

"The ones you keep looking at on your phone. You smile and look sad at the same time."

I nod, my mind already churning with how to say everything Sophia needs to hear. I only have a few days to figure out the right words, to show her I'm ready to embrace it all, especially the possibility of forever.

"Dad?" Hazel asks, suddenly solemn. "What if she doesn't listen to the episode?"

Sarah grins. "Oh, she'll listen. Between me, Blair, and Jess, we'll make sure of it."

For the first time in weeks, hope spreads through me. Now all I have to do is not screw this up.

Again.

forty-five

. . .

Sophia

I'M RUNNING LATE to lunch, but for once, I don't care. After weeks of back-to-back schedules between Vancouver and post-production on *Survivor*, it feels luxurious to have no urgent place to be—just a casual lunch with friends, catching up on all the life I missed while I was away.

The hostess leads me to our usual corner table at The Ivy, and I freeze mid-step. Sarah Hall's unmistakable laugh echoes across the restaurant, and I see her at our table. For a moment, I consider turning around, but she sees me first and waves, smiling warmly.

"Sophia!" She stands and pulls me into a hug, and I let myself sink into it. I've missed her—missed all of them—more than I realized. "I hope you don't mind me crashing lunch."

"Of course not." The lie comes easily, even as my heart constricts. Having Grant's sister here is like poking at a wound that hasn't finished healing.

Jess slides a glass of wine toward me when I sit. "You look good. Rested."

"Vancouver agreed with me." Another lie, but I'm getting better at them.

"Speaking of agreeing," Jess says, leaning forward with that mischievous gleam in her eye. "We were just talking about our favorite big romantic gestures in pop culture—Lloyd Dobler with the boombox, Noah building the house for Allie..."

"The airport scene in *Notting Hill*," Stella chimes in dreamily.

"Kat Stratford reading the poem in class," Brandon adds, earning a few raised eyebrows. "What? I watch rom-coms."

"You know what I love?" Stella sighs. "Those dramatic moments where someone realizes what they've lost and fights to get it back."

I take a slow sip of my wine. "Those only happen in movies. Real life is...messier."

"I don't know about that," Blair counters. "Sometimes, real life surprises you."

"Speaking of surprises," Jess says, straightening in her chair, "did you all see the speculation about Wonderland Studios maybe selling off their streaming platform?"

The abrupt subject change makes me tense. Any mention of the studio still does that to me.

"The press has been ruthless," Brandon cuts in. "Accusations about lack of transparency, questioning the studio's direction...brutal."

Sarah nods. "That's why Grant finally agreed to do press—he wants to clear the air about Wonderland's future. Address rumors head-on."

My stomach drops. "He's doing interviews?"

"Just one." Sarah watches me closely. "Personally, I love it when someone's willing to be vulnerable in front of the whole world. To just...lay it all out there."

"Like a podcast interview?" Blair asks, her tone a little too innocent.

Suddenly, it all clicks. Jess's podcast, this carefully steered conversation, everyone glancing my way like they're waiting for a reaction.

"What did you do?" I ask Jess, narrowing my eyes.

"He came to me," she says quietly, "said if he was going to talk about the studio's future, he wanted someone he trusted. Someone who'd let him tell the whole truth." She takes out her phone and slides it across the table. "Including setting the record straight about the relationship between you and him."

"Just watch," Blair urges.

The video opens on Jess's familiar podcast set, but in the guest chair is Grant. And Hazel. My heart stutters.

Jess's voice comes through the speakers with practiced clarity.

"Welcome back to On the Red Carpet. *Today, my guest is Grant Hall, head of Wonderland Studios, and his daughter, Hazel. Grant, Hazel, thanks for being here."*

"Happy to be here, Jess."

"Let's address the biggest rumor right away. Is Wonderland really planning to sell off its streaming arm, FlixPix?"

Grant exhales as though he's been expecting this.

"No, we're not selling FlixPix, despite what the tabloids and trade papers are saying. We're restructuring some of our

deals, but that's a far cry from a sell-off. I want to set the record straight on that."

"So, there's no truth to the speculation about financial trouble?"

"No. We're making strategic adjustments, sure—but nothing as drastic as a sale. The board and I are fully committed to the platform's future."

Jess flips through her notes and I can tell she's setting up to go all in.

"I appreciate the clarification. While we're on the subject of big decisions, there's been some whispering about your creative direction at Wonderland—particularly regarding the roles and projects green-lit under your watch. Some outlets have even suggested you hired actress Sophia Ford for personal reasons. Care to comment?"

Grant's jaw tightens slightly. He looks determined.

"Yes, and I'd like to be very clear. Sophia Ford was hired because she's extraordinarily talented. Any suggestion that she was given preferential treatment simply because of a personal connection is false."

"So, you're saying your relationship with Sophia didn't influence the casting decisions?"

"Not in the way people assume. I backed her for roles because she's right for them. Our casting team felt the same. Her success speaks for itself."

"Are you still in a relationship with Sophia?"

"Sophia has been an important part of my life and Hazel's life."

Jess smiles and glances over to Grant's side, winking at Hazel.

"*You mentioned your daughter, Hazel. Word on the street is she's been your sidekick at some studio meetings lately. Hi there, Hazel.*"

Grant smiles down at Hazel, proud of his little girl.

"*She's had some free time this summer, and she's made an excellent intern.*"

My heart aches when I see Hazel snuggle closer to him on the couch.

"*Hi,*" she says, hugging his arm. "*Dad said I could be here to show that not everything the press says is true.*"

"*That's very grown-up of you. So, Hazel, how do you feel about all of this? The rumors about your dad, Sophia— everything.*"

"*I think I'm lucky because I have a lot of people who love me. My dad, my mom, and Sophia, too.*"

"*It sounds like you are a very lucky little girl. So, Grant, I have to ask, are you and Sophia officially together?*"

Grant sits straighter, his expression changes.

"*Actually, Jess, I wanted to set the record straight on all of that. I've spent my career making calculated decisions, weighing every risk. But sometimes, the smartest choice is admitting when you've been wrong. Sophia Ford is one of the most talented artists I've ever worked with. And yes, we did develop a personal relationship, one that I let outside pressure and my own fears derail. That was my mistake, not hers.*"

"*You're being unusually candid.*"

"*Because I'm done letting speculation and rumors dictate my life—our lives. The press wants to know if I hired Sophia for personal reasons. No, I hired her because she's brilliant. Did our relationship affect business decisions? Only in that we both worked twice as hard to keep things professional. But here's what the press hasn't asked. Do I light up every time she walks into a room? Yes. Do I miss coming home and finding her and Hazel watching movies on the couch or the way she covers our fridge with pictures of everyday moments? Every day. Do I regret letting her walk away? Absolutely."*

Hazel shifts in her seat eager to talk.

"Dad's been kind of mopey since she left. He still makes her coffee sometimes in the morning."

Grant chuckles, squeezing Hazel's shoulders.

"Thanks for exposing me, kiddo. Look, I could keep trying to maintain this careful separation between personal and professional, but it's clearly not working. Sophia makes our lives better. She challenges me to be better, to take risks, to let people in."

He looks directly into the camera, his voice grows more intimate as he speaks directly to me.

"Sophia, I know you're probably wondering why I'm doing this on camera instead of showing up at your door. But there's a point to this. No more hiding, no more letting public perception stand in our way. I want everyone to know exactly how I feel about you. I love how you can command a production meeting and then spend hours helping Hazel with her science projects. I love that you make our house feel like home with your photos and your laughter. And I just...I love you."

"And professionally?"

"Professionally, I respect her too much to let anyone question her achievements. Every success she's had, she's earned. And if anyone has a problem with us being together, they can

take it up with me directly. Though they should probably know that our head of legal is firmly Team Sophia."

"Dad's still got all her favorite snacks in the pantry!"

Grant laughs at Hazel's interjection.

"The point is, I'm not here to apologize for falling in love with her. I'm here to apologize for not fighting for that love sooner. So, Sophia, if you're watching, I'm ready to do this right. No more hiding, no more letting fear win. Just us, building something real together in front of everyone who wants to watch. If you'll give me another chance, I promise to love you proudly, publicly, and completely."

Jess leans back, a genuine smile on her face.

"Well, that's quite a declaration."

"It is. And it's long overdue."

"You heard it here, On the Red Carpet. Until next time, listeners—stay tuned."

The video ends, and only then do I realize I'm crying. Sarah squeezes my hand.

"He recorded that last week," Jess says softly. "It goes live in an hour."

"I..." My voice cracks. "I can't..."

"Yes, you can," Blair says gently but firmly. "The question is do you want to?"

I think about all the reasons we fell apart and all the reasons we were so good together. "It might be too late," I whisper.

"Or," Sarah says, leaning forward, "it might be exactly the right time. Sometimes, we have to lose something to realize how much we want to fight for it."

My phone buzzes, and I glance down and see a text from Lucas with a link to an article from *Deadline* that recaps what Jess's podcast says.

LUCAS

Heads up. This is about to break. Do you want to comment?

I stare at the screen, my heart pounding. Everyone's watching me, waiting.

What do I want?

forty-six

. . .

Grant

I'VE GIVEN this party every year for a decade, but tonight, the familiar warmth of my Hamptons home feels hollow. The usual suspects are all here—industry veterans, old friends, chosen family—their voices creating that familiar buzz of connection and laughter that usually energizes me. Tonight, though, I'm just going through the motions.

"Hey, man, thanks for inviting us again," Wyatt says as he brings me in for a man hug.

I look behind him, hoping to see a familiar face. "Of course, man. Always." I'm just grateful he's been so cool about my public declaration for his sister.

"She didn't come with us. Sorry, man."

A week. It's been a week since I bared my soul on Jess's podcast, since I told the world—and Sophia—exactly how I feel. The silence has been deafening. Even Lucas has stopped offering reassurances.

I invited her tonight with a simple note.

You've always belonged in my inner circle. Please come. No pressure, no grand declarations. Just us.

She didn't respond.

I'm barely listening to my guests, so I slip out of the house and onto the back deck, which overlooks the ocean. The end of summer breeze carries a hint of coolness, and I can't help but picture a future where Sophia stands out here with me, telling me stories about her day.

"You're not being a very good host out here by yourself."

The chatter from inside dips for an instant like a wave hushed by the tide. I turn, and there she is.

As Sophia lingers in the doorway, the setting sun blazes through her hair. She's wearing a simple blue dress that makes her eyes look endless, and her hands tremble at her sides.

"Hi," she says softly.

I walk toward her, my heart pounding. We meet in the middle of the deck, close enough to touch, neither of us quite daring.

"You came," I say, my voice catching on the words. I've imagined this moment countless times over the past week, but nothing prepared me for the reality of her standing here.

"I almost didn't." Her eyes meet mine, and a storm of emotions swims in their depths. "I had this whole speech prepared about timing and trust, about how maybe we needed more space to figure things out. I rehearsed it a hundred times on the drive here." She lets out a shaky breath. "But then I realized something."

"What?" I take a tentative step toward her, afraid she might disappear if I move too quickly.

"That I'm tired of speeches. Tired of careful words and measured distances." She takes a small step closer, closing the gap between us. "I've spent my whole life learning how to guard my heart, how to keep people at arm's length. But with you..." Her voice cracks. "With you, I don't want to be careful anymore. I don't want to overthink every moment or question every feeling. I just want you—everything about you, even the parts that terrify me."

"Sophia—" I start, but she lifts her hand.

"Please, let me finish." Her voice trembles, but there's determination in her eyes. "You said on that podcast that you were ready to do this right. No more fear. That you wanted to build something real together. And I realized that's what I want, too. But I also want you to trust me, and I want to trust you. Not just the easy moments, but all of it—the challenges, the uncertainties, the beautiful mess of building a life together."

"I am. I do." I reach for her hand, unable to resist touching her any longer. "Before you, I thought I had it all figured out. I had my rules, my careful boundaries, this life I'd built that felt...safe. But then you walked in, and suddenly, safe wasn't enough anymore. You make me want things I'd convinced myself I could live without. When I see you with Hazel, or catch you looking at me across a room, or feel your hand in mine like this..." I squeeze her fingers gently. "It's like everything I was so afraid of losing becomes worth the risk. Because losing you?" My voice roughens. "That's the only thing I can't survive."

Tears slip down her cheeks, and I feel my eyes burning. "I spent so long protecting myself from exactly this kind of moment," she whispers. "From letting someone matter this much. But you and Hazel...you didn't just work your way into my heart—you became my heart. When I was in Vancouver, nothing felt right because home isn't a place anymore. It's wherever you both are."

"Move back home," I say, my voice rough with emotion. "With us."

"Just like that?" she asks, but I can see the yearning in her eyes.

"We'll figure out all the details later. The press, the studio politics, everything else. But I need you with us. Where you belong."

When I kiss her, it feels like coming up for air after being underwater. The applause and cheers from inside barely register—all I know is the warmth of her lips against mine, the way her body fits perfectly against me, the sense of rightness that settles deep in my bones.

The moment stretches, perfect and infinite, until we finally break apart, both a little breathless. She rests her forehead against mine, and I can feel her smile against my lips.

"We should probably join your guests," she murmurs, though she makes no move to pull away.

"They can wait," I say, but I know she's right. Keeping one arm around her waist, I lead her back inside, where our friends wait, their faces reflecting the happiness I feel.

The party flows seamlessly into dinner, with everyone gathered around the long table that's hosted so many meaningful moments over the years. As I stand to address the room, I look around at these people who've become family.

My heart pounds steadily in my chest, but at the same time, I feel completely at peace.

I clear my throat, tapping the side of my glass to draw everyone's attention. "Every year, I tell myself I won't ramble on about how much this tradition means to me. And yet... here I am again."

A wave of quiet laughter moves through the room.

"When I started hosting this celebration, I thought it would be a one-time thing—a way to connect with the people who'd helped me on my path. But I underestimated how much I'd come to rely on these nights. This room has no shortage of talent or inspiration, but it takes more than that to thrive. It takes creativity, yes, but it also takes genuine humanity and a willingness to lift each other up when things get tough. Those qualities are rare, and the fact that so many of you have shown up year after year tells me I've found them in you."

I pause, letting my gaze travel the room. "Some of you are here for the first time; some have been coming since that very first dinner. Either way, you matter to me, and you matter to each other. I've always believed the best moments are the ones we share with people who truly see us—and you've shown me time and again how powerful that can be."

I pause, letting that sentiment settle. Then I glance at Sophia, who gazes back with tears in her eyes. "This year, it means more than ever because, tonight, you're not just my inner circle—you're witnesses to one of the best nights of my life. The night I finally got it right."

A smile stretches across my face as I lift my glass higher. "Cheers, everyone."

Sophia threads her fingers through mine as I sit back down at the table.

"To new beginnings!" Jess calls out.

"It's not new; they've already been together," Lucas snaps at Jess. "If anything, it's a continuation of love."

"Whatever, Lucas. Raise your glass."

I laugh and raise mine. "To love, in all its complicated, beautiful forms."

The ocean crashes behind us, steady and sure. Sophia leans into me, dropping her voice so only I can hear. "How long do we have to stay tonight?"

"I already bribed the catering team to make this the fastest dinner they've ever served," I whisper back, leaning in to kiss her. It's a little indecent, and we break apart with matching grins just as servers appear with the appetizers. "Hurry up and eat, Ms. Ford. I'm ready for dessert."

epilogue

. . .

Sophia

Six Months Later – Oscars Red Carpet

THE RED CARPET at the Oscars feels different this time. Last year, I was desperately single and secretly drooling over being in Grant's proximity. Now, with Grant's hand steady on my lower back and Hazel bouncing excitedly between us, I feel like I'm exactly where I belong.

I spot Blair and Wyatt near the press line. Blair looks as stunning as always in emerald green. She catches my eye and winks, clearly noticing Grant's possessive stance. Behind them, I see Stella talking to a tall brunette I don't recognize— must be her friend Natalie, the one she mentioned was working the event tonight. Even in the server's uniform, the woman has an elegant presence that makes her stand out.

"You're killing me in that dress, Soph," Grant whispers, his lips brushing my ear. The cameras start flashing more frantically, and I can't help but grin. "You know what it does to me when you wear baby blue."

"Oh, I know. You had the same reaction to my dress last year," I tease back, smoothing my hand over his perfectly tailored tux. "Though, if I recall correctly, you were trying very hard not to stare at me then."

"And failing miserably." He winks at me and then crouches down to Hazel's level. "How're you doing, princess? Ready for your big red carpet moment?"

Hazel, in her miniature version of my dress, gives him a thousand-watt smile. "Ready! But Daddy, don't forget the—"

"Shh!" Grant puts a finger to his lips, cutting her off before she can finish.

I catch their exchange, but before I can ask what they're up to, Brandon appears, greeting Hazel with an elaborate bow that makes her giggle. "Your Highness," he says solemnly and then turns to me. "Sophia, you look incredible."

As Brandon chats with Grant about his latest film, I notice Jake hovering near the theater entrance. His wife's perfectly manicured hand grips his arm like a vice. The tension in his shoulders is visible even from here. Beside them, Jess and Lucas stand slightly apart from the chaos, their heads bent close together as they whisper, clearly having a moment.

Normally, I'd expect to see them snapping at each other—Jess with her sharp tone, Lucas with his trademark smirk—but something about this feels...different. Their body language isn't combative; it's intense and intimate. Before I can fully process what I'm seeing, Jess abruptly pulls back, and Lucas reaches out, catching her hand for a split second before letting it drop.

"Hey." Grant's voice pulls me back to the moment. He tugs on my hand, stopping us mid-walk. "Remember what I said on Jess's podcast? About how I wanted to love you proudly, publicly, and completely?"

"How could I forget? My phone didn't stop ringing for—"

The words die in my throat as Grant drops to one knee, still holding my hand. The crowd around us goes silent and then erupts in excited murmurs. Stella, who's tucked into Brandon's arms, lets out an audible gasp.

"Sophia Ford," he says, his voice steady but his eyes shining with emotion, "I fell in love with you right here on this red carpet, probably before that, if I'm being honest. You've made me happier than I ever thought possible, and you've given me the family I always dreamed of." He glances at Hazel, who's practically vibrating with excitement. "Since I already confessed my feelings to the whole world on Jess's podcast, I figured this was the perfect place to ask you to be my wife."

He pulls out a ring box and opens it, revealing a vintage diamond and sapphire ring. "Will you marry me?"

Tears blur my vision as I look from Grant to Hazel, who's now holding up a tiny sign that reads *Say Yes, Sophia!* in her wobbly handwriting. Through my tears, I catch Blair dabbing at her eyes while Wyatt wraps an arm around her shoulders.

"Yes," I manage to choke out. "Yes, of course, yes!"

The crowd erupts in cheers as Grant slides the ring onto my finger, stands, and pulls Hazel and me into a tight embrace. Cameras flash around us, capturing the moment for posterity. Our friends surge forward—Blair and Wyatt first, followed by Stella and Brandon, then Jess, who mysteriously lost Lucas in the shuffle.

As Hazel wraps her arms around us both and her giggles mix with the congratulations and chaos, I feel the perfect rightness of this moment settle into my bones. This isn't just a fairy tale ending—it's a beginning—our beginning.

Not ready to say goodbye to Grant and Sophia?
Scan the QR code to join my newsletter family and unlock
an exclusive bonus scene that wasn't in the book! You'll also
be the first to hear about upcoming releases, behind-the-
scenes peeks, and special offers. No spam, just bookish joy
delivered straight to your inbox!

The Backlot Series

Second Act – Available Now!
Center Stage – Available Now!
On the Record (Jess and Lucas) - Summer 2025
Behind the Scenes (Stella and Brandon) - Fall 2025
Off Script (Natalie and Jake) - Spring 2026

Thank you!

I hope you fell in love with Grant and Sophia's journey in
Center Stage! If their story captured your heart, I'd be

incredibly grateful if you'd consider leaving a review. Your words not only help other readers discover these characters, but they're also the lifeblood that keeps indie authors like me writing (and occasionally doing happy dances around the kitchen!). Thank you for being part of this adventure! 🤍

Keep reading for the first two chapters
of Blair and Wyatt's story in
Second Act
Book 1 in The Backlot Series

Available Now!
Read for free in Kindle Unlimited
https://amzn.to/41EHXFP

chapter one

. . .

Blair

"WHO'S THE HOTTIE?"

My assistant Stella leans over my shoulder to get a closer look at my searched images of Sophia Ford, the twenty-four-year-old best actress Oscar winner, and her brother. Sophia is on my list of dream clients to represent. With any luck, I'll convince her to sign with me before summer's over. However, her brother should have received an Oscar for his role as the popular guy in high school who can make you believe anything he wants.

"His name is Wyatt Bradford, and he's not that hot."

He is that hot.

Dark blond hair, short on the sides and a little longer on the top, but in this pic, it's slicked back. His eyes gaze into the camera and are the same ice blue I remember. Still tall and still working out, I see. That shirt is struggling to stay buttoned across his toned chest. His tan suit wraps around his body, hugging his muscular thighs, and is that a crease right there, or is that...

"Ohmygod, Blair, you can see the outline of his penis!" Stella shrieks behind me.

I slam the laptop closed, stand, and walk away from the desk to get a breath of clean, Wyatt-free air and shake his memory out of my head. I haven't spoken to Wyatt in twelve years. He looks good. Exactly like a selfish dick who would lead you on and then stomp all over your heart. But still undeniably hot.

"Were you able to get passes for the *Pink Slip* season two premiere?" I ask Stella as I grab my phone. She follows me out of my office as we head down to the conference room for our team huddle.

I discovered that Sophia is obsessed with the dark comedy about managers killing off employees who aren't meeting their potential in the office. I've seen a few episodes. It reminds me of a *Hunger Games* meets *The Office* mashup. It's dark but funny.

"Of course I did." She gives me a disappointed look for daring to doubt her. "I'll have a courier bring them to her tomorrow. You still want to go, too, right? And will you have a plus-one?"

I see the look of hope in Stella's eyes, always rooting for me and my "one day it will happen" plus-one. I both love and hate that she's a hopeless romantic.

"Just me."

"Well, I've got something better than a plus-one for you. Sophia agreed to meet with you. She's shooting at Everest Studios this week and can meet between her scenes."

"The greatest thing I've ever done in my life was hire you," I say while going in for a hug.

Stella started interning for me during her senior year of college, and I hired her as soon as she graduated. It's been three years now, and we've been inseparable ever since. She's my secret weapon, and some days, I think she knows me better than I know myself.

"Oh, stop it, Blair. I hate it when you get dramatic about things that are literally in my job description." She blushes, but I know she loves the praise.

As one of the top female talent agents in this city, I have a reputation as a girl's girl. I was in law school during the #metoo movement and had a front-row seat to the shift for women. The opportunities I had to impact and support legislature during law school were historical. Too bad I only realized I didn't want to be a lawyer after I graduated.

So, I moved to LA, and in a moment of right place, right time, I met Lance Wynn. He's the CEO of The Wynn Agency—a talent agency known around Hollywood as TWA. He seduced me with the idea that I could make a difference. As an agent, I could find and sell stories that might change the world, stories that might shed light on topics like poverty, discrimination, or injustice. Plus, my background and law degree would give me a leg up in the negotiation and contract process. Lance sold me when he grabbed my hands across the bistro table we were sitting at for lunch and told me he believed women were the future of this industry.

That was my first lesson about how this town works. Tell your client whatever they want to hear to close the deal. I do focus on women—I almost exclusively sign female talent—but getting Lance to take any of my projects seriously, or prioritize them, is getting harder. After the pandemic, it's like the

Hollywood mindset has reverted to "the good old days," and the scramble to make money has the industry leaning on the tried-and-true superheroes and sequels.

But I'm determined to prove the future is female. That's the reason for the Sophia Google search. Her current agent is an icon in the industry, and she's old school. Rumor has it she's retiring this fall and Sophia's looking for someone who can capitalize on her recent accolades and prevent her from being cast in stereotypical roles.

I want to represent her. I know I would be a perfect fit for her.

If Sophia agreed to meet, then it's my opportunity to lose. She wouldn't entertain the conversation if she weren't open to the idea of representation. I have some leads on a few significant projects I know she will be interested in, and I know I can convince her I'm the right choice. The premiere this week will help spotlight some of my contacts and relationships, too.

"Fine. But you know it's true." I take a seat at the large conference room table while Stella joins the other assistants in the chairs along the wall. The assistants are the lifeblood of this agency, but God forbid they get a seat at the table.

When I open my laptop, the image of Wyatt is still on the screen. The search took me right down the rabbit hole to Wyatt's bio. He works for his father's law firm, which isn't a surprise, but he had other dreams.

As general counsel, Wyatt guides the firm's attorneys on a wide range of matters, including client intake, legal ethics and professional responsibility, engagement management, and policy development and compliance.

Wyatt earned his Juris Doctor from the UCLA School of Law, where he served as an editor of the UCLA Law Review. *He graduated magna cum laude from the University of California, Los Angeles, with a bachelor's degree in political science and a minor in accounting.*

My investigative skills must be lacking because I could only find his bio on the law firm's website. It doesn't tell me anything about if he's single or dating or what he's been doing for the last twelve years. Would it kill him to get an Instagram account? I'd even settle for a Linked In account.

"Ok, please tell me we've booked Timmy to host the *SNL* season finale," Lance says, diving right in as he pushes through the door and sits at the head of the table.

"Done. And we've booked Olivia as the musical guest, too," says Brian, another agent and Lance's pet.

Lance looks up from his phone as a grin stretches across his face. "That's what I'm talking about. Teamwork makes the dream work."

It takes all my physical control not to roll my eyes.

"When does shooting begin on *Speed* 3?" I ask. "I may need Sandy for an appearance."

"In two weeks. Just let me know, and I'll see if we can make it work." Brian leans back in his chair, feeling cocky and comfortable. Another sequel for the win.

"Blair, what about Michelle? Were you able to lock her

into the lead for *Aquaman 3*?" Lance directs his question to me, but his attention is on the phone in his hand.

"Almost done. There's also a lead opportunity for her in Elizabeth's next untitled project." Yep. That gets his eyes up.

"Instead of focusing on projects that aren't a priority, perhaps you could focus on signing talent?" Lance stands and walks out before I can respond, and I take a sip of my coffee to regulate the rage bubbling under the surface.

"Ignore him," Stella says.

"Easier said than done." I grab my phone and coffee, and rise from my seat.

Stella is infringing on my personal space before I reach the exit of the conference room. "So, you gonna tell me the backstory on Wyatt?" She wiggles her eyebrows up and down, smiling at me.

I pick up my pace back to my office, trying to avoid this conversation. "I'd rather not," I mumble. Why does it feel like I can't breathe?

I'm quiet for a beat too long.

"Oh, my God—is he an ex? Did you sleep with him?" Her hands fly up to her cheeks.

I told you she knows me.

"It's ancient history."

"When? I know everyone you've dated." She puts her first and middle fingers of both hands up to air quote "dated."

"It's nothing. We went to high school together. I haven't seen him since." I play it off like it's no big deal, but my heart feels like it's being squeezed between Wyatt's metaphorical hands to remind me I'm still not over the hurt.

I've dated casually, been married—and divorced—and

had no trouble recovering and moving on with my life. But one mention of Wyatt Bradford has unlocked the secret compartment of emotions I buried a long time ago.

"Do you know Sophia, too?" Stella asks.

"I don't. Well, not really. I knew Wyatt had a little sister, but she was a lot younger than us. She dropped part of her last name, so I didn't put it together immediately." I think back to one of the few times I met Sophia. Her father signed her up for a junior golf camp at the country club where I worked. She joined her father and Wyatt for lunch that week, and I was their server. I doubt she would even recall the interaction.

"He probably doesn't even remember me." I sift through the files on my desk to signal the end of this conversation. Thankfully, Stella catches on quick and just smiles before she turns to go back to her desk.

"Actually, Stella? Cancel the courier and set the meeting with Sophia for tomorrow if you can. I'll hand deliver the *Pink Slip* passes. It'll be a great icebreaker to start the conversation."

There's no reason the topic of her brother should even come up, so we can keep it buried where it belongs until I've proven I'm the right agent for her.

chapter two

. . .

Wyatt

"SON! COME IN HERE FOR A SECOND."

I almost made it past him. My father is in the large conference room overlooking downtown LA, sitting in a white leather club chair surrounded by lights and cameras for his weekly *LawTalk* video web series. When in Hollywood, I suppose.

"Hey. What's the topic today?" I ask, feigning interest as I cross the room to see what he wants.

"Just a little update on California's new employment laws. You sure you don't want to join me for this?" It's the last thing on earth I want to do, especially with him.

"Can't today. Meeting Soph for lunch," I say. "Did you need something else?"

"Send her my love." He seems relieved at my rejection as he settles back into his hosting pose. "We have a new client coming in on Thursday, and I'll need you there. I'll send the details over." With a wave, I'm dismissed. He doesn't wait for questions because he doesn't allow them. Jackson Bradford has spoken, and now the conversation is over.

My grandfather started Bradford and Associates, but my father has turned it into one of the most elite law firms in the U.S. We employ over three hundred lawyers and have offices in six locations. We support a variety of sectors, but we primarily focus on mergers and acquisitions, corporate reorganizations, and shareholder activism.

Even though it's clear my future is to continue the success he's created and eventually lead the company, my father still expects me to earn partner. Too bad it's the last thing I want.

I make it down the stairs and out the door with no other interruptions and jump in the Town Car waiting for me. I haven't seen Sophia in a few weeks. She's been busy enjoying the perks of being an Oscar winner while also filming a guest-star spot on a new series for one of the streamers.

I'm so proud of her. She started acting in school plays as soon as she was able and pushed my parents to let her audition for a kids' network open call. When she landed the lead role for a new series at age twelve, it shocked all of us, but at the same time it didn't surprise us either. She was born to be in front of a camera.

There's no traffic as we wind down the side streets to Everest Studios, and I relax, knowing we'll make it there on time. She wanted to meet today because she's looking for a new agent and needs my advice. Dad and I work with a lot of the talent agencies in town, and I have some insight into the pros and cons of each one. I don't know many talent agents directly, though.

Except one.

Blair Barton. Actually, it's Bennett now. I can't believe she married someone. I used to believe that we would get married. Funny how things change. And how incredibly wrong I was.

The phone vibrates in my hand, bringing me back to the present.

SOPHIA

Almost here?

ME

Yep. What's craft services serving today?

SOPHIA

Something delicious I'm sure.

Sophia may be tiny, but she eats like a man trying to put on game-day weight. I have no idea where she puts it all.

ME

Everest catering never disappoints.

ME

Be there in 20. Love you.

SOPHIA

My phone buzzes again, and I'm expecting to see Sophia's name, but it's an email from my best friend, Jake. It's the itinerary for our annual Manmorial Weekend in San Diego—a weekend with a shit-ton of golf, whiskey, and debauchery. I look forward to it every year, but it looks like this year, Jake will be a little tame because he's engaged. He's been planning his wedding since we were in college, way before he ever had a hint of a fiancé. Jake just loves love. I shoot off a text to fuck with him a little.

ME

Is your mom joining us in La Jolla?

JAKE

What? Why would my mom be going?

ME

Oh, so she just created our itinerary then?

JAKE

Fuck you. You know I can't go to some places we typically go to.

ME

Right. You're in love. Or whatever...

I flinch, hoping I haven't reopened old wounds. I can't stand his fiancée, and Jake knows exactly how I feel. While he understands she's not for everyone, he's completely in love with her. I care deeply for Jake, and because he loves her, I do what any best friend would do—I support him the best I can.

JAKE

You should try it. Maybe someone would finally sleep with you.

ME

Hilarious.

JAKE

Where are you? Wanna grab lunch at Joan's?

ME

On my way to have lunch with Soph—raincheck?

JAKE

Tell Soph hi...

Jake was my roommate throughout undergrad and law school. He's one of the top entertainment lawyers in LA and close to making partner at Hays and Cole, one of the best entertainment law firms in town. It's where I'd love to work and where I will never get to work. Bradford and Associates is my legacy. The minute I was born, my destiny was preordained.

As much shit as I give Jake, I get it. It must be an incredible feeling to fall in love and build a life with someone. I just don't think it's in the cards for me. I've tried. I even lived with a girl during the pandemic. However, I hate flings and one-night stands even more. Luckily, I have a few arrangements in place when the need arises.

Speak of the devil.

BETHANY

Hey love, I'm in town this week if you have time for dinner.

ME

Can I let you know? New client starting.

BETHANY

Of course. If it can't work, I'll be back in a few weeks.

I run my hand through my hair and catch my reflection in the rearview mirror.

What am I doing?

I should lock in time with Bethany right now. A new client won't keep me that busy. But I'm not feeling it lately. I'm in a funk. Maybe it's because Jake is getting married and I'm losing my wingman. Not that he's been a wingman for a while now.

Or maybe it's because I already had my chance at love twelve years ago. When I watched it fail spectacularly, I knew nothing else would even compare to what we had.

Read *Second Act* for free in Kindle Unlimited. Available now in Paperback and ebook from Amazon and your other favorite online bookstores.

acknowledgments

TAKE 1: PRE-PRODUCTION
(The Early Stages)

My second acknowledgments! Still not over the magic of getting to write these—the novelty hasn't worn off, and honestly, I hope it never does.

First and forever, my family deserves the brightest spotlight: my incredible momma, Jamie, Ryan, Kristy, Matt, Emma, and the absolute center of my universe, my daughter Brooklynn. You all make me brave enough to put words on the page, even on days when I'm convinced they're terrible. Your unwavering belief in me is everything.

My heart overflows with gratitude for my ride-or-dies: Holly, who reads every single word I write—from messy first drafts to polished final pages—thank you for seeing the potential even when I can't. And Cami, who patiently listens to me untangle plot knots out loud, sometimes for hours. Your friendship is the safe space where my stories find their footing.

To the countless friends, colleagues, and extended family who indulge my endless book conversations and never once say, "Enough about your characters already!"—thank you for nodding enthusiastically even when I've told the same story three different ways.

TAKE 2: PRODUCTION TEAM
(The Technical Crew)

This time around, I found pure magic with my new editor, Nicole at Emerald Edits. Nicole, you turned my jumble of ideas into something actually readable! Your thoughtful feedback, brilliant suggestions, and gentle guidance transformed this story in ways I couldn't have imagined. I'm forever grateful for your keen eye and kind heart.

Eternal thanks to Jefferson, who graciously returned to The Backlot world for book two. Your meticulous copy and line edits make every sentence sing—and cleverly disguise me as a wordsmith and grammar genius when we all know better!

Staci, my cover designer extraordinaire—you've outdone yourself! I'm absolutely obsessed with this design and honestly can't imagine how we'll top it (though I said the same thing last time, so I trust your endless creativity!). Thank you for giving Grant and Sophia a visual home that captures their essence so perfectly.

Ellie, my visibility guardian angel, thank you for once again helping me get the word out and organizing the ARC reader signups. I'd still be shouting into the void without your expertise and network!

To my beta readers, especially Annie who came back for round two—your early feedback shapes these stories in profound ways. I treasure your honesty and enthusiasm in equal measure.

TAKE 3: SUPPORTING CAST
(The Industry Folks)

I loved working in entertainment and I love the people I met and worked with while in that world even more. I'll forever be grateful for my Disney, Turner, and WBD family and for those that still take my calls and cheer me on in this new role as spiller of all the secrets. Just kidding, ahem, it's all fiction.

TAKE 4: THE AUDIENCE
(The Reader Team)

To my newsletter subscribers—thank you for inviting me into your inbox. I promise to respect that privilege with content worth opening!

My ARC readers deserve their own standing ovation. Watching my social feeds fill with your thoughtful reviews and genuine enthusiasm brought me to tears more than once. You champion these stories with such heart, and I hope *Center Stage* lives up to your expectations. Please keep coming back for more!

To my Instagram and TikTok friends—every like, comment, and share helps these books find their people. Thank you for wielding your algorithm-magic on my behalf and creating community around these stories.

And to everyone I've been fortunate enough to meet at

signings and events—thank you for making time in your busy lives to come say hello. Those connections remind me why I write in the first place.

FINAL TAKE: THE SPECIAL EFFECTS
(The Behind-the-Scenes Support)

Finally, to everyone who's "just doing their day job"—you don't realize how profoundly you impact authors like me. To the incredible indie bookstores that took a chance on a new voice: Blush, The Plot Twist, Patchouli Joe's, Talking Animals, and Love Stories—stocking my books and hosting signings gave me legitimacy I couldn't create on my own. Your belief in my stories will forever hold a special place in my heart.

A heartfelt shoutout to Spotify for providing the soundtrack that fueled late-night writing sessions, and to the Dallas Stars for being the perfect background noise as Grant and Sophia found their way to each other. Bing Bong!

about the author

Kimberly Page is a contemporary romance author who loves writing about strong heroines and the irresistible heroes who fall for them. After a career spent crafting stories for major players in the entertainment industry, she decided to create stories of her own.

When she's not writing, you can find Kimberly planning for beach time, at a theme park with her daughter, or getting lost in a good sports romance book. Follow her on TikTok and Instagram for news and updates.

www.kimberlyjpage.com

9 798991 847230